The Half-life of Secrets

This book was previously
published under the title
Quiet Sins

The Half-life of Secrets

Holland Childhouse

For Gary, my husband, who brought me home.

CITIOFBOOKS, INC.
3736 Eubank NE Suite A1
Albuquerque, NM 87111-3579
www. citiofbooks. com

Hotline: 1 (877) 389-2759
Fax: 1 (505) 930-7244

Ordering Information:
Quantity sales. Special discounts are available on quantity purchases by corporations, associations, and others. For details, contact the publisher at the address above.

Printed in the United States of America.

ISBN-13:   Paperback   978-1-963209-72-3
            eBook   978-1-963209-73-0

Library of Congress Control Number: 2024903505

Table of Contents

Chapter 1

TASTE

As my son, the doctor, is fond of pointing out recently, the *Tibetan Book of the Dead* suggests that in the normal course of dying you lose your senses, or *"elements,"* one at a time. He says that in his experience as a physician, hearing is usually the last to go. He insisted on reading me a passage that speaks of "the sequence of the signs of death," each of which is related to one of the senses:

Now the sign of earth dissolving into water is present

Water into fire

Fire into air

Air into space

Thanks, Brian. I needed that, whatever the hell it means.

I would never admit this out loud, but I am finding this concept to be eerily correct, though these are not the words I would have chosen to describe it. Cancer is not the fun-filled vacation one might have wished for in their later years. There is a certain dissolution going on in me, a kind of melting and melding that I am powerless to stop Still I wonder if I didn't lose the best part of my senses years ago, and have been watching them slowly erode into my current state ever since.

It's a curious place I'm in. I have so little control over my body these days, yet in some ways that I've never experienced before, I feel more "sensitive" than ever. That's not necessarily a good thing; the things I do feel are exaggerated and elongated while everything else seems to slip through the sieve of my mind.

The mind I've got left is a pretty ethereal affair, partly hyper-conscious, partly adrift, partly asleep. And while I can't seem to get a good grip on the physical aspects anymore, my internal analysis of things seems very sharp to me. I'm just not sure that the outside world would see it that way. Not that I really care what my fellow inmates think, mind you. I never have before; why would I start now?

From what I can gather, there is a lot of activity going on around me that gives the basic (and quite correct) impression that I'm on the way out—"circling the drain" as they say. Bastards. If hearing is, after all, the last to go, they could at least have the decency to be quiet about it. I'm not deaf yet, not by any stretch of the imagination, even though they act as though I am. Nor am I nearly as incapacitated as they would like to think.

I lie here in utter disbelief that this final step could actually be happening to me— *me* of all people. It seems so unexpected, though one might speculate as to what I had realistically been thinking might happen as I got older. Still—Chronic Lymphocytic Leukemia, intermediate stage—quite a mouthful, and definitely not what I had pictured for the Autumn of my life. It rolled off my doctor's tongue like mercury. The news stunned me at the time, and I can't say that I've changed my original response to the announcement. Death defines and touches all of us obliquely, until the point at which it strikes straight and true instead of just tangentially. In the beginning, it's the death of others—the cruel snatching of mothers and uncles and sisters and friends, and even children—then slowly we come to accept that one day the bell will toll for us. We think about this time coming and dread its onset, never quite believing it. Most of us like to pretend it will not come, but it always does.

I used to pretend that it would somehow slide by me, miss me by inches, graze my face lightly, then move on to some other victim. If I just lay quietly, I told myself, not making any fuss, using my fear as a blanket, blending into the fabric of things, it might pass over me. It did not.

It's been viciously creeping up the length of my body, caressing my limbs one by one, alternately numbing and then jolting every nerve. This did not happen in a day. It has been days and weeks and months, maybe years in the coming, if I think back on it, though, now it seems reduced to hours. Now it seems agonizingly slow and insidious and chillingly effective. I had not expected such neatness and precision. Cancer is apparently very precise. Good to know the efficiency quota is so high.

More's the pity, I still seem to have some mental acuity left. While my mind is no longer working *normally*, it seems to be functioning on some new uber-level. It's more

like a command center now, reporting the various malfunctions as they occur. I try to assess my status. Hello, legs—are you still there? Roger that. They must be there—they hurt like hell. But then everything seems to hurt like hell. On some level that I can not quite define I feel more connected than ever before. The surreal life, no doubt.

I lick my lips to see if I have any feeling there. Affirmative. I have the vague sensation of cracked skin and a tongue that feels like sandpaper edging across it. Some days it hurts to move my mouth. Some days it hurts to move period. Other days, I seem to have a brief reprieve. Perhaps I should do a final audit of myself while I still have some mental faculties remaining. How long they will remain is anyone's guess.

I can still hear noises in the kitchen, and there is the occasional waft of either garlic or basil finding its way to my nostrils. Someone must be putting a meal together for me. I really don't know why they bother, but again, I am encouraged that my sense of smell is still intact. And I do still have a mild appetite though nothing like before Apparently I'm still alive, according to *The Book of the Dead*, or I wouldn't be contemplating the Chicken Marsala that lurks in my future.

Then a new thought drifts across the scattered landscape of my mind. I roll it over slowly, gauging its plausibility. It occurs to me that I want to re-experience my senses one last time before they all dissolve. I certainly won't get another chance at it; this could be my last shot.

I wonder if I have the time left for such blatant sentimentality. Probably I do. These final endings and last passages (a few of the many euphemisms I use now—even on myself) often seem to drag out long past one's predictions. If I remember correctly, it took Marvin bloody forever to die, not to mention Sylvia and Leonard, though Charlie was gone in a heartbeat, with barely time to contemplate his demise. This last pains me, as it always does when I think of Charlie, but I must push grieving into the background for now, as it may well take up all of my faculties and powers of concentration to dredge up my sensory memories. Not enough RAM left for a lot of multi-tasking, I remind myself.

I am thinking that I should take advantage of my foreknowledge of death—not everyone has this luxury—and savor each one of my senses, toss each one around in my mind for a while like a salad, play with it, love it a bit, then put it away for good. Then I suppose I will be ready. Then they can bring on the worst, whoever 'they' are. This preoccupation has the further benefit of prolonging the inevitable—a losing proposition, granted, but distracting nonetheless, which is what makes it desirable.

This sounds like a fairly academic endeavor now that I think about it. I only hope I can remember what my senses felt like when they were healthy. As I recall they were all quite luscious, perhaps the more so in retrospect than they were at the time.

I like this idea of mine; it sounds like an appealing alternative to the twisting, dark thoughts I've been having lately. Perhaps it will distract me from my current reality long enough to help me slip into the next phase. I need to look backward now because my present and my future are nothing but black holes. It's a good plan, a *sensible* plan, in the strictest definition of the word.

I must try to be logical and accurate and remember them the way they were. My senses—the fingers of my mind, the eyes of my soul, my last contacts with this world. I shall start now, one at a time.

Are you there, Olivia?

***

I was always very particular about my food. Even now, when everything they feed me feels bland and mushy, I am fussy about how it is prepared and served. My son has hired a cook to make meals for me. At first, I hated her just on general principles, but over time I've gotten used to the idea, the way humans get used to anything—the way water erodes rock, that sort of thing. Plus which, I think she has an interesting palate and an appreciation for the limits of the declining patient: no seafood, nothing too crunchy, easy on the saturated fats, lots of soft things, don't forget the fiber.

I originally despised the notion of someone feeding me, bringing me food like a baby, like an invalid, like someone who is dying, but again, we all learn to adapt over time. It's a bad sign that I sometimes have trouble holding my own fork, that I occasionally drool, that sometimes my lips hang slack while I'm fed and water just falls from my mouth when they put the glass to my lips. This last image makes me smirk just slightly though there's no one here to appreciate the movement. Yes, it's a very bad sign. Actually, I'm exaggerating a bit. I don't drool that much, and I don't always need help eating—it just sounds more dramatic to put it that way. But I have always loved hyperbole, so I suppose that accounts for it.

I think back to my younger days. No drooling then, at least not on my part. I was quite the lady, or so I thought. People have always said that I'm attractive—past tense, naturally. I suppose I was, physically speaking. Not now, of course, good God no, but then I was. Dark curly hair, amber eyes, smooth skin, broad forehead, long neck. I had a tall, trim, athletic body, the kind that women secretly envy. I could eat anything and never gain an ounce in those days, though that changed as I got older and I began to realize that your body can turn on you in an instant. In those days, I looked down my nose at women with fat on them. I secretly found them disgusting. Can't they control themselves? I would ask, curling up my lip. And then I became one of them; karma having finally caught up with me. My mother, when she got older, was a perfect example—the puffy hips, the fat pads behind the knees, the jiggly upper arms. I used to mock her behind her back—occasionally to her face. I used to say that I wouldn't be caught dead looking like that. What luck, for in the end I won't look anything like that I probably weigh about 95 pounds now. And not one inch of it is attractive. Oh well, better to die thin, no?

Louise, the cook, says she is constantly dieting, though it never seems to work for her—bad genes in my opinion. She could stand to lose at least forty pounds. And if she weren't such a glutton she would...but I digress, and I don't know why I'm being so mean, really. Maybe it's these drugs I'm taking. I wasn't always so judgmental; it seems to be a recent phenomenon. And in any case, I don't want to think about Louise; it only aggravates me, and I have no time for her. I want to think about me, my feelings, my life, my senses. Why shouldn't it be about me now? I'm the one lying here with pain shooting up my abdomen, not her, I'm sorry to say.

And then there's my daughter-in-law Lisa. She never seems to have any physical problems, damn her eyes. Just wades through life like a giant walrus in a tub of warm rice. How she ever managed to snag my son the Doctor I'll never know. She's got that never-ending genial expression of hers, Miss "everything is fine," "no worries here." I'd like to see her have some real problems, the way I have. Maybe she wouldn't be so complacent all the time.

I mean really, what does she know about struggling to survive? Miss "Private schools and Caribbean vacations?" She's never had her feet held to the fire, believe me, and if she did, she'd probably squeal like a baby. I have no respect for her, never have. She's got no stomach for the gritty part of life. Spends all her time making nice and glossing over everything—"taking the long view" she likes to say. "Don't sweat the petty things," she says, all smarmy and genteel—it's more like "don't pet the sweaty things," if you ask me. As though she even knows what the petty things are!

I know all about the small stuff—I lived with it most of my life. The devil is most assuredly in the details, or, at least, lurking in the small stuff; I can attest to that.

Of course, my son eats out of her hand, thinks she's "high-minded," says he loves the way she never gets ruffled. Spare me. I'd like to punch her in that ample stomach— just once—and see her flinch. It would give me great pleasure, even now. Hell, she probably wouldn't even feel it! The fat layers would act as giant shock absorbers and just ripple away the impact. Ahh, the things I'll miss...

I feel the corners of my mouth go up, and my eyes wrinkle at the mental picture.Lucky for her there's no chance of it happening—I'm far too weak. I missed my opportunity years ago. *Quel dommage*, as the French say. At least, I could speak a foreign language. What can she do that's useful? Scrapbook?

Suddenly I stop myself. As usual of late, my mind has meandered down a winding lane of recriminations and hostile thoughts – all of which give me a certain amount of pleasure, a certain *Schadenfreude*, as the Germans say. But on the other hand, my time is short, and I need to focus on myself, delicious as the deconstruction of Lisa may be. She is stealing my time and does not deserve my attention. Plus which I always begin to feel guilty after a healthy dose of ripping Lisa to shreds. I don't know what comes over me lately; what a terrible person I've become—especially when you take into account what I've done to her—it's unconscionable really. I should get down on my knees and beg her forgiveness. But let's not get into that just now. There'll be plenty of time for that particular trip down memory lane later—much later.

With difficulty, I push my mind onto a different path. Think about me, I repeat to myself like a mantra, she is nothing—a pebble on my beach, a grain of sand in my oyster.

Time to make pearls.

Now I see that Laila has arrived. Beautiful dark-skinned, doe-eyed, exotic Laila. She is my nurse now that I have been unwillingly deposited into home hospice care by my son. I love Laila—she's wonderful, she's great, but let's face it, we all know what being in hospice means, and I am not so clueless that I don't understand the finality of her visits. I hired her so that I could avoid the actual hospice nurse as much as possible. Laila is my private nurse and answers strictly to me, which is the way I want it. Still, I'm expected to churn out some lemonade from these miserable lemons they've handed me. I've decided to be as sociable as I can manage under the circumstances, and I turn over heavily to greet her.

"Hi, Laila, you're here, good. Things are bound to improve now. What's new with you?"

Laila comes over to the bed and rearranges the covers so that they look more presentable. She puts her hand on my forehead—always gently because she is a tender soul—and frowns slightly.

"You feel hot to me, Miss Olivia," she says, pulling out a thermometer.

"Just Olivia, please," I ask for the tenth time.

"Oh, sorry—it's tradition where I come from to be respectful. In Afghanistan you would be treated as my "aunty," but I will try to remember," she says smiling shyly.

I sigh and smile back at her as best I can muster, knowing that the request may be futile. She will undoubtedly call me "Miss Olivia" until my dying day, which is fast approaching, so I really should be more patient. Or maybe I'm not giving her enough credit; she does seem to be a quick study on most other things...

She plugs the thermometer into my ear and extracts it shortly after that. "99.5, a mild fever," she says. "Not good, but not terrible. Let's give you some Tylenol...Olivia."

She doles out the medication, then starts making herself comfortable in the room, adjusting sheets, arranging water glasses, fluffing pillows, writing in her notebook, presumably a notebook dedicated to my personal statistics. Fascinating reading, I'm sure. After all the fussing is finished, she sits in the overstuffed chenille chair near my bed. "So what are you thinking about today, my friend?" she says in a slightly sing-song voice that I find surprisingly charming. "I like to hear your stories; you have a way with words."

"Well, I was actually thinking about my daughter-in-law right before you came in, and it wasn't very nice."

"Oh?" says Laila conspiratorially, "all the more reason to tell me then. What were you thinking about her?" She flashes me a bright smile and cradles my hand in hers.

I size her up for a moment, then decide she might as well be privy to my stream of consciousness on this particular subject. If not now, when? It's not as though I have years to explain my feelings. I sit up in bed, marshaling my strength for our conversation.

"Okay, I'll bite. I was thinking about Lisa and the fact that she has never had to suffer the way I have. She's a doctor's wife now, aren't we grand—Doctor and Mrs. So and So. She'll never have to lift a finger again." Laila nods her encouragement on the subject, and since my thoughts have been gathering steam, I decide to let it all out. "Well, you can rest assured that Lisa never lived in a one-room apartment with only one bed in it and never shared a bathroom down the hall with other boarders. She's probably never had to share a bathroom in her life, except maybe when she goes to restaurants!"

Laila raises her eyebrows slightly, probably thinking about her own experiences with shared bathrooms. I make a mental note that I am coming off as rude, arrogant and snobbish, but I don't really care. It feels good to purge myself on the subject, I notice— self-absorption and insensitivity being the theme of the day.

I go on, full-throttle. "My mother and father could barely speak English when they came here from Poland. Marlena and Victor— fresh off the boat. It was all they could do to keep a roof over their heads. And it wasn't much of a roof at that. It was a squalid, miserable apartment that was permanently noisy and hot—except for when it was squalid, noisy and cold. I know because I lived there with them from the age of four. This was no romantic "attic loft"; it was just a rectangular room with a lot of ramshackle furniture in it that always seemed on the verge of collapsing."

Laila interrupts me. "For someone who's so sick, you certainly have a good memory."

"Well, I have no trouble remembering the past, it's the present that gives me fits, but I'm just getting started, thank you very much. I have much more to say on the subject."

Laila smiles indulgently. "Go on, then."

"Well, they were never quiet, my parents. They were interminably yelling and screaming at each other when they were together, or better yet, screaming at me. I think they had expected some gigantic apocryphal immigrant miracle to occur over here that would suddenly make their lives flow like honey, but it never happened. Instead, they just sucked the life out of each other until they both ran completely dry."

Laila holds up her hand as if to stop me. "You use words I have never heard before. They sound nice to me, but I have no idea what they mean. I would love to know because I like listening to you, the way you speak. It sounds so exotic to me."

I smile at her generously. "I'll print you out a synopsis at the end of the day, how's that?" I say, half teasing, half seriously. "You can look up the big words later. I imagine it was 'apocryphal' that slowed you down. 'Highly unlikely' probably describes it best. I've always had a love affair with words. I told you that when you first started— and the fact that I don't have much time left has only made me love them more, so you'll just have to put up with my floral language for a bit longer, okay?"

"Okay, deal. Now get back to your parents, tell me the rest of the story."

"Yes, well, they were like a black hole, these two. Their joyless existence filtered down on me, crushing me, depressing me and driving me into myself. Happiness was not a word I associated with either one of them, and certainly not something that ever described my childhood years. They never seemed to expect or anticipate happiness, and thus, they were never disappointed when it failed to materialize. They just seemed melancholy and resigned. A dark cloud hovered permanently over their lives, moving with them wherever they went, tracking them like a scout."

"They sound awfully depressing," Laila comments. "That would be an understatement. I think they were the reason therapy was invented. But that's another subject we can visit at some other time. To continue with the broad strokes…"

"Which means what?" Laila interrupts.

"It means, to continue with the overview, that's all."

"Okay, broad strokes, then."

"Right. So my father died when he was 49—some sort of bleeding ulcer they said—but I always thought it was more from being chronically irritated and pissed off and having a sense of anger and dread that simply carried him away. Naturally he never saw the doctor when it might have done him some good. For one thing, it would have cost money, which was in short or no supply at all, and for another, he never would have been interested in someone else's opinion, especially some over-educated snob who 'didn't know his ass from a hole in the ground'. By the time they figured out what was wrong with him in the emergency room, he was close to dead, and by the evening, he polished it off, with my mother wringing her hands next to the bed and whining nasally. Quite a send-off. It just made me feel even more isolated and alone than before."

"Were you actually there when he died?" Laila asks.

"Yes and no. I was there in the hospital, but they mostly kept me out of his room—well, it wasn't even a room, just a bed with a curtain around it, and I barely understood what was going on until it was too late. Then my mother was crying, and she dragged me into the room—where I did not want to go. It was all a bit of a nightmare." Laila nods as though she understands, and I continue. "His death of course made my mother even more furious—if such a thing is possible—a sentiment which she ruthlessly took out on me. Right or wrong, I was repeatedly verbally punished for the fact that my father, quote—left us in a goddamn mess, without even enough money to bury him decently—unquote. I had to agree with her."

"Still, she must have been very sad about his death, no?" Laila interjects.

"My mother spoke bitterly of his departure, not so much because she missed him per se, but because she now had to come up with the rent every month without any help from him, and her part-time job paid very little. She never forgave him for this breach of faith, nor was his memory ever honored in any way after his departure from our lives. He just ceased to exist one day and life got even more difficult than it had been before."

"Your mother must have been very strong to carry on like that."

"Yes, I suppose you could call it strength, though she just seemed to be in survival mode most of the time. But she was right about one thing: I shared my mother's anger at his deserting us. It did seem dreadfully selfish of him at the time. Thirteen was not a good age to lose your father, even if he was brutally self-absorbed, a terrible husband and father, and not much of a provider. I was unbearably unhappy, right alongside my mother. We were poor, we were foreigners, we were lonely, and we were lost. I thought my life could not possibly get any worse. As usual, I was wrong."

I stop suddenly, mid-thought, thinking how typically insensitive I was being. It occurs to me that Laila has herself probably experienced much of what I was describing. She is clearly a foreigner and undoubtedly has a story of her own to tell. And there's a good chance it's worse than mine, I think to myself.

"Laila, it occurs to me that I'm droning on about my past, feeling sorry for myself, complaining about this and that, and you probably don't want to hear any of it, or, at least, shouldn't be subjected to it just because you're hired to care for me. After all, you're not hired to listen to my palaver—my dreary troubles. I'm making it sound as though I'm the only one who's ever lived through such things, but of course, you must know what I'm talking about."

Laila seems surprised at my confession. "I do know," she says, "but it's not the same as the things you describe. Of course, I have my own story, but this is not the time for such things. Right now it is your story that interests me. I'm happy that you would confide in me. I think it's good for my patients—or for my friends—to share their feelings. It's good medicine for them. Don't stop."

"Well, that's kind of you, and I have to agree that there is something cathartic— that means it feels good—to talking about these things. It's been a long time since I've spoken of my childhood and my parents. Might as well get it out of my system, right?"

"Exactly. It's like breaking a fever," Laila says. "So where were we? Let's see, your father had died, your mother was upset, and you were unhappy."

"Right. That pretty much sums up my childhood. And much more succinctly than I would have put it, that's for certain! So my mother was trying to find a way to deal with the situation and in the end, her thought-provoking response to all of this was to go out and find herself a new man, which—all things considered—she did in record time. I have no idea how she actually found this man, Nelson, but find him she did. Never mind that she barely even knew him, let alone liked him, before accepting his marriage proposal. So, before I knew it, I was in possession of a big, bearded, strange-smelling stepfather whom I despised, and who apparently felt he had every right to treat me as his own."

"You mean he treated you like his own child? Isn't that a good thing?"

"Not in this case. Unfortunately, 'his own' were not treated particularly well Nelson's sole virtue was that he had a steady job and a decent home, which were the only two things my mother had bothered to check up on. His personality and habits left much to be desired, though I give him credit for being fairly even-keeled, and besides, my mother was hardly very demanding when it came to refinements. He lacked my father's mean temper and sharp tongue, but he was insufferably stodgy and opinionated."

"I take it those are bad things," Laila smiles.

I return her smile. "The short answer is: Yes. The day after their 'wedding' at City Hall, he moved us into his three-bedroom home in Seattle, where he installed each of us in separate, modestly furnished rooms. The place had two bathrooms, something my mother and I found deliciously excessive and wildly desirable. He treated both of us with a passing courtesy, but a certain coldness that left us both feeling nervous and insecure."

"But didn't this marriage somehow please your mother?" Laila questions me.

"Not really," I answer. "Their marriage seemed to please no one, and I asked myself repeatedly what on earth had ever prompted them to create such a loveless union. There had to be something in it for each of them, but it was not obvious to me at that age what that something was, especially for my mother. Or maybe it *was* obvious, and I just didn't want to see it through a daughter's eyes. I suppose, if pressed, my mother would have pointed out the roof over our heads and her escape from being a feckless widow, and that's probably the end of it."

"Well, I don't know what a 'feckless widow' is," Laila says, "but I get the general idea. It seems pretty straightforward on her part, but what was in it for him—besides the obvious?"

"All I can hypothesize for him is that he gained a fairly handsome woman—albeit a moody one—to run his house and visit his bedroom, and a toothsome ready-made step- daughter to complain about to his peers and titillate him in general. What took place in their bedroom I did not want to know, and to this day I have my doubts that any normal marital activity ever went on in there. But then, I'm sure all daughters think that, and furthermore, I'm not sure what 'normal' is, so perhaps it's irrelevant. Also, judging from his behavior, it seems unlikely, but that's a different part of the story."

"What did Nelson do for a living?"

"He was a businessman of some sort, worked for an import/export firm, and Mother was never sufficiently interested in getting many of the details. As a teenager, I couldn't have cared less what he did as long as he stayed out of my hair. Mercifully he left the house every morning at eight and didn't return until at least seven at night, so that seemed reasonable to us. Isn't that what businessmen should do? You could set your watch by him. He worked out of a small storefront and had a handful of employees to push around, so this seemed to occupy his time during the working day."

I glance at Laila to gauge her interest, and note that she still seems to be listening intently, so I continue. "But his return in the evening was when the trouble always started. Nelson made it clear from the outset that he expected a piping hot gourmet meal to appear on the table shortly after his arrival in the evening. He was providing his part of the deal, and now he expected some return on his investment if you see what I mean. In addition, he thought his newly acquired 'family' ought to dine with him and ask him polite but superficial questions about his day—something along the lines of: '…How did your meetings go, dear' or '…Sales going well, are they?'

Laila giggles and I continue my story.

"While the questions were expected of us, the answers were anything but forthcoming. We barely listened, in any case, on those occasions when he deigned to describe his day. Really, we couldn't have cared less."

"I can imagine," Laila says knowingly.

"My mother was capable of mediocre chit-chat when forced, where, at the time, I was not, though her grasp of complex English was limited. My English was exemplary when I chose to use it, but the two of them hardly inspired me, and no one seemed to notice or care that I sat sullenly at the table, the epitome of the petulant adolescent."

Laila reaches for her notebook. "How do you spell that word you said before petulant, I want to look it up."

"E-p-i-t-o-m-e. The perfect example. But feel free to look it up, it's good for you. "

"I will, trust me," Laila says. "But so here you are a petulant teenager—I know what that is, believe me—and you're living with your mother and Nelson now, and then what happens?"

"Well, life happens, the usual events in a teenager's existence, I suppose. But the thing I remember most is the story of the cooking and how that evolved and what it brought with it."

"How do you mean?" Laila queries.

"Well, the cooking started out as a chore that originally fell to my mother and me, but since my mother was inherently lazy, I ended up doing the brunt of the work, with her barking orders. I could be found every evening in the kitchen chopping and dicing so that Nelson—who it turned out had very sophisticated tastes, don't you know—could have his fancy epicurean meal served to his liking."

I smile wanly at the memory and notice Laila jotting down another word in her notebook. "My mother was a decent cook, but her repertoire was pedestrian— common—at best, as she and my father had been too poor to afford fancy food, and no one had ever pushed the issue. Her dinners consisted largely of stews, soups, and noodle casseroles. This was not what Nelson had in mind. He was nothing if not demanding. My mother, of course, wanted to rely on the dishes she had learned to cook in Poland, but Nelson had his own ideas on the subject and had no problem telling us exactly what he expected. He had an eclectic menu in mind—that means varied, extensive—much to my mother's chagrin."

Laila smiles and writes again in the notebook.

I pause for a moment, then continue. "Mondays he might want steak with parsleyed potatoes, Tuesdays could be lamb chops with mint jelly, noodles Romanov and salad. Beef Bourguignon with wild rice would do nicely for Wednesdays, prime rib with horseradish and shrimp cocktails on Thursday, grilled trout seasoned with dill on a bed of scalloped potatoes on Friday and so on and so on, until mercifully, the menus were repeated.

"I can't believe you remember all that," Laila says.

"I know, strange, isn't it, but I do—long term memory is the most reliable, I've found. My mother just stared at me at first when she heard what was expected of her, hoping to find some relief from me. I shrugged my shoulders and told her I would start looking up the recipes in The Joy of Cooking, the book he had bought for just this purpose. This seemed to appease her, and I set my mind to the task."

"Wow. That sounds like an awful lot of work!" Laila says.

"You have no idea," I intone. "And then there were the desserts that he made a list of; he wanted Baked Alaska, double-crusted cherry pie, blueberry cobbler, crème brulée, and chocolate layer cake, all made from scratch, of course, and he expected to see something sweet appear on the table after each one of his prized entrées. We started following the recipes from the book, with me taking the lead and my mother providing cursory support. Her talents as a sous-chef were limited, but we somehow managed to produce a series of meals that over time became more accomplished."

"I guess the sous-chef is the helper?"

"Exactly. We had a few tricks up our sleeve that worked as long as we didn't

repeat them too often; we would occasionally manage to slip in a pastry from the corner bakery, but we were careful to top it with something from our pantry so that Nelson wouldn't notice its origin, as store-bought sweets were verboten—forbidden."

"Got it," Laila says.

I pick up the thread. "Nelson was on the portly side— overweight—and had every intention of staying that way. My mother, who had heretofore been slender, began to develop a sizeable gut and went from being marginally attractive to joining the ranks of most post-menopausal women of her day. But this was the currency of their marriage; he provided the money and stayed mostly out of our way—we served as a fancy bistro for him in the evenings and on weekends."

"So you had to cook like this for him seven days a week?"

"Well, no. Only six, thank God. Sunday was our day of rest. On Sundays, we cobbled breakfast and lunch together from leftovers and then he grudgingly took us out to dinner, a rare treat for the two of us, who were sick to death of cooking and grateful to have a moment of respite—a moment's peace. "

"Oh, and did I mention the liquor that went along with all of this fancy fare?There were pre-dinner drinks for him, and during-dinner wine, and after-dinner liqueurs. My mother eventually joined him, figuring there was no point in resisting, and certainly no point in being sober while he was drunk, so the two of them would be thoroughly inebriated by the time they were ready for bed, which usually coincided with the end of the meal. This left me to clean up the enormous mess the two of them made. You can imagine how thrilled I was with this stellar routine."

"Mmm, I'm sure. Thrilling," says Laila with a sly grin.

"Add this to the typical angst of a newly-teenage girl and it was a recipe for seething misery. I was a bouillabaisse—a soup—of predictable adolescent emotions: anger, frustration, resentment, loneliness, alienation, shame, sorrow, and unrequited (that's unfulfilled) desires. The girls' school I attended—a school that sounded classier than it was—and that Nelson paid for, made me feel more than ever like an outsider and I longed for the attention or even the appearance of boys my age."

"Boys! That's a new topic. What boys?" Laila asks, wide-eyed.

"Well, actually, no boys at that point in the story, sorry to say! That came later. At this point, there was only Nelson and my mother to think about, as I had very few friends at school and no one I could confide in. I found Nelson mostly insufferable, I only barely tolerated my mother, and I despised their overdone nightly dinners. I couldn't wait to be alone in my room, with the door firmly barricading me from the two of them and the outside world."

"I can see why," Laila says, reaching her hand out to mine.

I nod in agreement. "In my room, I would dream of a nauseatingly romanticized Prince Charming, who would help me slide down the balcony into freedom. Or I would be whisked off to foreign lands by some land-rich baron besotted with my youth and beauty. This was long before cell phones, remember. I went through cheap romance novels like corn chips, devouring their treacly plots—that means overly sentimental—imagining myself in every bodice-ripping scene. Anything to escape the monotony of my reality. My life seemed so humdrum that I was content to project myself between the covers of my books. I read and re-read some of them eight and nine times, carefully hiding them under my mattress so no one would find them or take them away from me."

Laila smiles and jots another word down in her notebook.

"Are you sure you want to hear all of this nonsense about my teenage years?"

"Absolutely, I do. I'm loving your story. I want to know what happens next," she says looking at me sincerely.

"Alright, I'm taking you at your word then. But stop me if you get to the point where you can't take it anymore. It's good for me to blather like this, takes my mind off always thinking about my present situation…"

"Exactly," Laila concurs. "Besides, I'm enjoying the vocabulary lesson."

"I doubt that, but we'll keep moving forward nonetheless. Now where was I? Ah, yes, talking about the cooking wasn't I? It turns out there was an upside to all of this, one bright spot amongst all of the frustration. Oddly enough, I began to realize that the cooking somehow pleased me. Not in the beginning, to be sure, but over time, once I became adept at it, I started to like it. I was a quick study, after all, and left my mother in the dust after a few months of on-the-job training. Another positive was that neither my mother nor Nelson even bothered complaining about my schoolwork as long as I was cooking or cleaning or shopping for them. Their own selfish needs vastly outweighed their interest in my school or my future, or anything remotely having to do with me. And in a strange way, this suited me. Schoolwork wasn't a problem for me anyway. I found it easy enough, no particular challenge there."

"Lucky you!" Laila says, shaking her head.

"Yes, lucky me," I reply wryly. "But the cooking was different. I surprised myself by coming to enjoy the art of it, the creativity of cooking. It was one of the only milieus—sorry, areas—in which I was allowed to express myself without restraint. It was strangely empowering to create something from scratch, present it nicely on a plate and have it be admired and fussed over. This, at least, my mother and Nelson were vocal about. There was no question that I was learning to cook, and to cook well. Both adults had the good sense to compliment me on my cooking—though this did not extend to any other phase of our relationship. I guess they realized that it was in their best interest to do so. Thus, I was lavishly praised for the first time in my life and took a liking to the flattery."

"Don't we all," Laila interrupts, smiling shyly.

I smile back; message received. "So as it turns out, I had an instinctual flair for matching flavors, knowing when to season something and when to hold back. I came to understand which textures worked well together, which colors blended pleasingly, which kinds of berries or liqueurs or spices would enhance a dish. I had no limits on what ingredients I could use, so I began to be a knowledgeable shopper, picking only fresh items that I knew would augment the flavor of the recipe, just from their natural goodness."

Laila nods knowingly. "I like to cook myself. There's something comforting about it, don't you think?"

"Absolutely. And I learned a lot from that experience. I learned when the strawberries were at their peak of ripeness, when the tomatoes were the sweetest, when the corn was most succulent, when the sugar peas were still young and firm, when the steak had been aged long enough and which chickens were still plump and fresh. I surprised myself with my attention to detail."

"I found that the old man who worked in the produce department at the corner store—Armine, I think—was all too happy to help me choose my fruits and vegetables. He taught me how to select them, how to roll them around in my palm, how to tap them, and when to buy them. He was pleased to share his knowledge with someone eager to learn. And learn I did under his tutelage…"

Laila grabs her notebook again and stops.

"Tutelage, right?" I say.

"Yes. Does it mean he was teaching you?"

"It does. See, you're figuring out the words just from the context aren't you?"

"I suppose," she says, looking pleased with herself. "Go on, though; I'm doing fine."

"Well, I discovered over time that where Nelson was parsimonious—that means stingy—about everything else, he was reliably generous when it came to money for the grocery shopping. He was indifferent to my pleas for clothing or trinkets, but never denied me cash when it came to preparing new meals for him. Even at that age, I was a realist, and I had a good head for numbers. I learned to pad the expenses, siphoning off money for my secret purchases— silk scarves, small but expensive perfumes, soft argyle socks, and, of course, the paperback novels I craved. He never suspected, or if he did, he never let on."

"I'll bet he knew," Laila's eyebrows flick up.

"Perhaps. But it would have been counter-productive to complain. My mother was so thrilled to have escaped the monotony of shopping that she gladly turned the job over to me, despite the fact that it cut her out of that particular money loop. But she had her ways of coaxing money out of Nelson—best not to think too long on what they were. I did not begrudge her the money she slipped out of his pockets, the 'home improvement' projects that cost substantially less than she told him, and various other less than above- board tactics. Actually, I picked up several useful tricks from her." I smile wryly at the memory.

"Sometimes on Saturday nights, after a particularly dazzling dinner, Nelson would wax philosophical during dessert, especially if it was one of my more viscous affairs, like the custard éclairs with hard sauce. I would make the hard sauce myself, using at least twice the amount of liquor the recipe called for, but I would surreptitiously—that means secretly—buy the éclairs ahead of time from the local bakery. Then I would unpack them—always hiding the pink boxes carefully in the trash—and drizzle them generously with my hard sauce, topped with an abundance of juicy red raspberries and whipped cream. He was convinced that I was a gifted baker, sent from heaven specifically to indulge his sweet tooth."

"Your trick always worked?"

"Always. I remember one night he said something to the effect of: 'My God, you have created a masterpiece tonight, Olivia. I swear we should open a bakery just to showcase your talents!' "

"I told him as sweetly as I could muster: 'No need, Nelson, I make them just for you, not the general public.' My mother gave me a crafty look as though she somehow shared in the accolades—the praise."

"What was Nelson thinking?" Laila asks.

"Well, my read on it is that it made Nelson deliriously happy to think that I had created the entire masterpiece from scratch just for his dining pleasure. For him, there was something wildly luxurious and perhaps sexual—though I'm only guessing—about eating large, home-cooked meals. I say this not because he said so, but because I could sense it in him. I'm sure his mother lay at the root of this proclivity—you may have to look this one up, Laila, as part of your on-going education—but I had no interest in exploring his reasons, lest I find out more about him than I had the stomach for."

"I think I understand," says Laila with a coy smile.

I go on. "My mother wasn't nearly so gullible as to think that I was the genius behind all of these treats, but would never have dreamed of exposing me on this issue, fearing that it might somehow be traced back to her with disastrous results. All three of us derived our own benefit from the unwritten contracts that came to exist."

"I can see what you mean," Laila says sagely.

"Yes, well on certain occasions Nelson would congratulate me on my confections by pulling me—carefully—onto his lap and dropping the plump cherries—or whatever bonbons happened to appear on the plate—directly into my mouth. I say 'carefully' because he took great care to situate me on his two knees in such a way as to prohibit suspicion on anyone's part that there was anything salacious—scandalous—about the pose."

Laila nods to show that she understands.

"We all pretended to find this amusing and laughed slyly at his childish antics. In fact, I encouraged him in this behavior when I discovered that quite often he had secretly stuffed a five dollar bill into my pocket while I was dangling over his legs. Five dollars was good money in those days, and I gladly tolerated this indignity when I realized the reward awaiting me. I also figured out that the longer I sat willingly on the sharp bones of his knees, the more likely I was to find my payment."

"And your mother, did she have any reaction to this?" Laila asks.

"Not really. My mother appeared to take no ill notice of his actions and treated this as though it were normal fare. I sensed no jealousy or anxiety on her part, though if she had known of the pay-off, *that* would have made her jealous—not the fact that he had touched me or paid attention to me. I think she would have demanded her pound of flesh—her share. But I was careful always to conceal my gifts. Nelson and I had an unspoken understanding. It was perfectly clear to both of us what was happening and why. It was a symbiotic relationship at that point, *quid pro quo*—you give me this, I give you that. We apparently both got something we wanted, and that was fine by me. Do you understand what I am saying?"

"I do," Laila answers. "I'm not as naïve as you may think. I understand everything you are saying, and I'm fascinated with your story. Thank you for sharing it with me."

"Oh, my pleasure. It's good to get it off my chest. I rarely get a chance to talk about the past like this. And I hope you aren't offended by any of it; it's a bit personal I realize…"

Laila interrupts me. "I'm not the least bit offended. I feel as though I'm watching you paint a picture and I can't wait for you to finish it so I can see the entire portrait. I get the feeling that you are leading up to something, and I want to know what it is."

"Ah, well, you would be correct in thinking that this path is leading us somewhere—though I'm not sure I should take you there with me…"

Laila suddenly glances at her watch. "I need to make your lunch, Miss—no, just plain Olivia! Louise will have left me food from last night that I can use. Let me go fix it; I'll be back in just a bit, and then we can continue, no?"

"We'll see. Not all stories are meant to be shared you know. I've plunged you into the middle of this one, but I'm not sure how much farther I can go with it."

Laila looks disappointed. "I didn't mean to push you," she says.

"No, of course not, I didn't mean it that way," I say apologetically. "Let's see how I feel after lunch, okay?"

"Okay," she says, uncurling herself from the chair she's been sitting in. "I'll be back soon. Why don't you rest?"

"I will; I'll do exactly that," I say, laying back on the thick pillows and closing my eyes, hoping to quell the rush of images in my brain. But my thoughts immediately snap back to the years I had been describing to Laila. These were chapters of my life I had not thought about for decades, and now suddenly here I am, drenched in the memories of my mother and Nelson, the smells and tastes of those days suddenly igniting in my mind. It seems so vivid to me now. I find myself relaxing into a time warp.

By now I was fifteen, going on sixteen. All of my senses were beginning to ripen, one by one. I found that I suddenly had all kinds of appetites I had never been aware of before. I was hungry for just about everything: new sights, new sounds, new tastes, new feelings. I felt like a stew with juices rising in me, ready to boil over. I was very much like one of the heroines of my cheap novels, but with no target for all of my new-found lust and desire.

I began to notice men watching me on the streets, at the market, when I shopped. I saw them watching me slit-eyed as I walked to school in my uniform, all fresh and dewy. I would occasionally glance at them coquettishly, as I believed the women in my books did, testing the concept, trying to get the right angle to my chin and eyes. When they responded, as they inevitably did, I would blush crimson and cast my eyes down, still too awkward to engage them in kind, and instead would rush hurriedly past them.

In those days, flirtation was more of an art, where today it can be a dangerous behavior. But I was innocent then, only biding my time for some future that I had concocted from the soggy pages of romance novels. I could feel it coming; I knew the moment was near, like the crescendo of a wave. I felt it in my gut—soon I would make contact. Soon all of my senses would detonate. But there were other elements unfolding then, circumstances colliding in my direction that I had not anticipated, and they would all converge on me in the next year, pushing my life in different directions, bypassing the sugary plot I had cast for myself.

If one were looking at a chart of my life at that time, one would have seen the points on the chart where the horizontal line suddenly jogs up, plotting a course at an angle away from the original trajectory. My father's death created one such angle, the introduction of Nelson into my life another.

But what, if anything, does this have to do with my original quest regarding Taste, I ask myself? Before I can come up with the answer, I find myself drifting off to sleep.

By the time Laila returns with my lunch, she does not have the heart to waken me. So she leaves the plate there on the night table, adjusts the covers around me, and then tip-toes out, on to her next assignment.

I dream fitfully of lost youth interspersed with gourmet meals, designer scarves, and wasted opportunities.

***

When I finally wake up, it's the middle of the night—the worst of all times to be awake. I can hear the wind and the sleeting rain outside colliding against the windows. Dear God, now I'll never get back to sleep, I think to myself. My mind snaps back to the last place it had been, catapults back to the days of Nelson and my mother and the epicurean debacle. It is so fresh in my mind, it seems like yesterday. I can remember every detail as it washes over me to the rhythm of the relentless rain. Probably just as well Laila is not here to share this with me, I think—too many unsavory details, too many dark memories. Best to travel this road alone. But I remember it all vividly.

Once a week Marlena would venture out at night. Her friend Rose—from the "old country"—would host a bridge party at her home, and my mother would take a taxi to Rose's apartment on the east side of town. Occasionally one of the other ladies would pick her up and return her home, usually by ten o'clock or so. Mother could be counted on to leave our house directly after the last crumb of dessert had been cleaned off her plate. Then she would clumsily force herself up from the table, grab whatever sweater or coat she could find, and start pinning up her hair and patting on some special pink rouge for her outing.

"I'll be back in a few hours," she would yell up the stairs as she left. And indeed, she would return like clockwork by the end of the evening.

Nelson didn't seem bothered by these sorties, and I was just as glad to see her leave, as it removed me from her line of fire. He probably felt the same way, though we certainly never discussed it. He would normally scuttle off to his room in the back, not to be heard from again until he turned up the next morning in his tattered robe demanding hot coffee. I was usually deep into my kitchen cleanup by the time I noticed my mother was gone. Once the dishes were finally dispatched, and the leftovers carefully wrapped up and stored in the refrigerator, I often liked to take my bath.

Late evening seemed like the perfect time for bathing. No rushing to school, no shopping, no cooking, and the homework could certainly wait. One of the true luxuries Nelson had unwittingly provided was our second bathroom. This seemed like an indecent, mind-boggling extravagance to us after so many years of sharing with virtual strangers.

Now my mother and I shared the smaller bathroom situated between our two rooms, and Nelson, naturally, had appropriated the larger one down the hall by his bedroom. We were not bothered that he had the larger room, as he had used it prior to his marriage, so it seemed reasonable that this order be preserved.

Mother's and my bathroom was pleasant in an old fashioned way; it had those quaint old white subway tiles, with small diamonds of black trim, as was the style in those days. There were bright colored tulip drapes over the windows that must have been chosen by Nelson's sister Dorothy—that would be my new "Aunt Dorothy."

She had apparently lived with him in the house for some years, which made sense, as I couldn't imagine Nelson taking the time to pick out something so decidedly feminine. The shower curtain was equally cheerful and unexpected, along with the green throw rugs and color coordinated towels. I had always meant to ask Dorothy if she had decorated the room, but never managed to remember when she was visiting. No matter, it was a comfortable room.

There was a bathtub and a shower stall, but I preferred the bath. I liked to fill the tub as high as possible with hot steamy water, pour in the lavender bath oil Mother had given me for Christmas, then climb in and soak peacefully until my skin turned a rosy peach color. I would have a short pile of fluffy towels stacked up next to the tub, ready to jump into when I finally forced myself out. On top of the towels I would place a small bowl of fruit or nuts or some pastry to nibble on—sometimes the remnants of dessert from dinner. This was done less because I was hungry than because it seemed more decadent to me, and therefore highly desirable.

Usually, I brought in one of my well-worn paperbacks which I would read while marinating myself. Occasionally, I would accidentally dip the book into the scalding water, which accounted for their thick, raggedy appearance. But nothing was more sacred and highly anticipated by me than that solitary bath. It made me feel so grown up, so spoiled, so pampered to luxuriate in that tub by myself. There I was, sculpted by large clumps of frothy white bubbles and wrapped in an overwhelming floral scent. It was a private pleasure and a sensuous one. I must have known unconsciously that there was something erotic and sensual about it, but I had not yet explored these areas enough to put it into words. I simply knew that I was happy there.

I remember one warm summer evening in particular, after my mother had left early for her bridge party. Nelson had not been home for dinner that evening, so I had the rare luxury of not having to cook. My mother and I had fixed a large plate of leftovers from the night before, warmed them up and eaten quickly at the table, happy to be spared the usual fanfare. After she had left, I cleaned up in record time and made plans for my long-awaited bath. I arranged the towels in the room the way I liked them, positioned my latest novel on the edge of the tub, lit a large candle and placed it opposite the books, then began to run the water while I undressed. I dropped my clothes unceremoniously on the floor around the tub, then pulled the white terrycloth robe off of its hook behind the door and folded it on the edge of the bath so that I could slip into it the moment I got out without getting cold.

As always, I waited until the water was as high as I liked it and the bubbles thick and creamy; then I eased my way into the bath, one foot at a time. I sank down slowly, acquainting myself with the new temperature, adjusting to it as the water surrounded me with its liquid heat. I craned my neck and head back onto the folded towel on the rim of the bathtub so that only my face was clear of the white foam beneath me, and sighed with pleasure. This was such a self-indulgent exercise, a strange envelope of time when I never felt lonely, despite the fact that loneliness was one of my most difficult and constant companions. All my life I would love this ritual.

I languished in the tub for easily forty minutes while I read my novel, polished off whatever delicacy was on the plate that night, and finally made myself get up. I remember drying off and slipping loosely into my terrycloth robe, still damp, shiny and over-heated from my bath.

Before I had managed to tie the sash of my robe, I heard a noise at the door, and then through the steam and vapors, I suddenly saw Nelson standing there with a startled look on his face, staring intently at the vertical slice of naked flesh created from my untied robe.

I screamed once, then pulled the terrycloth tightly around my body. I was deeply humiliated and more than that, horribly surprised.

"My God, what are you doing in here, Nelson?" I shrieked, searching for some possible logical explanation.

He seemed as shocked as I was. "I, uh, I didn't realize you were here—I was looking for your mother and…"

"Since when do you simply barge into our bathroom when the door is closed?" I asked indignantly, using a tone of voice I was not normally allowed, either with him or with my mother. But this was new territory for me and my blazing eyes seemed to hold him at bay.

"I swear it was an honest mistake," he stammered weakly. "I'm so sorry, truly, truly, my apologies." He was backing up now towards the doorway, his eyes averted. "Please forgive me," he said, putting his head down and pulling at his beard. "I had no idea you were in here…"

He appeared to be genuinely apologetic and shaken, so much so that I actually felt sorry for him. No harm had been done after all, and it seemed to be an uncalculated blunder, nothing more. Perhaps I had over-reacted, I told myself ardently.

"I'm sorry I screamed like that; it's just that I didn't think anyone was in the house, and you scared me. Never mind. I suppose it's nothing really. Let's pretend it never happened," I said, still blushing crimson from the embarrassment of being seen by him.

"Yes, yes, it never happened, and it will never happen again," Nelson said muttered, shaking his head as though to rid himself of the image.

By now he had backed out into the hall, and I was standing near the doorway, my robe tightly wrapped around me. My flushed cheeks were beginning to calm down though my heart was still pounding with shame at the thought of his eyes on my body, brief though it may have been. Still, it had been nothing more than an accident, I reminded myself, and, after all, we did live in the same house, so it's not impossible for such things to happen on occasion.

"This is certainly not worth mentioning to your mother," he said sheepishly as his eyes met mine.

"No, of course not. There's nothing to tell, after all," I said thinly, wishing he would move out of my path. Mother would be the last person I would want to tell in any case.

Nelson stayed planted where he was. "No, nothing to tell. Again, you have my sincere apologies."

With this he began digging into his pocket, then his hand emerged with something crumpled in it. He moved towards me, then pressed his hand into the large pocket of my robe before I could protest. Finally, he turned on his heel and whisked himself down the hall to his bedroom, closing the door firmly behind him.

I looked after him with confusion and fear written on my face. Then, overcome by curiosity, I pushed my hand down into the wide pocket where his hand had just recently been. I saw the crushed twenty dollar bill he had put there. Now I simply stared down the hall at his closed door in disbelief. When I had recovered somewhat, I padded quietly into my room, shutting the door tightly behind me and locking it.

I pulled the twenty dollar bill out again and flattened it out on my desk, straightening the corners. When it was as smooth as could be, I traced its shape affectionately with my fingers. Twenty dollars was a lot of money to a girl my age at that time. I could buy a lot of things for myself that I had not anticipated being able to afford.

I stared at it for several minutes, asking myself what it really meant. Was it a simple apology, was it a bribe, or was it something darker still? I was not sufficiently worldly to understand all of the nuances of that "something", nor was I completely naïve, despite not having the words to explain it.

Nonetheless, my mind seemed to rebel at the direction it was heading in. Stop this nonsense, I told myself. This was a one-time occurrence, and both of us should simply

put it out of our minds. As far as I was concerned, the money was well-deserved. He owed me an apology, and this was his way of making it. There was probably nothing more to say about it.

I remember feeling uncomfortable around him for several days after the incident, avoiding contact with him whenever possible, and then, as the weeks slipped by, the event began to pale in my mind.

Like all young people, new thoughts and ideas began to supplant the old ones and my mind darted forward rather than looking backward. Like water covering sandy holes on the beach, my thoughts rearranged themselves until the surface was smooth again. It was as though it had never happened. Life lurched forward again at its usual pace.

If Marlena noticed anything out of the ordinary, she certainly never mentioned it. Nelson acted as he always had: courteous, remote—for the most part inscrutable. He gave no indication that he even remembered the occasion, and so it vaporized along with a thousand other discarded moments. Our lives continued in the same pattern as before. I was lonely, I was disturbed, I felt a storm rising in me, but the landscape of my outer life barely changed.

At least two months had passed since the incident with Nelson. July had morphed into September; the air in Seattle had cooled considerably, and the trees were beginning their kaleidoscopic transformation from greens to reds and yellows. I had been coerced into practicing making pumpkin and mince pies in anticipation of Thanksgiving, along with baked quail and Cornish game hens.

Little had changed in our home. I would hardly call it our "happy home," but things were relatively stable there, and I had managed to stay under the radar for most of the summer. No one had rocked the boat any more than usual.

Then one night my mother left the house for her bridge party fairly early in the evening. Nelson was at home as he normally was at that hour, presumably in his room, and I, not having changed my habit of bathing after dinner, readied the bathroom. There had been no further hint of impropriety on Nelson's part on the many evenings when my mother was gone, and I had taken my baths as usual. I had by now blocked the initial incident from my mind. There was no lock on the bathroom door, else I would have locked it, but I had no reason to feel paranoid.

Once again I found myself buried to the chin in hot water, my eyes half closed, one hand grasping the book I soon intended to read. I had not been as lavish with the bubbles as I usually was and the foam had dissipated to some extent so that my body was partially visible through the green-tinted water, my breasts peeking out from the surface. My limbs felt like rubber. I was so relaxed and enervated by the heat.

Suddenly, with no warning whatsoever, the door was pushed open, and Nelson stood in the archway, his eyes slightly lidded but staring directly at me. I instinctively crossed my arms over my exposed breasts and tried to turn my body towards the wall of the tub. I remember whimpering slightly and being frightened of his next move. I crouched in a kind of fetal position against the porcelain, mute, anguished, feeling trapped by this man who was supposed to be my guardian.

I'm not sure what I expected to happen next, but it was certainly not what actually happened. Apparently, he could see that I was frightened, and he took several steps backward to show me that he was not going to come any further into the room. He said not a word. Then he opened up one of his hands, and I saw money folded up in his palm. He slowly placed the folded money on the edge of the sink, then—without moving—gave me a long steady gaze.

I instantly understood the game and the rules. He would look, he would pay, I would acquiesce. Silence was the trump card. I also understood at that moment that he did not wish to hurt me in any way. His eyes told me that he expected no more than this and that I could refuse to play if I wished. I relaxed my legs just slightly from their tightly held position, but only enough to make myself more comfortable, not enough to make myself more visible.

"Goodnight, Nelson," I said in a high thin voice, not trusting myself to say any more than that.

He nodded slowly then backed out of the room and quietly shut the door.

Thus began a sordid pattern that was to go on for years. Nelson was not particularly imaginative, nor did I have any interest in refining or expanding his amusement, so the ground rules remained the same and the circumstances changed only occasionally. There would be moments he would catch me dressing in my closet, or crossing the hall to my bath or brushing my teeth in my slip – all accomplished behind my mother's back though I often think that she would have been a willing accomplice if she had seen some financial incentive waiting for her.

My respect for Nelson had hit rock bottom shortly after the first incident, so his chronic bad behavior had little effect on his standing in my eyes. My own self-respect, however, was at an all-time low, and I saw myself as the rankest form of opportunist. I often wondered how far I would have gone if Nelson himself had not kept the bar where it was. Still, my well-hidden bank account was getting fatter by the month, and my new- found wealth made me feel both powerful and seductive.

One day after school I sat with a small cluster of girls on a bench in the park near my house. We had only recently learned about prostitutes and "women of the night," as they were called then. My friend Lillian told us that she had heard her father joking with her mother after dinner one night. He said to her:

"So this guy says to this woman in a bar: 'Would you sleep with me for one dollar?' 'Certainly not!' she said indignantly. 'Then would you sleep with me for a million dollars?' She hesitated, 'Well…' 'Ah, good,' he said, 'now we've established that you're a whore, and we're just dickering over the price.'"

I squirmed as the others giggled, perhaps understanding the joke better than they did. It's only a matter of degree, I said to myself. But then, prostitution comes in many forms, and only some of them are sexual. I understood this. I understood it profoundly and spent a lifetime seeing the various forms that it could take, both in my own life and in the lives of others. I never said a word to anyone about it though, not a single word. It was both an observation and a revelation.

Nelson belonged to me now. I sensed the power I had over him, even though, practically speaking, he was the one in control. While I should have been the slave to his master, in fact, the roles seemed reversed. His need to see me accelerated, while the circumstances necessary for our encounters became increasingly difficult to maneuver. My mother became more erratic with her outings and could not be counted on to stay away for prescribed periods of time. It had nothing to do with her being suspicious; she was just less interested in her card playing as time wore on.

On the one hand, this inaccessibility suited me, as I secretly despised our sessions; but on the other hand my greed pushed me into needing our game to fuel my ever increasing appetite for the money I was accumulating. Both Nelson and I became more irritable, the inner conflict of self-interests flagellating both of us in different ways. We both felt our own aspect of guilt and yet neither was willing to forsake the reward. Neither of us seemed inclined to resolve our moral dilemma, and so for several years nothing ever really changed.

Since my mother was primarily interested in her own comfort, the fact that both her husband and her daughter seemed unhappy was not an overriding concern. What did concern her was the fact that her husband was becoming so preoccupied that he gave her even less attention than before, and was less interested in the stories she concocted in order to divert money her way.

She was observant enough to notice that I seemed to be capturing more of Nelson's attention than she was, and this was not a good thing in her mind, since there was no payoff for her in such congress.

She also slowly began to notice that I had a more self-confident tone to my voice, that I did not seem nearly as cowed as before, and that I seemed less intimidated by Nelson than I had been in the past.

It was clear that Marlena instinctively guessed that she had somehow been cut out of the loop, but could not quite wrap her fingers around the details. She seemed to keep a closer eye on the two of us, but only when it suited her. When she could not come up with anything concrete, she appeared to lose interest.

We went on in this fashion for another year and a half, the three of us, nursing our own narcissistic interests, and pulling further apart from each other as those interests intersected. And then, finally, the tectonic plates of our lives shifted against each other, bringing about the probably inevitable collision that we had all hoped to avoid.

It was a Thursday night late in the summer of my seventeenth year. School was out for me, so my time was my own, save for the part-time job I had babysitting the neighbor's toddler. I had been out shopping by myself that afternoon, searching for just the right jacket to go with the cream colored linen skirt I had bought the week before. Not only had I become skilled in the kitchen, but I had also begun to teach myself fashion and design. The same principles that applied to cooking—as far as pairing colors and textures—were true, I had discovered, in clothing and décor. I had determined to become a woman of substance and style, and I was acquiring the means to do so, or so I told myself.

My collection of Vogue magazines was growing, and I could almost envision myself on one of its glossy pages, vamping for the cameras, one hand plastered to my jutting hip. My biggest problem was convincing my mother that I had managed to bankroll my new wardrobe with my babysitting money. She seemed skeptical, but never having managed to keep track of the hours I worked, she was always a little befuddled when I came home with yet another new outfit.

Since I periodically and purposely brought home well-thought-out presents for her, she restrained herself from complaining too often. She admired my taste and had no intention of refusing my generosity. I convinced her that I was a genius at finding clearance sales and once-in-a-lifetime bargains at thrift shops. Ever the opportunist—like daughter, like mother—she preferred to believe my stories rather than delve into their veracity. Nothing had changed as far as that dynamic was concerned.

This particular night I needed to stop off at the market to pick up the remaining ingredients for our dinner. Nelson had requested something different, and I decided to surprise him with freshly caught rainbow trout which Armine (now ensconced in the fish department) had told me would be coming in that afternoon. I walked up to the counter and ordered three of the fish displayed on the ice, marveling at the firmness and tone of the translucent white meat. I placed the wrapped fish carefully in my basket and proceeded to the vegetable counter.

There I bought two bunches of thin green asparagus spears, along with fresh basil and fennel which I couldn't resist pressing to my nose and inhaling, and finally a pound of small red potatoes and a container of heavy cream for the sauce. A bright pink box of Napoleons completed the purchases. I had, over time, persuaded Nelson to eat the occasional bakery treat, convincing him that there were certain feats that even I couldn't accomplish as well as a pastry chef. The other ingredients were already at home waiting for me. Mother's bridge club was tonight, so I fully expected her to eat and run.

It seemed to take hours to prepare the meal, but finally, it was ready, and I called my mother and Nelson to the table. The trout was exquisitely cooked; I remember that even now. It was light and flaky, coated with a lemony herb sauce that accented the tender fish without overpowering it. The flavors blended perfectly with the crisp young potatoes laced in fennel and the fresh asparagus with hollandaise. All three of us seemed pleased with the results.

"You're such a fabulous cook, Olivia, I'd never have thought it," my mother said, putting down her fork after finishing off the potatoes.

Nelson was just in the process of complimenting me on the trout as he placed a forkful of fish in his mouth.

"This is without doubt one of your finest meals," he was saying, or something to that effect when, without warning, he began coughing as though something was stuck in his throat. He coughed and coughed and soon no noise came out of his mouth. My mother and I both looked at him expectantly, waiting for him to clear his throat. But he did no such thing. He put one hand up to his mouth and made a gasping noise as he tried to pull in air. Then he grabbed his throat with the other hand. He tried to say something, but it was so garbled we couldn't understand him though we grasped the fact that he was choking.

This was long before the Heimlich maneuver had been devised. We sat transfixed, staring at him helplessly, thinking we should do something, but unable to articulate what that something was.

Finally, my mother stumbled over to Nelson's chair and began to vigorously slap his back, which seemed only to make matters worse. He looked terrified; his eyes were wide and wild, his face pallid and damp. He clutched at my mother, clearly imploring her to help him, but she seemed paralyzed now that her feeble attempts to rescue him had failed. I was equally petrified and seemed incapable of moving.

"What should we do?" I screamed, hoping that just this once my mother would rise to the occasion and solve the problem.

She just shook her head back and forth, her mouth open and slack, her eyes glued to Nelson's face, her hands waving uselessly in the air. He tried to grab her again, but she pulled back from him as though he were a devil trying to pull her into his web of sin.

"No, no, I can't help you," she screamed, "I don't know what to do. I don't know, I don't know..." she keened over and over again, still backing up from him.

By now, Nelson's face was contorted, his skin turning from a dull, pasty color to a slowly emerging blue pallor around his lips. Terrified, his face was frozen in fear. Finally, in desperation, I jumped up, pushed my mother out of the way, and began to shake him violently in the hope that somehow this would dislodge what I assumed was a bone stuck in his throat. But this had no effect on him except to make him look even more panicked. It seemed as though hours had gone by, though in fact it could not have been more than a minute or so. Pushing my fear aside, I tried to pry his mouth open with my fingers to see if there was anything obvious that I could pull on, but I found nothing.

Now his eyes were bulging. I turned my face away; I found it unbearable to watch him. I somehow ended up on my hands and knees crawling from the room, anything to get away from his horrific face. My stomach was churning wildly, and I tried to fight the nausea but could not stop myself from being sick on the carpet outside the dining room.

My last memory of that night was of my mother slumped in a chair near Nelson's inert body, her head down and her hands over her head. The silence in the room was perhaps the most disturbing thing. There was no sound coming from Nelson and none from my mother. The two of them were shrouded in silence. I was incapable of speaking.

I eventually staggered into my bedroom and threw myself onto the bed, where I sobbed uncontrollably until I finally fell into an exhausted sleep. My mother must have eventually called someone because I heard voices and scuffling long into the night, and when I awoke the next morning, unbelievably, all traces of Nelson were gone.

Someone had cleaned up the carpet where I had been sick, the dining room had been cleared of dishes, the kitchen was completely straightened up, and Nelson was just simply—not there.

Implausibly, for years to follow, my mother and I never once spoke of the events of that night. Not once. When people question me about this, I cannot explain it except to say that neither of us could bear to bring up the subject. There was a funeral and a small wake, and a flurry of phone calls from relatives and friends stunned to hear that Nelson had passed away at such a relatively young age. But my mother never uttered a word to me about what had happened that night, nor did I ever broach the subject again myself, so it lay between us like a festering sore that never heals.

It was another one of those memories that we shared only because of our physical proximity, not because we had connected in any meaningful way. It was many years before she would revisit the events of that night.

The cause of death was listed simply as "asphyxiation during meal." When people asked Marlena how Nelson had died, she always said that he had choked on a fish bone and that she preferred not to discuss it. Everyone always presumed it was too painful for her to recount the details and immediately backed down. And that was the end of it. That was also the end of my elaborate meal preparations and obviously the end of the arrangement between Nelson and me. It was also, concomitantly, the final nail in the coffin of my innocence.

I stayed in Nelson's home with my mother for another six months after that, then headed off for college, which was paid for by some money he had left to me in his will. I was always stunned that he had taken the time to remember me in that way. Strangely, he ended up providing for me better than my parents had, and I remained grateful to him for the decency of that small kindness. After all, in the end, who is to say that Nelson was more depraved than I?

I knew that in his own twisted way he respected me, despite the fact that he had used me. I also knew that on some extremely subtle level I was responsible for his death, I just couldn't figure out what that level was. I knew that on the face of it, I was not to blame, and yet something inside of me remained unquiet.

But it depresses me to think of Nelson again and the whole sordid fish story. Perhaps I should move on to a more pleasant topic that has nothing to do with taste buds. I'm sure I can find one buried in there somewhere. Time to dust out some of the more remote, unused corners of my mind, places where no broom has been in years.

The collision of my life with Nelson's pushed me onto a path I might not have chosen without him. Unwittingly, he gave me a taste of some of the finer things—things I probably would not have had access to without him. Post-Nelson and post-university, I became a connoisseur of fine foods, fine wines, and stylish clothes, and I developed an appreciation for the beauty of textiles and fabrics. I came to recognize good art and well- crafted writing. In short, the liberal arts college education that Nelson paid for so dearly had fulfilled its goal. I was ready to unleash myself upon an unsuspecting world.

The net effect of all of this rehashing of the Nelson years has finally taken its toll, and I find myself—at four a.m.—drifting back into a much needed, richly deserved sleep. Not yet the sleep of the dead, but close to it.

Chapter 2

SMELL

Seattle rain has a habit of pelting down on the roof—not just a coherent drip-drip- drip, the way it might sound in California, but a heavy, smacking, forceful sound, as though it wants to pierce right through the shingles and enter the room. Out of the corner of my bedroom window I can see that the late afternoon sky has turned to a murky, pewter color, and, along with the sky, my thoughts begin to darken. I can hear Lisa stirring in the kitchen and think I can detect the aroma of freshly brewed coffee, a smell that I used to adore but which now has a tendency to make me feel nauseated.

Why she's making coffee at this hour, I couldn't say. Certainly not for me, that much I can tell you. As for nausea, chemotherapy has that effect on you: a certain residual metallic taste that lingers in your mouth long past the time when it first filters into your blood. Laila has been giving me pills that deliver the toxic potion to me systemically. I prefer it to the intravenous method, so I don't complain.

Lisa suddenly pokes her head around the partially opened door. "Olivia, can I get you some coffee?" she asks cheerfully.

I take note of her carefully coordinated taupe outfit, the layered look at its best, thinking how like a Doctor's wife she looks. I also take note of the fact that she is clearly trying to be nice to me.

"No, thank you, dear," I say in my most courteous voice, "I couldn't keep it down if I tried. Maybe some milk if you've got it?"

"Milk it is. Let me get it for you," she says, her tone as civilized as mine.

A few minutes later she reappears, milk in hand. "How are you feeling today, any better?"

I debate whether I should tell her how I really feel or simply deliver the sanitized version. Choosing to be magnanimous, I opt for the latter. "Oh, not so bad, every day is a new adventure, I guess. It's kind of you to ask, though. I do appreciate the thought."

I impress myself with the faux graciousness. Even Lisa seems surprised that I have said something so genteel. She raises an eyebrow in silent response, then takes up the thread of the conversation. "Is the milk because your stomach is still upset from your chemotherapy?"

"I assume that's the problem," I respond noncommittally, thinking to myself how little appetite I have for repartee at the moment, especially with my daughter-in-law— though to be fair, she's behaving rather well today.

Sensing my lack of enthusiasm, Lisa starts to back out of the room. "Well, I was going to heat up some left-over lasagna for your dinner, since Louise isn't here today, but if you're not interested…?"

I suddenly remember being told that Louise is off on Thursdays, hence the appearance of Lisa. "I think I'll pass on the lasagna. It's sweet of you though, but don't bother with my dinner tonight. Go on home, be with your family. I'll manage, really," I say, as congenially as I can muster. "I'll fix myself a snack later, something that appeals to me."

"Okay, then. But don't tire yourself out too much," Lisa says, looking relieved. "I'll be by tomorrow to check up on you. Maybe I'll bring Tad along with me. He keeps saying he wants to see you."

"I'd love to see Tad, hear how's he's getting on with school. Tell him I miss him too. He's so grown up these days…" I say ruefully, unable to think of anything else to say to promote our discourse.

Lisa seems amazed that we are even having this conversation. "I know, I can't get over it myself. I wish I could keep him in a bottle; if I had my way, he'd stay our baby forever, but I guess that's not very realistic, is it?"

I shake my head in agreement, understanding her desire to freeze the present.

"If only it worked that way." I say. "I'd bottle up everything, everyone, but I'm a little late to the game. I should have started long ago." Lisa stares at me and I meet her gaze. We are both thinking similar thoughts, our minds jumping to the chasm between us that we never discuss. This is as close to a real conversation as we have had in years, but neither of us has the energy or the nerve to continue it.

"Yes, well, these are problems we can't solve today," I say, rather cryptically, sinking further into the bed and longing for solitude and a stomach that doesn't flutter every ten seconds. The very presence of Lisa always makes me feel guilty, and I find myself hoping for her quick departure so that I am not forced to confront the roots of my remorse.

"Okay, tomorrow then; we'll both come over." With that, Lisa turns abruptly, partially closing my bedroom door behind her.

I hear a few more random noises in the kitchen, probably dishes being put away, then the sound of the front door closing with a distinct thud.

The silence slowly sweeps over me, both friend and enemy. I welcome it, and I fear it, all at the same time. But this evening it seems more benign than usual, and I decide to embrace it.

My choices now seemed limited: I could read—my favorite pastime—but that would probably irritate my eyes and put me straight to sleep. I could watch TV, but the thought of some cheerful sitcom with a laugh track makes my stomach feel even more acrid. I could sleep (perchance to dream?), but then I would most likely wake up at some ungodly hour in the middle of the night and wish to hell I had waited for a proper bedtime. Faced with no pleasant choices, I finally opt for just plain vegetating—my default mode. Perhaps I should take up my review of the senses, I think to myself. After all, I suppose it's encouraging that I can still smell anything at all, even if *it does* make me feel nauseous. In its own way, it could still be seen as a positive sign, given my deteriorating state.

I make a conscious effort to organize my thoughts. Think back, I tell myself; what do you remember?

On reflection, I can remember a bouquet of smells and scents and fragrances and even the occasional stench over the span of my lifetime. I read once that smell is the strongest sense tied to memory and, when I let my mind meander backward like this, I believe it. I think it must be true that this is the most evocative of all the senses.

I vividly recall the smell of our garden—Charlie's and mine—when we were still young enough and strong enough to tend it. We had deep red Diva roses with such a heady scent that when the windows were open, you could smell them from inside the kitchen. The night-blooming jasmine that had attached itself to the trellis in the backyard made you swoon, it smelled so strong and sweet.

Then there was the herb garden on the side of our house. We used to snip the rosemary to cook with lamb or chicken, and the sharp, spicy scent would cling to our hands for hours. We would cut fresh basil for our pasta. I loved the feel of its soft waxy leaves. The pasta always tasted fresher and more "Italian" that way—the Italian part was for Charlie, not me, but I came to appreciate the fine romance of Italian cooking just by loving Charlie as I did.

"You smell like Genoa," he would say when I was chopping garlic and basil. We used to vacation in Italy when we were younger. When we were just starting out, we would go to Rome and Florence. Later, we became more eclectic and went to smaller places like Perugia and Cortona. We loved the ancient untouched villages so impossibly perched on the angled rocks, with their steep stairs and terraced gardens. All of Italy seemed to us to smell of bread baking in the oven and herbs drying on a sunny countertop.

Lake Como was our favorite place by far, though you could hardly call it an eclectic selection. It was like one of those velvet paintings brought to life—the ridiculously cerulean lake, the ring of majestic mountains around it, the pudgy white clouds, the slightly tart smell of the water and the foliage mingling together in the heavy air—heavy because it always seemed to rain just the perfect amount in the late afternoons. The air would be misty and thick and smell like greenery. Better wordsmiths than I have described it, but we always thought it was the most beautiful place on earth.

But back to my garden. The lavender we had planted so lavishly in the front yard by the porch always made me think of Provence and the perfumes from that magical place called Grasse, high in the hills overlooking Nice. Just the mention of Provence catapults me through memories of a French countryside in bloom, a marketplace redolent with the sharp odors of fish and cheese and tart citrus. The smells of France could form an entire novel unto itself; they are stored in an easily accessible portion of my brain. Is there anyone more attuned to the senses than the French? Possibly, but not easily found.

I can still remember the smell of my son's hair and skin when he was young, signaling an inexplicable promise of youth that would last forever. I remember the fresh powder smells of my family's laundry, the rich aromatic meals I would cook, the antiseptic smell of tiny wounds being cleansed, the smell of just-blown-out candles at a birthday party.

And I remember how much I liked the way Charlie smelled. Not sour and sharp like other men; he had a salty, piquant kind of smell that I found enchanting. That must be the universal sign that you're in love when you like the way your lover smells when you bury your head in his shirt or his armpit or his chest—something to do with pheromones, no doubt.

Charlie was a tall man with broad shoulders, dark eyes, and a healthy head of brown hair. He was athletic and insisted on running to keep his weight down. I, on the other hand, found exercise distasteful and succumbed to his influence only occasionally, which always amused him. He was a generous man, both with his money and his affections. He loved to take me in his arms and kiss me for no particular reason, just because we were there. He had an appreciation for the present moment. It didn't matter if we were doing something special or doing absolutely nothing, as long as we were together he thought we were having the time of our lives. And we were, there was no question. I loved everything about him. And he was just as besotted with me. It was the one thing I got right in my life. Nothing and no one ever came between us. Nothing— until his accident; and that was the single thing we were both powerless against.

But I digress. Thinking about Charlie only makes my throat constrict and my heart pound. But then everything reminds me of him, so I suppose it's best if I try to change my focus. But don't be surprised if I veer back this way.

So where was I? Ah, the sense of smell.

I remember when Brian and Lisa got married, Lisa carried gardenias in her bouquet, and their strong, powerful fragrance clutched at my heart, pulling me back to the funeral home when my mother was laid to rest. That day at Brian's wedding, I ping-ponged back and forth between happiness and grief, caught in the vortex of other bittersweet memories. Gardenias, with their heavy perfume, have always reminded me of both weddings and funerals. It's a sensation that lingers in my mind. It makes me think of my own funeral, my own death, my own decaying ripeness. I feel a hint of nausea as my thoughts cascade over this pungent flower and the emotions it always extracts from me.

I remember, too, the smells of all the animals I have had in my life. There was not a one of them I didn't love fiercely for its sweetness and innocence. Before I got sick, I would often graze my face along the silky fur on top of Merlin's head on a hot day and notice the way it reeked of sunshine or ozone or whatever it is that reminds one of burning sidewalks and sandy beaches. I don't seem to avail myself of that pleasure nearly as much as I used to, and yet it's always there for the taking.

I had so many animals over the years, and each one touched a separate piece of my heart—though Merlin may well be my favorite cat, probably due to his Cheshire smile and his slanted blue eyes. At this rate, it's clear he's going to outlive me, There's a fine statement: my days are numbered, but Merlin's will stretch out languorously for years to come, assuming of course that Brian tends to him properly, which is another conversation I need to have with him. But that's too depressing a trajectory. I prefer to think back on all the animals I have known, not a one of which has ever disappointed me—something I can hardly say for the humans in my life.

I remember the song about Bo Jangles and how his dog "up and died" and how "after 20 years he still grieved." *Only 20*, I always thought?

I miss them all, every one of them, and wish I could hold them close to me again, my head nuzzled against their velvety ears, breathing in their rich flavors. I thought every one of them smelled delicious, and I love to pretend that they will be waiting for me when I die, padding softly over that ridiculous "rainbow bridge" that they like to talk about in Hallmark cards and at veterinary clinics. I don't care about the bridge or the rainbow, but I hope they all start running towards me when the time comes and jump into my arms. Ah, to hold them all next to me again. That must be part of heaven; it simply has to be. I like to believe that—it comforts me to believe it.

I remember the way Charlie would smell after working all afternoon in the garage on some carpentry project—a sticky, tart, musty smell that I found strangely attractive. But as I said before, I liked pretty much everything about Charlie, so it's hardly surprising that I liked the way he smelled even after he was working. He always smelled like a man I could love. To this day, I have kept his shirts in my closet because even after being freshly washed there is still some trace of him that I find there that brings him wafting back to me. When he first passed away, like many a widow before me, I would bundle up one of those shirts, put it next to me on the pillow, and imagine him next to me—all the while weeping into the fabric until every crease became damp. Just thinking of it now makes me yearn to hold him again and makes the tears spring up in my tired eyes. Oh, Charlie, how is it possible that you're gone?

Of course, there is no point in asking that question. But I must ask Laila to bring me one of his shirts. I had forgotten how they comforted me when I was at my worst. And what better time to pull him close to me than now, when I am approaching my final destination? I could wrap myself in those old memories and maybe feel his strength flowing into my limbs. He helped me then; perhaps he can still help me now. Perhaps only the dead can help me. Such a dismal thought.

I suppose it is inevitable if I'm to have a discussion of the sense of smell that I come around to the subject of my mother's death. It's just that the whole thing seems so tawdry, so cartoonish, I shudder at the thought of going there, but every sign points in that direction.

First, you have to understand Marlena—if this is even possible. She was such a strange soul. Even if she was my mother, I need to say that. Certainly, I loved her in my way—the same way that all children find a way to love their mothers—but I cannot say that we were close or that we relied on each other or even that we trusted each other, because that would simply not be true. I believe that she loved me, but I think she needed me more than she loved me—which is much the way I think she felt about my father. Nor can I say that there was much overt affection between us. There was a blood bond, and a familiarity bond, but I'm not sure much else kept us tied together.

She was always distant, aloof—with everyone, not just with me. She was one of those people who felt that they had been cheated in life and that the inherent unfairness of it all was a great burden on her. My father felt that burden and tried to carry it but, having neither the moral nor physical strength to keep lifting, he just collapsed under the sheer weight of her neediness.

Marlena was always on the outside looking in; she never felt that she had a seat at the table. And yet that was not strictly true because, in fact, her life had not been so very terrible on the face of it. The problem was that it felt terrible to her, and that was all that mattered.

She felt that she never got the love or respect that she deserved, and she held it against the universe. When I was born, I think she thought that I would be her savior, would bring her into the "club" she so longed to join. Now she had a daughter, a comely one at that, and it should have brought her some joy, some connectivity, some camaraderie; but I never felt those things from her. Not that she didn't love me, because she did, in a desperate sort of way; but she often saw me as an adversary, occasionally as a threat, and, on a few occasions, as an enemy. I think the one person she adored in her life was her father, and he had died young when she was in her twenties, so he remained almost a fictional figure in her life, yet an important one. No one else ever came close to filling her elusive need to be loved.

When I watched my father and mother together, it was the antithesis of what a young girl wishes for in her parents. They were sullen with each other, rude, demanding, unchivalrous, and selfish. The only thing they seemed united on was their mutual grievance against the world. My father always thought he got a "raw deal" (that was the way he always put it), and my mother saw her fate linked to his. I'm not sure why they thought they should have had some dispensation from the hardships of life, which, after all, most people suffer, but they believed that life had treated them badly, and that was the end of it. There could be no happy conclusion to their story. How could there be? If you were cheated and robbed from the get-go, what satisfaction could you possibly have?

They both shared this self-fulfilling prophecy and lived their years believing that they would never get what was coming to them, only the dregs, the leftovers, the hand- me-downs. Just describing them disheartens me. I often wonder how I managed to lift myself out of their melancholia. But I did; I broke free. Still I see tinges of them in me. Whenever dark parts of my mind surface, I ascribe it to them. Their mental imprints, their taboos inhabit some corner of my mentality. But for the most part, I have managed to keep them at bay.

After my stepfather Nelson died, and I went off to school, my mother was forced to create a new life for herself. However, the new life wasn't very different from the old one. Its only notable feature was the absence of Nelson. She collected his pension and social security check with great relish, so it wasn't as though she was out on the street. But she stayed on in that dreary house that held so many unpleasant memories for both of us. I can remember the conversations we had during this dismal period.

One day, when we were sitting in her living room, I said, "Why don't you just sell this place and move into a one-bedroom condo, or get a small apartment on the other side of town?" She'd been there for many years at this juncture.

"Now why would I do that?" she asked, scowling at me. "It would be nothing but trouble and a lot of extra expense. Do you think I'm made of money?" she said rhetorically. "Forget it. Besides, I have everything I need here. And, by the way, since when are you interested in my living situation?"

As usual, she was missing the point that I was trying to be helpful. But I went on. "Well, things are looking pretty dismal here. You've always got the drapes shut, you barely turn on any lights, the furniture is getting dingy, the…"

"Well, listen to Miss Uptown, then!" she interrupted me. "What—is this place not good enough for you now? Maybe you don't like the décor anymore? It seemed to suit you just fine when you lived here with Nelson and me and when you were always buying new clothes and new scarves and new shoes. It was good enough for you then, wasn't it?"

This too seemed like a rhetorical question, and I saw no percentage in answering it. Also, I was beginning to see that no good would come from expanding this conversation.

"Things might be a sight better," my mother continued, "if you hadn't seen the need to polish off my husband, the only one paying the bills around here…"

There, she had said it—for the first time—unbelievably, considering that it had been years since Nelson died.

The silence hung heavily between us for a moment.

Finally, I looked at her sharply. "You know that was an accident. We both know it. You can't possibly think otherwise." I said this uneasily, shocked and unnerved that she had brought it up after all the time that had passed.

"Do I?" she said softly, cocking her head at me, her eyes narrowing.

I felt my face flushing uncomfortably. "Yes, of course, you do! We all ate the same thing that night. How was I to know he would choke on a fish bone? It could have been me; it could have been you…it should have been no one at all. You can't believe that I had anything to do with it! It was just a tragic accident; that's all – a terrible accident! Nothing more."

I felt out of breath. "And since you bring the subject up," I went on, "why didn't *you* call someone? Why didn't you know what to do? I was young, what did I know about such things? You were the adult. You should have done something. You should have saved him. You did absolutely nothing. You just sat there moaning uselessly. Why was that *my fault*?"

"All I know is that things weren't so bad with Nelson," Marlena pouted, ignoring all of my questions, as was her usual wont. "At least, I had some security and someone to talk to occasionally—at least, I had a *husband,* lived like other people live, had some affection, and then you just had to make it all disappear, didn't you?" Her face had darkened.

"Mother, I can't believe you're saying any of this to me! Aside from the fact that I had nothing to do with his death—short of simply being in the room when he died—I never got the impression that you even liked Nelson, let alone loved him, so let's not play the hearts and flowers card too much."

"What the hell do you know about it, hmm? I liked him just fine!" she fumed. "He was my husband, not yours though you sometimes seemed to act as though he was yours, with all your flirty little ways. Don't think I never noticed, because I did."

I was shocked into silence for a moment and could feel my face reddening again. Finally, I said, "I can assure you, I was not 'flirting' with Nelson, and had no designs on him. What a ridiculous thing to say." I wondered vaguely if my discomfort was as obvious to her as it was to me. "He's the last man I would have wanted as my husband, make no mistake," I added, narrowing my eyes at her.

I secretly wondered just how much she knew, but my instincts told me that Nelson would never have revealed his actions with me to her, so I kept my silence. No point opening doors that had been long shut. Some secrets are meant to be kept.

"Well, something was going on there. I don't claim to know what it was, but I know this much—you were more than happy to spend his money—going to that fancy school, pretending that you were interested in getting an education—all of that stuff. That money could have been mine, should have been mine..."

"Ahh, so *that's* what this is about!" I said, suddenly understanding everything more clearly. "Silly me. Well, it's nice to know you begrudge me an education and are jealous that your husband left me a little money. That's very maternal of you. Why am I not surprised?" I said, pursing my lips together as though there were something bitter in my mouth.

"Olivia, sometimes I can't stand the sight of you. Just leave, why don't you?"

"Gladly, Mother. Have a nice evening," I shouted over my shoulder as I slammed the front door.

This was the tenor of our relationship. It had always been so, and time had done little to change it.

We didn't speak to each other for several months after that. Then I remember I drove by her house one spring evening when the trees were just beginning to bloom. I noticed an older, fairly beaten-up white sedan parked in her driveway, covered with blossoms that must have blown off the trees in the high wind. I didn't think much of it until I drove by a second time a few days later and saw the same car, again parked in her driveway, still covered in blossoms, as though it had been there for some period of time. I filed this away in my mental notebook but said nothing to her about it.

When Mother's Day rolled around, I relented and picked out a fairly generic greeting card, wrote "Love, Olivia" under the saccharine sentences on the card, and mailed it. I followed it up a few days later with a phone call, telling myself that it was time to break the silence. She was, after all, the only mother I had.

"Hi, Mom, how are you?" I started out innocuously enough, hoping futilely that she wouldn't make things too awkward, yet knowing full well that she would.

"I'm just fine, Olivia, thanks for asking," she said in a mildly sarcastic tone, which I decided to ignore rather than challenge.

"So what's new in your life, Mother? Got any new friends?" "What makes you ask such a thing?"

"Well, I had occasion to drive by your house a few times and I…" "And you couldn't bring yourself to ring the bell?"

"No, what I was going to say is that I was on my way to a friend's house both times and couldn't stop, but I did notice a white car in the driveway. Is someone visiting you these days?"

"Not that it's any of your concern, but yes, I have had a friend visiting recently. What of it?"

Marlena's tone seemed somehow defiant, as though she was waiting for me to argue with her. But I restrained myself, instead saying, "Well, that's good. It's nice that you have some companionship. We all need someone to talk to occasionally. What's her name?" I said.

My mother hesitated. "It's not a her; it's a him, and his name is Albert." "I see—Albert. Well, where did you find this Albert?"

"I met him at church, and he's turned out to be a very good friend. We have a lot in common, Albert and me. And besides, he's taken care of some repairs around the house, so he's been quite helpful. He's done some painting, patched up some of the walls, you know, that kind of thing..."

"Really? A friend named Albert who fixes the house during the day and visits you in the evenings then?"

"Olivia, I refuse to have this conversation with you. You are hardly my keeper, nor do I owe you any explanation besides what I've already told you," she said, her voice tightening with each word.

"No need to raise your voice, Mom, I get it. It's your business, of course, I was just curious, that's all."

"Well, be curious on your own time," she said sharply.

"So when do I get to meet this Albert, or is that not part of the plan?"

"You'll meet him when I'm good and ready; that's when. Anyway, so nice of you to call every year or so. But I've got to get going. Bridge, you know."

"Yes, bridge. Okay, Mom, have it your way. Maybe we can have a meal together one of these days."

"Fine, let's do that. Only let me do the cooking this time," Marlena said, twisting the knife just slightly as she hung up.

After that conversation, we saw little of each other for the next six months. I would make the occasional perfunctory call, ostensibly to see if all was well, but really more to make sure that some small, albeit rudimentary, line of communication stayed intact between us.

I went to her house at Christmas, and she did indeed cook a meal—and a good one at that—which surprised me, but not nearly as much as the fact that the elusive Albert had also been invited. I had not expected that he would still be part of the landscape, but there he was, perched on the living room couch, looking fairly comfortable.

The mysterious Albert was of medium height, stockily built, with thinning brown hair and soulful dark brown eyes. He was much younger than my mother—possibly in his forties, whereas she was in her mid-sixties by then. I would guess he was Hispanic or maybe Middle Eastern, but while he had a slight accent, I couldn't quite manage to identify his ethnicity. Not that it mattered to me one way or the other, but my mother had always been, shall we say, "socially challenged"—not one to associate with people outside of her immediate circle—which had always been remarkably narrow. So I was surprised on several levels.

He seemed pleasant enough, stood up when I came into the room, introduced himself, shook my hand and pulled the chair out for me when I sat down at the dining room table. He participated minimally in the conversation, making ancillary remarks, agreeing with things my mother said, throwing in a line or two of explanation here and there, but overall, he was noticeably subdued and seemed to defer to my mother. He seemed intimidated by me, or, at least, that's the way I interpreted his behavior.

We managed to get through the meal without incident, all of us obviously on our best behavior and trying hard to get along with one another, it being Christmas and all.

My mother had cleaned up the house for the occasion, built a nice fire in the fireplace (or probably had Albert do it), and the place was bright, warm and inviting, in contrast to its usual drab appearance. We talked mainly about the food, the weather, and my new job as an editor at a fashion magazine—something I was inordinately proud of, but which they seemed completely disinterested in, so I finally just stopped talking about it.

I wanted to ask Albert what he did for a living but couldn't find a suitable way to bring it up, so I left it alone, nor did he volunteer anything that might have helped me put two and two together.

I bowed out early, having an uneasy feeling about the evening without being able actually to pinpoint any one thing. As I drove away, leaving Albert and my mother together in Nelson's old house, I felt something discordant and unsettling, but I shrugged it off and drove back to my cozy place and my increasingly pleasant life.

I did not see my mother again until Easter though we occasionally spoke on the phone—always superficially—what's new? Nothing; how do you feel? Fine—that sort of thing. This particular Easter she invited me to come for a special dinner of lamb stew and potato pancakes, a dish she had clearly perfected, much to my surprise, given her natural reluctance to cook. I had not yet met Charlie at this point, but I was seeing a man, so I brought him along, just to run interference and perhaps hoping to smooth over the awkwardness that had developed between my mother and me.

When we arrived, Albert was there and, as before, he was appropriately polite, though it was not clear to me what role he saw himself playing. I assumed that my mother had invited him because it was Easter and she thought it was a nice thing to do.

At some point my date—Robert I think his name was—casually turned to Albert and said, "So what do you do, Albert, to make ends meet?"

"Oh, I'm between jobs right now—construction jobs. You know how that is. Still looking, though, always looking, right?"

"Right," Robert agreed, casting a glance at me.

I felt nervous in my mother's home, as though it was a foreign place where I did not belong. Stranger in a strange land, I thought to myself. At some point, I excused myself and wandered down to what was now the guest bathroom, the one that had been hers and mine so many years ago.

Once inside, I saw the old bathtub that I used to bathe in, and all the memories came flooding back to me. I saw myself in the white bathrobe, the scent of lavender in the air, Nelson's eyes boring into me; I saw the crisp bills tucked inside my pocket. I felt the shame wash over me, a feeling I hadn't had in so many years. A wave of distaste came over me as I remembered our tawdry dalliances. What was I thinking then? More to the point, what was *he* thinking?

I shook my head in an effort to clear the murky soup of memory from my mind. I moved to the sink and began to splash cold water onto my face, hoping to snap myself back to reality.

As I looked at the sink, I noticed a man's razor dangling from the toothbrush holder that was attached to the wall. I noiselessly pried open the medicine cabinet. It was filled with men's deodorant, shaving cream, razor blades and the like. I snickered to myself. So he's moved in, has he? Well, that's a cozy little set-up. The old lady and the young stud, is that what we're featuring here now? Is that the matinee? The thought of my mother and this man together in Nelson's house, in her bedroom, struck me as so wrong, so degrading.

But then I checked myself, thinking: I'm a fine one to talk about degrading. Prostitution comes in many forms, remember? Live and let live. And why was I so judgmental? Must be something deep and primal having to do with children and their parents—something I didn't feel like exploring at that point in time. I tucked it away in a corner of my mind to be retrieved at some later date and said nothing to my mother.

We finished the meal and after a decent interval said our goodbyes and left.

Life reeled forward after that, with my mother keeping to herself for the most part.

We mended our relationship to the extent that we resumed being civil with each other, and as long as I didn't question her about her living situation, she remained relatively benign. Life as we had known it finally resumed without incident.

Shortly after our reconciliation I met Charlie, and from that point on, he was all I could think about. My life seemed to expand to the point where every conceivable inch of space and oxygen was taken up by him. I forgot about my friends, my co-workers, my mother, Albert; they all just faded into the background. Charlie became my universe. I was thirty-two years old, and I was head over heels in love. Could anything else have mattered? Right or wrong, it did not.

Eventually, I decided it was time to introduce him to my mother— not something I was looking forward to, just something proforma that had to be done. I called her up, gave her the broad strokes of our relationship, and suggested that she come to my apartment for dinner to meet Charlie.

"I assume Albert is welcome as well," she said assertively when I broached the subject of dinner.

"Well, yes, I suppose…" I said, feeling annoyed that she felt the need to bring Albert with her. "What's going on with you two, anyway? I mean, this can't really be a serious relationship—or is it?"

I could sense my mother bristling, and could literally feel the negative charge in the air at the other end of the phone.

"I'd say that's none of your business, Missy. You've got your life; I've got mine. Let's leave it that way. If you want me to meet this new man of yours, fine, but I hope he knows he's getting a real snob and a busybody in the bargain. A busybody who has very little time for her mother, but plenty of time for her new romance. That's about the size of it, isn't it?"

"Nice, Mom, really nice. Do you think you could ever say something supportive about me? Or would that be too much to ask? It's a wonder I have any confidence at all, the way you treat me. And by the way, I am neither a snob nor a 'busybody,' as you call it. It's just that your relationship with Albert strikes me as pretty bizarre and…"

"Why bizarre? Because he's younger than me? Is that all you've got? How incredibly trite. Please tell me what that's got to do with anything?"

"Alright, touché, forget about the 'younger' part. How about the fact that he has no job—and he's living off of you?"

"First of all, you don't know anything about it. And second of all, even if it's true, what's it to you? What makes you think you can judge me just because I'm trying to get a little pleasure out of my life. Don't I deserve that? Haven't I suffered enough? Haven't I been alone long enough, thanks to you?" She let the sentence hang in the air for a moment, then continued. "He likes being with me, and I like the company. It's no skin off your nose, so leave it alone, Olivia. Just leave it alone, you hear me?" By now she was practically hyperventilating.

I took a moment to gather my increasingly defensive thoughts and then tried— somewhat in vain—to temper them in an effort to get through the conversation. "I hear you, Mother, alright? Calm down. Sure, fine, your business. Let me just say one more time, I did *not* kill your husband, as you insist on insinuating, and I'm tired of your trying to lay this guilt at my feet. I'm not taking it on, simple as that. I am not personally responsible for the vagaries of the world. So please—think what you want and do what you want, but don't expect me to cater to this guy or treat him like some member of the family. He's not and never will be. Capiche?"

Marlena's mood had darkened, both at the tone and the content of my speech. "Don't be too sure about that. He'll be whatever I want him to be. And I expect you to treat him with respect or you're really going to hear about it from me. And don't you think I can't make your life miserable because I can..."

I forced myself to take a deep breath and reminded myself that it was best if we both left each other's choices alone. Besides, why did it annoy me so much? She wasn't bothering anyone with her lifestyle, not even me, if I was honest. Why on earth was I so agitated by all of this?

I sighed deeply, my frustration evident, and forced myself to lower my voice. "Okay, Mom, have it your way. There's no problem. I accept your decisions."

I pushed down my irritation and tried to find a more pleasant tack. Be civil, I told myself. You need to put up with her and then maybe she'll do the same for you. Quid pro quo. "Bring him along, then," I said, "I don't care."

"Alright then," she said quickly rebounding, sounding triumphant, as though she had just won both the battle and the war. "I'm glad we can see eye to eye."

"Yes, eye to eye, that's it, Mom." I gave a final exasperated sigh. "I'll expect both of you at seven o'clock sharp Saturday then."

To make the conversation seem more normal, I added: "I'm

making a roast with finger potatoes. Lemon meringue pie for dessert."

"Fine, we'll be there," Mother said curtly. I could almost see her shaking her head in disapproval though there was really nothing to disapprove of.

And so, that Saturday, we had the requisite dinner party to announce the acquisition of my latest love interest. The evening was strained, much as I had expected. In spite of myself, I secretly longed for my mother's approval, so I wanted everything to be perfect. To cover up my nervousness, I talked too much. At the same time, as usual, I couldn't help wondering why I cared whether she approved of me or not. A daughter's dilemma, ageless but predictable and true.

Albert said almost nothing, content to eat heaping portions of food without comment. Charlie was as charming as was possible under the circumstances and ended up endearing himself to my mother by flattering her and being overly attentive, which of course worked like magic—though I don't know why this surprised me when I thought about it. It was a fairly simple formula for getting along with my mother.

Marlena was openly impressed when Charlie told her that he was a reporter for a well-known magazine. Apparently Marlena believed this gave him a certain cachet (one that I—merely an *editor* at a magazine—apparently did not possess). No doubt she was hoping some of it would rub off on her. I found this highly unlikely under the circumstances, but it was her fantasy, not mine, so I left it alone

. We survived the dinner, and Charlie and I heaved a gigantic sigh of relief after they left.

"Thank God that's over with," I said, putting my arms around his waist and looking proud. "You handled that like a pro. Thank you. Engaging with my mother and her paramour is definitely yeoman's work, and you just took it on."

"Oh, she's not so bad, Olivia. Marlena's a bit of a battle-ax, and difficult to pull out of her shell, but underneath all of that, she's a woman who wants some attention and wants to feel attractive again.

I get it. That Albert's a piece of work, though. I wonder what he gets out of it—besides the obvious room and board. It's not easy entertaining someone like Marlena all day every day. It's not like he goes off to work in the morning. I mean, what on earth do they talk about? What do they do?"

"Damned if I know, and quite honestly, I don't want to think about it. It's a bit too icky if you ask me. I prefer to pretend that it's all platonic. Makes it easier on my imagination," I said, feeling uncomfortable even talking about it, and feeling hypocritical at the same time. Since when was I such a prude, I asked myself, wondering when I had somehow fallen into all of the conventional traps that I had sworn to avoid when I was younger. I sighed, mentally noting that it was time to have a serious conversation with myself—preferably not tonight.

"Let's talk about something more pleasant, like you and me, for example."

"I'm all for it, Liv. You and me; let's talk about us," he said, tickling me gently at my waist and grinning.

In fact, that was the last we spoke of them for quite some time. We were far too immersed in our new love affair to concern ourselves with them. We were like two giddy teenagers, lost in each other, oblivious to the outside world, thrilled with the cocoon we had woven for ourselves.

It was a good four months before I saw my mother again. I called first, then stopped by the house one afternoon on my way home from work. I couldn't help but notice that she looked different somehow. Her face seemed heavier, her eyes more lidded, her skin more sallow. Had she looked like this before? I asked myself. It was hard for me to remember. I knew I had to navigate carefully, or I would bring down her wrath.

"Are you okay, Mom? You look a little tired," I started out tentatively.

"I'm fine. A little rundown maybe, but I'm good. Thanks so much for the compliment. I'm not a kid anymore, you know. Can't expect me to be running around like a twenty-year-old," she said, coughing at the end of her sentence.

"No, of course not. What's up with the cough though, do you have a cold?"

"Oh, I've had some bug on and off for a while now," she said, coughing again. "I can't seem to get rid of it."

"So, go see Dr. Nash, why don't you? Maybe you've got bronchitis-like you used to get when I was younger."

"Maybe so. Could be. Yes, I'll go. But you know, all they do is give you those antibiotics..."

"Well, what's wrong with an antibiotic now and then? Especially if you've got some infection that's making you cough. Go look into it; get rid of it," I said.

"Yes, doctor. I'll get right on that."

"Have Albert take you. He's got the time."

My mother shot me a quick glance to see if this was meant as an attack. She decided to let it go. "I'll ask him. Now leave it alone," she said, coughing again and sounding even worse than before.

***

Marlena eventually recovered from her cold but continued to look worn down and still suffered from the occasional coughing spell. I suppose you have to factor in the reality that she was in her sixties now and not one to avail herself of any of the latest technologies or lotions and potions to help stem the tide of old age.

Seeing her growing older and more frail actually make me feel more sympathetic towards her. Nonetheless, our relationship was as precarious as ever, like walking on river rocks instead of a smooth path.

But by this time, Charlie and I had begun to plan our wedding, and my own narcissism kept me too preoccupied to be concerned with Marlena and her problems. The wedding was nothing too elaborate, but still there were hundreds of details to be taken care of, especially since, in addition to the wedding, we were buying a new apartment for the two of us to start our married life. Between finding a property, securing loans, buying new furniture, sending out invitations, and planning a menu for the reception, we had little time for our usual social interactions.

I would call Marlena occasionally, but as always, my mother wasn't particularly interested in the specifics of my life, including my upcoming nuptials. Nor did she seem enthusiastic about our upcoming union—which didn't surprise me in the slightest, and I didn't even question her as to the details of why that was the case.

And so, I saw very little of her during this period. I preferred to stay out of the range of her negativity. Skies were brighter where I lived, literally and figuratively—it was as simple as that.

Charlie and I swam in a haze of excitement; our minds focused solely on each other and our forthcoming wedded bliss. What with our newly minted lust and the love that came along with it, and the frenzy of all the new feelings and legal documents and possessions, we barely managed to do our professional work, let alone tend to more fragile structures like friendships and relatives.

We squeezed out just enough energy to do our work sufficiently, but it was hardly noteworthy, as far as quality went. I remember thinking, thank heaven for indulgent bosses. Both of our employers cut us enough slack during this period to give us the time we needed, and we took whatever extra time we could wheedle out of them. We would later make up for this, working like dogs for years, but at the time, our work was fairly low on the priority list.

It was without question the happiest time of my life, a period I would look back on in darker times in an effort to try to siphon some of the joy and sweetness of those days into the more bitter times that were to come. But that frenetic chapter of my life with Charlie was arguably the most delicious, sensual, and exquisite of all of them.

I find that my life is easily divided into chapters; isn't everyone's? Some chapters are defined geographically—the move to Washington, or the change of residences, for example. Others are defined by the people in it, and those are undoubtedly the most important and salient ones.

I had those fairly regrettable childhood chapters and the Nelson years, the college chapter, and then the Charlie Years—that was to take up more than half of my life and would include various sub-chapters—like the birth of my son, and others that fell under major headings. In the book of my life, those were the sweetest chapters of all, and in my mind, I marked them with velvet bookmarks, worn down over the years from constant touching. There were dark, grief-filled chapters as well, but they were to come later and were best not revisited.

It was about three weeks before the wedding when it happened.

A fierce storm brewing over the Pacific had come pounding down over Seattle that winter. It included thundering rains, blustery winds, and a gray icy chill that hung over the sky and wouldn't let go. During one of the worst storms, large blocks of houses lost electricity as trees came crashing down, pulling power lines down with them. Crews scrambled to restore the power, but it took days, going into weeks, to fix them all.

Charlie and I got lucky in our separate apartments and managed to avoid the blackouts, but the area where my mother lived was not so fortunate.

I didn't think to call her, though in retrospect, of course, I should have. In fact, in hindsight, there were many things I should have done but didn't. My self-absorption during this time was epic, and in my later years, I came to understand how people can be drawn into a vortex of egocentrism. But I didn't see it then; I can only see it now. And I regret it now. But the die was cast, and in any case, nothing I could have done would have changed the outcome.

But back to the storm. One dark, freezing evening in the middle of this storm, around nine o'clock at night, Albert called me—Albert, who barely had a place card in my mind. He had never called me before, and at first, I didn't realize who he was. His voice sounded strange to me—not so much the accent, but the tone of his voice. He sounded nervous, tense.

"Olivia, it's Albert, you know, Albert—I live with your mother?" he said, by way of identifying himself.

"Oh, okay, Albert. Right. Is there some problem?"

He hesitated. "Yes, there's a problem. I'm not sure how to say this, but I needed to call you," he stammered. "It's about your mother."

"What about my mother?" I said, starting to feel uneasy. My mother—my only mother, who on some level I disliked, but who on some more primal level I still loved and had always loved—as we all love our mothers, no matter what we say.

There was a long pause at the other end of the line. "She's gone."

"What do you mean 'she's gone?' Gone where? Is she missing? Did she leave you?" I asked, my tone betraying my anxiety.

"No," he said slowly. "You don't understand. She's gone from us. She's just gone." "What are you saying, Albert?" I said, my voice rising, my attention now riveted to the phone. "Where is my *Mother*?"

Charlie, who was with me, heard my new intonation and stopped what he was doing. "What's going on?" he said. "Is something wrong?"

"That's what I'm trying to determine," I said to Charlie with an edge to my voice that he rarely heard. I put the phone on speaker so he could hear as well.

"Albert – talk to me!"

After a long pause, he said in a low voice, "She passed away tonight. Your mother is dead."

The silence was palpable as I attempted to digest what he had just said.

"Dead? What do you mean dead? How could she be dead? She wasn't sick; there was no accident. How can she possibly be dead, Albert? What are you talking about?"

Is there anyone on the face of the earth who doesn't say "No, No, that's not possible!" when death is first announced? Isn't denial the universal response? Sadness comes later, but first, we deny, deny, deny, as though saying "No" will somehow undo everything. As though as long as we say "No" we can put ourselves back to the point before which it all happened. No, you didn't say that. No, it didn't happen. No, I am not having this conversation. No, everything is just the way it was before you started talking. And if I keep saying No, it will hold back the tide. And no, my mother isn't dead!

"I'm trying to tell you that there was an accident," he said, now starting to hurry with his words. "Look, I'm going to explain this to you. Your mother—she fell asleep on the couch this afternoon. She had been coughing…It was so damn cold in that house; you know how it was. The power has been out for two days now. All the windows leaked cold air, none of the weather stripping worked. The heater couldn't keep up with it even when it worked. We had been burning wood in the fireplace; then we ran out. We had some charcoal left over from the summer and thought that would help to keep us warm, so we lit some, and she laid down on the couch to take a nap. Then I went out to find some wood and get something for us to eat. It took some time because of the roads and the snow. I never knew it was a problem. I had no idea, I swear to you, I didn't know, I never knew…"

"Didn't know what?" I screamed, my mind not really functioning properly.

"Didn't know it would kill her, that's what! Didn't know about carbon monoxide until they explained it to me. I didn't know! I swear to you! I get home, the fire is out, and it smells really funny, like a barbeque maybe, and I open one of the windows, but I didn't think much of it, and she's still lying on the couch and I go over there to wake her up so we can eat and I touch her, and she's so cold. Then I touch her face, and her face is cold! I can't believe what is happening. I can't believe that she might be dead. I don't know what's happening. Like you, I don't know how it's possible."

When there was no response from me, he took a deep breath, then continued.

"So I don't know what to do—I call 911, and in five minutes three guys show up. They come over and look at your mother and hook her up and try CPR and do all kinds of things to her and keep asking me all these questions, like 'what's in the fireplace,' and 'how long has she been sleeping,' and all of this stuff. They open all the windows and air the place out and start yelling at me about how 'you can't burn charcoal in an enclosed space like that, don't you know that? Haven't you ever heard of carbon monoxide?' They make me sound like a complete idiot, but I didn't know..."

"And I tell them, 'No, I didn't know, or I wouldn't have done it!' And then they're telling me I need to call you and tell you. They say that they will be calling you themselves after they've gotten her to the hospital or morgue or wherever they took her. I don't know. They just took her away. And then they said there would be an autopsy and that the police would be contacting you and talking with me. I don't know what to do. I'm here all alone. I just don't know what to do. They just took her away now. I'm sorry, Olivia, I'm so sorry."

At this point Albert seemed to fall completely apart, having managed to relate this entire tale to me without stopping. Somewhere along the line, I had dropped the phone and never even heard his final whimperings. Charlie found the phone, hung it up without saying a word and took me in his arms.

The rest of this chapter in my life—a separate sub-chapter called

My Mother's Death—is mainly a blur. All of the things that happened were dreamlike. I felt as though I were watching an episode of *Law and Order*—one that I had seen several times before, but through a clouded lens.

My mother was dead. I felt bereft; I felt orphaned, abandoned, and somewhere inside my head I felt guilty, though for what I could not tell you. More than guilty I felt angry—at Albert, at my mother, at myself, at the charcoal. I mentally jumped from target to target, never staying too long with one suspect before moving on to the next.

I wanted to blame someone, and Albert was, of course, the best foil, but somehow I blamed my mother as well. It would be just like her not to know, and just like Albert as well, though I had no real insight into his mind. But I knew my mother. She was not one to pay attention to warnings or read up on things. Perhaps she didn't know. Perhaps he didn't know. The effort of thinking about it constantly exhausted me until I finally stopped and decided to simply accept it for what it was.

What followed was a blur of police reports, autopsy reports, fire investigators, insurance investigators. A thousand questions, a thousand answers—none of them really satisfactory—but they all fell into place like bits of a jigsaw puzzle until all the pieces had been pushed together to form the final picture and the story was simply over— complete with signatures, piles of paperwork and final checks issued to the beneficiaries.

My mother was gone and she was not coming back. End of chapter, end of story, end of her book.

Surprisingly, Marlena had made up a will. Albert—conveniently enough—knew exactly where she kept the will and produced it with a flourish several days after her demise. It looked legal enough, seemed to have her signature on it and had been duly witnessed and notarized, so there was not much I could argue about.

Much to my chagrin, and somewhat to my surprise, Marlena left Albert the house and virtually everything in it that didn't belong to me, which amounted to a few boxes in a closet and some clothes in a dresser. In addition, she had taken out an insurance policy in his name, leaving him $50,000. This last left me breathless; her final act of indifference towards me hurt me to the core. Well played, Mother, I thought. I guess you showed me, didn't you? Or maybe—and more likely—I should congratulate Albert on his quick and efficient work. Good job, Albert. Kudos. You pulled it off, didn't you?

It took some time to probate the estate, but when all of the dust cleared, I inherited about ten thousand dollars from her various accounts and her wedding ring from Nelson, plus a few other trinkets that Albert "graciously" threw my way. That was it.

It felt ironic to have Nelson's ring, but I kept it anyway, tucking it away in an old jewelry box in case I ever found a use for it.

I went so far as to call the insurance company and demand to see a copy of the paperwork, which they did indeed forward to me. The signature looked correct and was duly witnessed, so I had no real recourse. I had seen her sign many documents, and this looked no different than the others. Before issuing the check to Albert they had done their own cursory investigation and concluded that the autopsy finding of

"Death by accidental carbon monoxide poisoning, with underlying COPD" was plausible. They had no reason to take it any further than that. And certainly I had no proof of anything else; I just had this nagging feeling…

Somewhere in me, I was sure I knew the truth. And so did Albert. But I knew there would never be a reckoning. This was just another one of those stories that end badly and leaves a sour taste in your mouth. My mother never saw it coming, but in fact, the day he walked into her life was the beginning of the end—the end of all her chapters. I never spoke to Albert again.

I had Charlie call him and arrange to clear out what few things belonged to me from the house. I purposely took more than I wanted, just to annoy Albert and make life more inconvenient for him. I couldn't stand the sight of him. The day I came to take possession of my belongings, we stared at each other with a palpable hostility, but spoke not a word. I knew what he was, and he knew what he was. What else was there to say?

As I have thought many times, it occurred to me again that prostitution comes in many forms. Is there one of us who has not bent to the task? Perhaps. Someday I would have to ask Charlie this question. I never thought of him in that role, but nothing is impossible in life. Yes, I would have to ask him.

That is what I was thinking as I left Marlena's house so many years ago. I should have been thinking about her—thinking about my mother—thinking about our life together as mother and child, but I wasn't thinking about any of those things. I was thinking about how people use each other and how they step on each other like cobblestones. I was thinking about what a sad and ignoble ending my mother had to her life, and what kind of conclusion I should draw from it. I was wondering if she ever had any real joy in her life, or if it was all just various shades of gray. It was another question that would never be answered.

Somehow it all leaves a terrible taste in my mouth—worse than the metallic after- taste of the IV drip I used to get on Tuesdays, before I switched to pills—and a smell that I cannot identify, but that I know is not pleasant. And somehow, too, I sense that the topic of Smell has come full circle.

Chapter 3

LAILA

Laila is looking after me during these dreadful days. I was lucky to get her, believe me. I knew that I would have an occasional nurse sent to the house through hospice, but I wanted more than that. I called the private agency, and they sent over three different prospects. The first two made me cringe and had me feeling even more depressed than before they came. Both wore starchy white uniforms and squishy shoes. One had even donned the fortune cookie hat for good measure, but it was lost on me. Too rigid, too uptight, too mainstream for my taste. It was no contest.

Laila wore street clothes and approached me very gently but with an inherent dignity that I immediately appreciated. The agency told me she was born in Afghanistan but had been living in the States since she was ten, so her English was fine. She was young, maybe twenty-three, and exotic looking—coffee colored skin, large almond shaped eyes, thick black hair parted in the middle, slight of frame, and she had what looked like light scars or birthmarks on the left side of her face.

These did not bother me in the slightest, but I could tell that she was self- conscious about them by the way she tended to favor her right side when talking. She had a certain gentility about her and a light in her eyes that made me recognize her as someone who is "present" and compassionate. I knew immediately that she was the one for me. I snapped her up before anyone else could hire her and had no regrets then or now. She is a treasure.

Laila has been with me for several months now, and you might think that I barely know her, but you would be wrong. Something about sickness and caring for someone on an intimate basis puts relationships on a fast track in a way that nothing else can. She has bathed me and turned me and stroked me and held me up. More than that, she has talked to me; I know this woman well.

There are some people in life who speak to you in ways that have nothing to do with conversation. She is one of them. I was drawn to her the first time I saw her. She soothes me mentally and physically; the soft tone of her voice calms me. She gives me something to look forward to in the day, and God knows there has been very little else to make me feel that way.

I think it was the third time that she came to the house—after I had finally dissuaded her from calling me "Mrs. Calvert"—that I was able to look more closely at the scars that were usually hidden by her abundant hair. Naturally I said nothing, but I knew there was a story behind them, and I waited for her to find the right time to tell me.

Several days later, to wile away the hours, I asked her to be Scheherazade for me. When I saw the puzzled look on her face, I proceeded to tell her the tale from Arabian Nights of the Persian sultan who believed that all of his wives would be unfaithful to him.

"Each day he would pick a new wife, bed her, then kill her the next morning so that she could never betray him," I told Laila, ignoring the astonished look on her face. "And then one day he picked a beautiful woman named Scheherazade to be his wife, and it turned out that she was far more clever than her predecessors—the ones who came before her. On the very first night that they were together, she skillfully began to weave an elaborate tale that so captivated the king that he allowed her to live for one more day, just so that she could finish her story."

I saw Laila nodding appreciatively and continued. "Of course, one day turned into two, and two into four, and so on. In order to save herself and all the other women who would come after her, she never quite managed to finish her story. And so for one thousand and one nights, she unreeled her tale until finally the king relented and allowed her to live without conditions."

"That's incredible. I had never heard that story before," said Laila, wide-eyed.

"No. I'm sure most girls your age don't know about the Arabian Nights, but my mother told it to me and I think her mother told it to her, so it's been around for many a year. But now the point of all this," I said, rather dramatically, "is not finding foolproof methods of infidelity; it is that I want you to be my Scheherazade. It's a tall order, but now you must follow in her footsteps and tell me tales to distract my weary thoughts— give me something to think about besides myself."

Laila took a moment, then nodded indulgently and said she would try, though she thought it a bit theatrical that she should play the role of a Persian Queen. I pointed out that I loved drama, so there was no problem there. I told her that the melody of her voice pleased me and I was happy to listen to whatever she might conjure up. I said it was unlikely that she would be called upon for the requisite thousand and one nights. She appreciated the irony, which made us both smile.

She began by telling me stories of being raised in Seattle with her adoptive parents: how difficult it was for her to fit in at first, but how much she missed the home they had shared, now that she had her own apartment. She recounted how she had come to love the city, how much she came to admire her new parents, how important it had been to her to get her nursing degree.

Over the weeks, I asked a few leading questions as to how she came to this country, and what her life had been like before, but she always just shook her head quietly and made it clear that she was not ready for such topics yet.

"Perhaps another time," she would say quickly. Then she would push her dark hair to one side and sigh deeply. It was clear that heat and emotion were lying just behind the stone wall of those particular stories. A sadness would come over her, a shadow across her eyes—a sudden glimpse of her discomfort that stopped me from pressing her further. She would stand up and bustle around the room, straightening sheets, fluffing pillows, pouring fresh water, clearly attempting to dispel her feelings by executing mundane chores.

She would chatter then about her high school days, or her nursing school trials, anything but address the subject of her origins. Still the weight of it was palpable. She held it inside, like a dark secret, and I—who had enough secrets of my own—simply waited.

I knew she would eventually share her story with someone, and why not me—a dying lady, not long to keep her secrets, not likely to disperse them far and wide, someone who understood melancholy and loss—surely I was the perfect choice, no?

I waited patiently (for me), thinking to myself that, unlike most people, I really didn't have forever…still, it was her story, not mine, and she, not I, was the keeper of the key.

And then the day came, as I knew it would. I had mumbled something to her by way of a request for water or Kleenex or something pedestrian, and she turned her head so that she was closer to me and said, "I'm so sorry, but I don't hear well on this side. Could you repeat that please?"

"Oh, it was nothing," I said, "I was just looking for something to wipe my forehead with. Not to worry. Which side do you have trouble hearing on?"

"It's my left side," she said. I could see her turning something over in her mind. Finally, she pointed to the skin near her eyes and said, "See the scars here on my forehead?"

"Yes. I see them," I said honestly, "but how are they involved in your hearing?"

I could see her hesitate, as though she had pried open the edge of something without really meaning to do so. "Well, that's quite a long story," she said slowly. "And it's something I don't much like to talk about. It's…well, it's a very painful subject for me, a very private subject."

"I'm sorry, Laila, I'm not trying to push you into anything. You certainly don't have to share it with me—or anyone else for that matter. It's fine, really, I don't mean to meddle," I said, stumbling over myself in an effort to be sensitive to her.

"—No, no, it's not your fault, really it's not," she said rubbing her arms nervously. "I feel so torn about it. I rarely talk about it because it upsets me so, but at the same time, in some strange way, I know that I want to talk about it. I almost long to tell you about it, and I don't know why that would be, although maybe you are the perfect person to tell it to. I keep it so bottled up inside me. But it's not something I can tell to some girlfriend or someone on a plane or some boy on a date. I talk to my parents about it sometimes because they understand—but no one else. It seems like too big a box to open. Do you know what I am saying?"

"Of course, I know. It's Pandora's box and too many demons fly out when you open it up, am I right?" I asked.

"Well, I don't know anything about Pandora but yes, the demons fly out along with all the emotions and all the blackness, and I get too swallowed up in it. And then a depression comes over me, and sometimes it takes days or even weeks for me to find my balance again."

I nodded, all too familiar with the process. "Well, I certainly don't want to be the cause of your depression or sadness, Laila. By all means, keep the box shut if that's what you need to do. We don't have to open it here."

I smiled at her kindly, knowing full well the dangers inherent in trapping deep feelings and captive thoughts and hoping she could find the courage to release her demons. "It's completely up to you. Do whatever makes you feel comfortable…"

She looked at me directly this time with no veil over her eyes. "But maybe we do need to open it—maybe I do. Maybe you're exactly the person I should share it with…"

This seemed to make her blush, as though she realized, as I did, that I was not someone who was likely to be disseminating her story. "Maybe if I opened the box more often it wouldn't hold such power over me," she continued. "Do you think talking about it would bring me some relief?"

"Oh, Laila, I can't say. Sometimes letting your feelings out can be cathartic—do you remember this word?"

"I think you told me once, but tell me again." Laila said.

"Let's see," I paused. "It means that you feel better when you finally express certain strong emotions that you have kept bottled up for a long time."

"So do you think it would work?" Laila looked at me imploringly as though she thought perhaps I could solve her problem.

"I don't know. It might help—or conversely, it might only make you feel worse. It's hard to say. Certainly it won't solve anything to talk about it. But it might take some of the sting out of repressing your feelings all the time. There are no guarantees, though."

Laila looked thoughtful but said nothing. I continued. "Sometimes you tell your story, and it's like reliving everything all over again. If the story is a sad one, it pulls you in, and it can flood you with memories. That's the way I feel when I talk about my husband—Charlie. You've heard me talk about him from time to time, yes?"

Laila nodded assent, and I continued. "On the one hand, I ache to talk about him, because he was the sun and stars to me, and I loved him so, but at the same time, his absence is like a knife in my heart. So which is it, I always ask myself, pleasure or pain?"

I paused for a moment, feeling chilly and pulling my robe more tightly around my shoulders. "Bittersweet is the true answer: a little of both. The rush of adrenaline that floods me when I think of him is usually offset by the realization of how much I've lost now that he's gone. I seem not to be able to have one without the other. So that's the final question to myself: should I never think of him or speak of him, knowing that after the joy comes the sorrow? Or should I accept this as the human condition and consider it the reasonable price of remembering?"

"And what is the answer to that question, do you know?" Laila said looking at me with great concentration.

I took a moment before answering because the question deserved a thoughtful response. Finally, I said: "I think that the memory is too precious, too important, and too authentic *not* to be shared. I think the sorrow is a heavy price, but a fair price, nonetheless. I talk about Charlie because he was real to me and his story is my story as well. I can't just put all my memories in a drawer and never look at them again."

I sighed at the thought. "That would deny his worth to me, and that would be wrong. It would be like hiding every picture of him so that I would not have to feel sad when my eyes swept across them. No, I keep the pictures out. I look at them, I smile when I see them, and sometimes I remember how it felt to be happy. Sometimes the tears well up moments later, but as I said, I cannot seem to have one without the other. So I take my gift and lay down my money. I guess what I'm saying is that it's worth it to me. I cannot speak for you. It's a question you have to answer for yourself."

Laila exhaled, the weight of a thousand thoughts on her breath. "Sometimes I think the things that happened to me were a dream. Sometimes I question whether it really happened at all, but then I look at my skin, I touch my ear, I put my fingers on the scars beneath my hair that you can't even see, and I know that it was no dream. A nightmare maybe, but no dream. I'll try to tell you. I don't know how far I will get today, but I can, at least, begin to show you where I came from."

"Take your time, Laila," I said gently. "Tell me whatever comes to mind, and if you want to stop, just stop. No need to explain."

She nodded gratefully, then perched herself on the edge of the bed, facing me. "I was born in Afghanistan," she began slowly, "in Kandahar province, Panjwai district. It's a poor area, I know that now, but I did not know it then. But no matter, it was home to me and all I knew."

"My father had a food stand—a stall I guess you'd call it here—like many of the people living there, and my mother worked with him cooking the kebabs that they sold on the street. It was nothing fancy, nothing special, but he made a living and supported his family."

"My parents were good people, simple people, and they were kind to me. My father used to call me 'Lida,' which means 'beloved' in Pashto (our language)—and I was. I had an older brother, but he died from some type of infection when he was six. I never knew exactly what it was, but it was always a source of great sadness for both my mother and my father—but especially my father because in our culture it was so important to have an heir to carry on the name. And, well, the truth of it is that boys are always more important than girls in our society."

I nodded ruefully to show that I understood, and she continued.

"We rarely spoke of my brother after that, but he was never far from our thoughts. In any case, life continued after his death, but was never as sweet as it had been before."

"Did you go to a school? I don't really know what's normal over there."

"I did go to a school though sometimes my mother would make me help in the stand when she had errands to run. Then I would miss the classes, but usually, I went. It was my mother more than my father who insisted that I go. The Taliban elders—a few lived near my village—did not like girls attending school. But there was a small unmarked school in my area where ten or so girls showed up every day, despite the Taliban's warnings. We were told not to talk about our school to other people and certainly not to strangers."

"My mother said it was important that I learn to read and write. She wanted that for me even though most girls did not get this opportunity. It was slightly dangerous, and it cost them some extra money, but they sent me anyway. I didn't mind; on the contrary, I liked school and preferred it to the boredom of my chores at home or the food stand. So I got some basic education, even learned some English, which turned out to be fortunate for me in the end."

"But my life was just normal. We were pretty much like any other poor Pashtun family struggling to live, having little in the way of extras in our life, just food and a roof over our head, some heat in the winter, and a few games in the summer."

She paused for a moment, as though to gauge my reaction.

"Go on, Laila; you're doing fine," I said, nodding to encourage her.

"Well, everyone in my village lived this way, so I had nothing else to compare it to. We lived in a compound of sorts—I guess that's what you would call it. There was a large wall surrounding a group of houses—well, they were mud huts more than houses really, and they were very basic, nothing like your houses here. Then there would be another wall around another group of huts, and so on. The families in each compound were often related to each other and tried to help one another."

"My parents were Muslim, as were most people in the region, but they were not particularly religious, which was unusual. All I knew was that we were different from the Taliban, who were scattered around the area. They were not like us at all. They were very strict, very religious, fanatical, really—that's a word I learned quickly in English after I came here—and we did not associate with them by choice."

I nodded again, encouraging her not to stop.

"But they had authority over us," she continued. "I never really understood why that was, but they seemed to be in charge much of the time. I suppose they had power because they took it. They claimed their power in the name of religion, but I never saw it as a religious thing, in fact it seemed far away from religion. It seemed mostly that they ruled with fear and threats. We were simply afraid of them. The men could be cruel and often singled people out for punishment."

"They wanted everyone to follow a long list of rules that they would announce or post on the walls: 'Do this; Do that; Pray at this time; Cover your head; Cover your face; Don't speak; Don't laugh; Don't go here; Don't go there.'"

"The rules went on and on. Especially for young girls. We were always being watched and told to mind our ways. We…"

I interrupted her. "This is so incredible to me. The Taliban have always just been a concept to me, a bogeyman—the really bad guys in a bad movie. I can't imagine that you lived with them, rubbed shoulders with them, served food to them…"

"Oh, but I did—on a daily basis. They were a part of our everyday life. We didn't like them or their endless rules, but they called themselves the holy leaders, and, for the most part, we obeyed their rules. It seemed less threatening that way. As I said, I don't really know why; it just was how life was over there. And still is today, I think…"

She stopped for a moment before continuing, as though seeing a glimpse of her country in her mind. "My parents did not make me wear the hijab, but I had to dress very modestly—scarves and long skirts—and stay in the shadows. That was the best way to stay out of trouble, or so they told me, and I was very obedient—I never made waves. Girls in Afghanistan, especially young girls are taught not to cause trouble or bring attention to themselves, and for the most part, we did not."

"The people who lived next door to us—distant cousins of my father—had a relative who was Taliban and he would visit their house sometimes. When he did, we would keep to ourselves and try not to let him see us. We were all afraid of him."

I interrupted her with a question: "So the Taliban allowed your school to continue, even with girls in it?"

"Well, it was not so much that they allowed it as that we just somehow managed to stay unnoticed. Most of the boys in the village went to a different, larger school, which was sanctioned—I think that's the word—by the Taliban. Ours was just a tiny little place in a hut down the road, just a room really, not a formal schoolhouse, so you wouldn't really notice it. But our teacher was smart and he knew how to be discreet. He helped all of us with our subjects and especially wanted us to learn to read. When I think back on him now, I realize what a courageous and important man he really was. But for him, I would have had no schooling, never would have learned to read, never would have picked up English."

"I knew even then that I was lucky to be in that school with that teacher, so I kept quiet about it. My father would always grumble to my mother that he didn't see what good sending me to school would do, and he didn't like having to send money with me once a month for the teacher. He thought it was dangerous and almost subversive—that's another word I learned here—but I think deep down he was proud that I went."

"In any case, that was the sum total of our lives, just what went on within that complex and at my father's stall, on those streets with all the bicycles and the vendors and the dirt and the animals."

I interrupted her again: "Were the Americans there yet?"

"Not at first. It wasn't until around 2001 when American soldiers started turning up in our district. I was still little at the time, maybe seven or eight. After they came, there was always fighting going on—new noises, new sights, new conflicts. We hated all of it, as you can imagine."

"Actually, it's hard for me to imagine, but go on…" I said, shaking my head at the thought.

"Well, life became so much more complicated after the Americans arrived. Not that things had been wonderful before they came, but at least it had been familiar to us. But then after they came, everything changed. A war had begun. We were always on edge, always frightened, always uncertain of where we stood, always terrified of the gunfire and the sounds of war, worried sick that we would lose our food stand, even more petrified that we would lose our lives on some unlucky street that turned out to be a battle site."

I stayed silent, and after a long sigh, she continued. "On the one hand, we never liked the Taliban, but on the other hand, they were part of us, they were Afghan, they spoke Pashto—we knew them, and they were part of our landscape. But the Americans were so foreign to us—another culture, another language, another religion; they were so... 'not us,' I guess you would say."

"We were torn between wanting to be rescued from the Taliban and at the same time hating the people doing the rescuing. I'm sorry to say this in front of you, but it is the truth."

"Laila, don't be sorry. This is your story. You don't have to worry about whether I approve or not. I can well imagine that having complete strangers show up in your village with guns and army tanks is not a pleasant sight. Anyone would feel the way you did. I understand in a way that I never did before. You are making this painfully real for me, and I truly appreciate your sharing all of this. What a picture you have painted—one I never saw before."

Laila took a deep breath. "I wish it was just a picture for me. But it became our life on a daily basis. We had nowhere to turn, no one to turn to; we felt powerless. This new frightening way of life was simply thrust upon us, like it or not. And we did not like it. There was nothing about the war that helped my family in any way."

"I can understand that. So then what happened?"

"Well, what happened is that the Americans were always trying to find Taliban commanders among us. They were always spying on us, breaking into our homes to search for them with no warning. They especially wanted the leaders. And when they found them, they would engage in battle with them, no matter where they were or who they were with."

"For the American soldiers, it was hard to distinguish between ordinary Afghans just living their lives and the Taliban, who were their sworn enemies. *We* knew the difference, we could have told them, but they rarely asked us, and we did not offer any information. Usually, they just started pushing and shooting. And of course, even if they did ask, we often wouldn't tell them the truth because nothing good would ever come from it as far as we were concerned. All it did was put our own lives in danger from the very people they were going after. In one sense we were glad to see them go after the Taliban, but the reality of it was that they were so interspersed among us that rooting out the one often destroyed the other, if you see what I mean."

"I do."

"I mean…they didn't seem to care much who got hurt in the crossfire. Sometimes it was wives or mothers, sometimes children who happened to be there when they showed up. Sometimes they would kill the men they were after or wound them, or sometimes the Americans were the ones killed or wounded."

"But always, always, the fights brought destruction with them. There would be gunshots, explosions, fires, broken furniture, dust, blood, horrible smells, sickening scenes. It was a nightmare for us. We hated it. And we hated the Taliban just as much for bringing all of this ruin to our doorstep. But it was the American soldiers we feared the most, because we never knew what to expect and we didn't know how to communicate with them."

"How did the Taliban react to this American incursion—this intrusion?" I asked.

"These men were not stupid. They were cunning; they knew how to fight, and they knew how to hide, and they often made us help them evade the Americans. We feared for our lives with them as well. They would shoot you or torture you if they found out you had given any information to the Americans. So if the soldiers came into our compound, we were terrified that the Taliban would think that we were somehow involved. Sometimes the Taliban would booby-trap certain parts of the walls around the compound so that they would explode if U.S. troops tried to come over them."

"Certain people in our village would hide various Taliban members if the Americans came through looking for them. My own family never did but, as I told you, the people in the house next to us often sheltered one of the Taliban leaders. This used to make us so nervous and anxious because we didn't want the Americans anywhere near us. We didn't want the U.S. soldiers to come barging in, questioning us the way they did some of our neighbors."

"We began to live in a state of constant fear. I remember how much we all wished things would just go back to normal, but there did not seem to be a 'normal' anymore. There was just war and fear and destruction. That became our normal."

She took another long breath, as though exhausted just from the telling of it.

"Laila, we can finish this some other time. You've told me so much already; I'm just trying to digest it all. I can't imagine how frightened you must have been; you were just a child and a girl-child at that…"

"No, I don't want to stop. That was not the hard part—that was just the background for this story. The hard part is coming…"

I remember feeling shocked to know that there was worse to come. "Alright. Take your time. Drink some water," I said, sympathy in my voice.

Laila got up and poured herself a glass, then repositioned herself on the soft cushioned chair next to my bed. "Okay, now for the hard part. It's mostly a blur, and it has taken me years to reconstruct the story so that it makes sense, but I think I have most of the facts now."

"You remember I told you about the Taliban commander who sometimes stayed next door to us? Well, he was someone the Americans really wanted to find—what they called a 'High-Value Target' or 'High-Value Individual.' I guess they had been gathering intelligence on him for some time, and they had come to the conclusion that he was living in our compound."

"Oh great," I said.

"Right. Nothing but trouble for us, coming and going. One of the U.S. Special Forces soldiers had gone to my father's stand with an interpreter and asked him some questions about whether or not he knew this man named Azlan. My father, of course, said nothing—said he knew nothing of Azlan, and then they left. But my father told us he thought they did not believe him. And then, sure enough, one evening, long after dark—I don't know how they got in or who helped them—but there they were at our door. They banged on the door and pushed their way in—without my father's permission, of course—to question him again about this man, Azlan."

"The Americans were all tall and scary-looking to me, with long, black guns in their hands, thick camouflage uniforms and ferocious looks. They wore helmets with night lights on them and had all sorts of military gear attached to their uniforms—I have no idea what all their gadgets were—but they kept talking into their radios and had an Afghan translator with them. We were absolutely petrified."

She stopped for a moment to let this sink in, then continued. "My parents grabbed me and pushed me behind them. I was clinging to my mother's skirts, shaking with fear. Then my father spoke to the interpreter. When he questioned my father about Azlan, my father insisted that no one in our house was Taliban and no one we knew was either. 'You have to believe me; I tell the truth,' he said. He was so nervous; I could tell by the way his voice was shaking. The interpreter asked him whether the neighbors next door were hiding Azlan."

"My father didn't know what to say. He was as frightened of the Taliban as he was of the American soldiers. Either way, he was taking a risk, for the Taliban did not tolerate us pointing a finger at them, and at the same time, the U.S. soldiers could be brutal if they thought you were lying to them."

"We had heard a lot of stories about these Special Forces—we all talked among ourselves. We knew that many of them were good and had helped our people in various ways, but we had also heard stories about the bad ones, and that was what had us choking with fear. How could we know if these people meant us no harm? What if they thought my father was lying to them, then what? Would they take him? Would they hurt him? Would they hurt me?"

She paused, to try to evaluate my reaction. I finally said, "I can see why you were terrified: damned if you do and damned if you don't, right?"

She let out a breath, seemingly pleased that I understood the dilemma. She nodded. "Exactly. So my father stuck to his story that he didn't know any Taliban, that the neighbors were just like him, simple shopkeepers, nothing more; he didn't mention that we were related to them. What else could he say without putting all of us in danger? 'Keep your mouth shut' was what we had all learned to do."

"There was no percentage in ratting out someone to the Americans. Then you were shunned by your own people, or worse, punished by the Taliban. So we decided to cast our lot with the devil we knew." She smiled at her phrase. "That's something Ben would say; he talks like that," she said, interrupting her train of thought. "But we'll get to him later."

She continued. "Where was I? Oh yes, the night they came to our house. That night seemed like it lasted a year, but in fact, they were only in our hut for about fifteen minutes or so. For whatever reason, the interpreter claimed to believe my father's story and said to the man he called Captain: 'There's nothing here to find, these people know nothing.' The two of them exchanged glances and shook their heads."

"Then the Americans talked on their radios for a minute or so and, looking rather disgusted, finally, just left. We were so relieved to have those men out of our house—I can't begin to tell you. I was crying by then, and my mother took me in her lap and rocked me until I stopped."

"She looked at my father with gratitude and he just nodded at her, relief all over his face. 'I did what I had to do,' he said. 'But they may come back, you know, especially if they find out what's going on next door. You'd better keep your guard up, be prepared,' he said to my mother."

"She closed her eyes and shook her head as though she couldn't quite believe that any of it had happened. But it did, and we all had the uneasy feeling that we had not heard the last of this story, which of course turned out to be true. So we…"

The phone rang just then, and I answered it. "I'll have to call you back, Howard, I'm in the middle of something right now. Hold that thought, though; I'll get back to you." I didn't think it was the right time to interrupt Laila with some legal drivel, just when she was getting to the heart of her story.

"If you need to talk to him, I can certainly wait," Laila said.

"Howard will keep. You can't stop now; you've gotten this far. Go on with your story, Laila."

"Well, let me think where I am. So…the soldiers had come to interrogate us; then they left, and we didn't hear anything more about it for maybe a week. All the other neighbors had been questioned as well, and all of them had stuck to the same story we had used: 'We know nothing,' they all said. Nobody breathed a word. Whether the Americans believed us or not, we had no idea. Probably not, was our guess, but we tried to put it behind us."

"Finally, Azlan himself paid us a visit one night after the U.S. soldiers' raid. He was staying next door. He came inside our house and sat down at our table, pretending to be friendly at first. Then all of a sudden he stood up and grabbed my father by the arm and started twisting it. 'You tell those American bastards one word about us, and you'll have me to deal with,' he said, his eyes blazing. He looked like he wanted to kill my father. 'Do you hear me? Do not betray me or I promise you will not live long enough to regret it,' he said, squeezing my father's arm even more tightly and baring his teeth."

"'I understand,'" my father had cried, wrenching his arm away from the man. 'I told them nothing. Keep your secrets; I want no part of them!'"

"'Don't speak of my secret! I have no secret! There is no secret! Do you understand my words?' my father said. Azlan's eyes were almost popping out of his head as he stared at my father, and it was clear that he was as frightened as we were."

"My father screamed at him: 'Leave us alone, Azlan, You don't need to come here to my house to tell me this. Go back to your family, do whatever you are going to do, but don't involve me, don't speak to me, don't drag my family into your story. I have nothing to say to the Americans, and I have nothing to say to you. Now leave my house!'"

"My father's face was red with anger, and his forehead was beaded with sweat. Normally you did not speak to the Taliban in this way, but on this night, Azlan seemed to accept it. He gave my father another fierce stare and then stormed out, slamming the door behind him."

"We all felt as though we had been thrown into a boiling river of anxiety and that we couldn't escape from it on either side. We hated the Taliban, and we hated the foreigners in our country, even though they were supposedly there to help us. We had no good options. All we could do was lay low and hide and hope this darkness would somehow pass over us and let us return to the daily routines that used to make up our lives. My father feared for his business—such as it was—and knew that there would be no peace in our village as long as the dual threats remained."

Laila paused to drink more water, searching my face for a reaction.

"Go on," I urged, fascinated with her story.

"Well, as it turned out, our troubles were only beginning. Apparently the Americans continued their surveillance, despite the fact that no one in our area was giving them any information. Still, there may have been informants that we did not know about. Certainly there were people who could be bribed for the right amount of money, especially in an economy as terrible as ours. We will never know exactly how they zeroed in on the Taliban leader, but they eventually figured out that he was staying in one of the houses in our compound. "

"They also apparently found out that the wall behind us was wired with explosives—another good tip that the man they were looking for was nearby. Our house was maybe ten feet from the compound wall. My father and mother's bedroom was nearest to the wall, while mine was opposite theirs, on the other side of the house."

Laila stopped for a moment and broke her gaze. She put her hands in her lap and stared down at them for a long time before she spoke again. The air in the room seemed heavy with tension. I could feel her anxiety and sensed that we were finally coming to the "hard part."

Finally, she took up her story. "It was in December of 2001—of course, I remember the date—a cold night in Kandahar, a night that changed my life. We were all asleep, as it was late."

I nodded at her to continue, fearing that I could already guess some of what was to come.

"Most of what I will tell you is not my memory of it; it is what I was told later because I remember so little of what actually took place. But the Americans had finally decided that their intelligence was correct and that their target was living in our compound. As it turned out, though their intelligence was good, it was not perfect. They believed their target was living in our house, not the house next to us. "

"Somewhere around midnight, they scaled the wall on the other side of the compound so that they would not set off the trip wire. Then they snuck up behind our house and attached some sort of explosive to the back wall of our hut. This was the wall of my mother and father's bedroom. When the explosion went off it made such a sound that it blasted me from my sleep and set me directly to screaming. That is all I remember of that night. Perhaps that was a blessing—and perhaps not—because I never saw the faces of my father or mother again."

She looked down at her hands, and I could see the tears slowly seeping out of her eyes. Her voice was very low and thin now.

She paused for a few moments, then continued. "They were killed instantly by the explosion—I learned later that it is called 'overpressure.' Their bodies were broken— blood everywhere. Our tiny house was destroyed."

I swallowed hard and shook my head in disbelief, the visuals of her story playing in my mind. I looked at her closely to see if she wanted to stop there, but clearly she was not finished yet.

Laila took a Kleenex and dabbed at her eyes. "Really, I'm okay," she said in answer to my unasked question. "Apparently I was thrown onto the floor of my bedroom, wounded by debris and the shock of the impact, but obviously not killed."

"No, mercifully not," I said.

"One of the soldiers—the same Captain who had interrogated us—saw that I was still alive and gathered me up—I found this out later of course—and took me back to the U.S. Army base where doctors worked to save my life."

"I had a ruptured eardrum, a traumatic brain injury, and wounds on the side of my face that had not been protected by the pillow. The blankets had helped shield much of my body from the shrapnel but I still had a ruptured spleen from the shock waves as well as wounds on my shoulders and arms, plus I was bleeding from several wounds on my face and head."

"When I woke up the next morning I had no idea where I was. I was a child, alone, terrified, in pain, disoriented, in a strange place with strange people all around me. I cried for my mother, not knowing that she would never answer me again. I cried for my father, but no one came for me. Finally, an American nurse came and bent over me and touched my forehead, pushing some of the bandages back in place. 'Poor child,' she said in our language, though I could hardly understand her accent."

Laila stopped to take a breath.

I just stared at her, at a loss as to what to say in the face of such tragedy. Finally, I said, rather weakly, "I'm so sorry all of this happened to you, Laila. How incredibly awful. How did you ever survive?"

"Well, I had no choice, really, did I? The nurse left me to fetch the American soldier who had rescued me because apparently he had asked to be kept informed of my progress. She came back with an interpreter and the Captain. They told me his name was Ben— Captain Ben, they said. He was indeed the same man that had come to our house to question my father. "

"He terrified me. I remember shrinking down into the bed in an effort to escape from him."

"'I am not going to hurt you,' he said very slowly. 'Can you understand me? Do you speak English at all?'

"I understood him, but I did not want to speak English with him, so I shook my head no. Through the interpreter he told me, 'I understand why you are afraid, and I'm very, very sorry that this has happened to you. It was all a terrible mistake. I need to try to explain this to you. What is your name?'"

"In Pashto, I told him my name was Laila. I said I wanted to go home, and I wanted to see my mother and my father, and that I did not want him in the room with me. "

"The man named Captain Ben took my hand though I did not want him to; I tried to pull away from him. But he held it tightly and looked me right in the eyes. I could see tears start to run down his face, and I was even more scared than before. Then he told me he was sorry again. "

"Sorry for what?" I asked him in English, which surprised him.

"He started to speak again in English, but I shook my head, and the interpreter told me what he was saying. It was something to the effect of: 'Sorry to tell you that your mother and father are gone. They were killed last night. It was the wrong house Your father was not the man we were looking for. We found out afterward. We made a terrible mistake and now you are paying for that mistake. You will never know how sorry I am, how sorry we all are for what happened'—something like that."

Laila was staring off into the distance now, her eyes glassy and locked on some other place and time, the memory of that terrible night washing over her like a dark sea.

I felt that I should say something but couldn't think what that could possibly be, so I stayed silent.

Finally, Laila took a few ragged breaths to regain her equilibrium. Tears rolled down her face, but she maintained her composure. Then I could see her consciously straighten her back, pull her shoulders back, and inhale slowly. It was clear that she had learned to compose herself physically when necessary. "I didn't hear most of it, only the part about my parents being killed. That I heard. I started wailing before he had finished. He tried to comfort me, touch my face, but I wrenched my hand out of his and turned my head to the wall."

I nodded, understanding the gesture.

Laila continued now, sounding stronger. "I was inconsolable. I could do nothing but cry. I was horrified that he had touched me. But more than that, the thought of living without my parents was inconceivable. I was just a child…My soul was crushed."

I could only nod, feeling my tears welling up at the thought of her complete desolation.

"It was several days later when I finally saw myself in the mirror of the bathroom. It was the first time I was allowed to get up by myself. My swollen face was a mass of scars and bruises, particularly on the left side. My skin, which was once so soft and smooth, now looked like a pockmarked dirt road. "

"I stared at myself in total disbelief. So, not only have they taken my mother and father from me along with my home and all my possessions, but they have taken my beauty as well, I thought to myself. They left me with nothing, absolutely nothing; that was all I had. And now I am an orphan. This thought kept coursing through my mind like the chorus of a song, looping over and over again."

She shifted in her chair, looking small and overwhelmed. "My misery was so deep and so complete that I remember little of what happened from that time until the time my wounds had healed sufficiently so that they could release me from the hospital. I barely spoke, and then only when necessary. My hatred of these people could not have been measured."

She gave me what could only be described as a guilty look, as though to apologize for her feelings.

"You needn't apologize to me," I said. "You had every right to feel the way you did, the way you probably still do…"

"Well, my feelings are much more complicated now than they were then. At that time, there was only hatred and despair. Now, so much has changed, but that's another whole story—for another time, maybe."

"Fair enough," I said, "But what became of you after you left the hospital? Who took you home, who cared for you—you were just a child, right?"

"Yes, just a child. A child who turned into a woman in a single day, I think. My aunt and uncle had visited me at the army hospital, brought there by the American, Ben, who continued to check up on me on a daily basis, despite my protests. "

"But I hated him too much to ever speak with him. He would try to have a conversation with me when he came by, but I would just motion for him to leave. I knew at some level that he felt bad about what had happened, but really, what difference did that make to me? My life was so shattered that his feelings or his presence were of no consequence to me. My bitterness was too deep to take in anything outside of me. "

"I suppose I should have been glad to see my aunt and uncle but, in fact, I had nothing to say to them either, just turned my head to the wall and cried miserably, humiliated that they should see me looking the way I did. Among the long list of problems I still had was the fact that my hearing was practically gone in my left ear. But no matter, there was nothing I wanted to hear."

"But what did your relatives say to you?" I finally asked.

Laila answered: "Eventually, they came back and said they were going to take me to live with them. I wanted nothing to do with them, but I had no one else. I was so young then, and so deeply depressed, I didn't know what to do or say. I told them I was 'too ugly' to live with anyone, and they said: 'No child, you will come with us, we are your family—there is no other choice. You will come.'"

"They had seven children and a hut no bigger than ours had been for the three of us. My despair was complete."

I shook my head in acknowledgment.

"Before I left the army hospital, Ben came to my room again with an interpreter, as he had almost every day. And every time he came, I shunned him. But on the last day—before I left with my aunt and uncle—I finally spoke to him."

"Incredible," I said. "What on earth did you say to him?"

"Spit at him would be more accurate," Laila retorted. "I remember using broken English and saying something dramatic like: 'I will forgive you never!' Then in Pashto, I told him: 'You have taken my life away. I have no mother, no father; I have no future, no home. You have ruined my face and taken away everything that ever meant anything to me. You have done this to me. Why do you bother to say to me: 'Sorry?' It is only a word, and it changes nothing.' I remember picking up a book by my bed and hurling it at the Captain."

I smiled wanly at the passion of this little girl—in a room with the man responsible for the murder of her parents—baring her feelings.

"He picked up the book from the floor and put it carefully back on the table. Then he said to me through the interpreter, 'I do not want to speak to you in English because you might not understand what I have to say, and it is important to me that you understand every word.'"

Just then an alarm on Laila's cell phone jars us back into the present.

"Oh, goodness, it's time for your medication, Olivia," Laila says grimacing and pulling herself with some difficulty out of her past self.

I shake my head, "It's not important anymore. Let's not talk about me."

"Yes, it is important," she says getting up stiffly from the chair and doling out three pills into my hand. Then she pushes a glass of water in my direction. "It is very important to me that you take these right on time. It's my job to see to it that you do, not to be sitting here forcing you to listen to my sad story."

I gulp the pills down, realizing that it is important to her that I do so. "No one is forcing me to listen. And this is more than a sad story; it's a tragedy and a shameful catastrophe that no person— certainly no child—should ever have to endure. I feel as though I should apologize for my country's part in this..."

"No, please don't say that; it's not your fault, you had nothing to do with it. Besides, I have reached a place in my life where I have come to terms with what happened."

I raise my eyebrows in disbelief.

"It was a war, it was a mistake, it was fate, and it was terribly cruel and unnecessary. I see the bigger picture now though it doesn't change my sorrow or my hatred of the situation. But I have spent many years dealing with my anger, and I finally decided that it was consuming me. The only way for me to escape the prison of my anger was to let go of it and accept my new reality. "

"I know now, objectively, that those soldiers meant me no personal harm. While they ruined my life, they actually meant me no harm. Can you see the irony there? It was not their intention to hurt me. That's how I see it now in hindsight, for much has happened since then. And when I look at some of the changes in my life, I have to be grateful for many of the good things that have happened. Nothing can ever make up for the loss of my parents, but I have to accept that they are gone and will not be coming back. And they would want me to live, and live well; I know that. You know I…"

"But how did your life change after all that? What happened after you went to live with your relatives?" I interrupt her, unable to contain my curiosity. She smiles at my intensity, forcing herself to return to her story. "Well, I went to live with them as planned. And it was as depressing as I had imagined it would be, if not worse. There was no room for me, no time for me, no money for me, and my cousins resented my presence for all of those reasons and more. Add to that the fact that in the village where I was now living I was taunted for being different—the scars, both physical and emotional—made me a constant target. I was an orphan, my face looked hideous, I had trouble hearing, I was depressed, I didn't seem to belong anywhere, and I had no friends. It was like living in hell."

"But then just when I thought my life could not possibly get any worse, something happened that I hadn't foreseen. Once again, these soldiers changed my life."

Laila glances down at her watch, then looks up in horror. "Oh my God, I had no idea it was so late! I've got to massage your legs and then get to my next client. I've been taking up all of your time…"

I interrupt her and tell her not to worry about my legs.

"Laila, you were so brave to tell me this. I hope you won't regret sharing this with me. I promise to be a good guardian of your story. You can trust me. Go now; we'll finish another time, I promise."

"I'll go, but take one more pill—no wait, two more and we're done," she says, handing me a glass of water and two new capsules.

And then she was gone, and I sit with my thoughts of her, reforming the sounds and the pictures she has painted, awash in a canvas so foreign to me, and yet so immediate because of her presence in it.

Chapter 4

SCHEHERAZADE

The next day dawns like any other. I slept fitfully through the night, chased by dark amorphous shapes, nothing concrete—just a generalized sense of unease and foreboding, neither of these feelings terribly unusual these days.

Ever since Charlie's death, I have found those moments just between sleep and wakefulness to be the most disquieting. Waking up is the moment at which I realize yet again that he is gone—as though right up until then, just before consciousness rises in me, just for a split second, none of it is true; as though if only I hadn't awakened, I might still be in possession of that luminous life I had once led—the one where I woke up every day with him beside me, looking forward to the day's unraveling. But consciousness always breaks the spell. It signals the death of the daydream, the beginning of the nightmare.

Snap out of it, I chasten myself, and stop feeling so sorry for yourself. You'd think you were the only one with problems in this world. Just think about Laila and what she went through—what so many refugees go through—people suffering mightily all over the globe. You've never experienced that level of hardship, not even close; have some compassion, get some perspective…OK, so you're dying, but at least the majority of your life was pleasant, no?

I shake my head, trying to get a clearer focus, cobwebs flying in all directions. You need to get a grip, Olivia. You've got a ways to go before you can completely give up, a ways to go before you sleep.

I drag myself heavily out of bed, clutching the sore spot on my back and trailing my old flannel robe behind me as I walk. I peek through the partially closed shutters currently holding back the day. Grey and cloudy outside, chance of rain, I tell myself, much like yesterday and probably the same as tomorrow. Sunny and warm would make for a well-deserved change once in a while, don't you think? But that won't be happening; no chance of that anytime soon. Grey and cloudy it is then. Bring on the gloom and the shade—suits my mood perfectly.

I lay back down on the bed, pulling the robe around my thinning bones. No point getting dressed. What on earth would I dress for? My rendezvous with the cook? My phone call with Howard? The sponge bath I can anticipate from Laila? The two-minute encounter with my son and daughter-in-law? Brian says there is no longer any point in having more chemotherapy, so even that is out. No, nothing worth dressing for.

In fact, I should probably start thinking about how to streamline my possessions, starting with my closet. What am I saving all this finery for? There's no chance that I'll be seen in any of these outfits again. Just think of it: no need for the sequined jacket, no need for the fur-lined coat (faux fur of course—having been a fervent environmentalist all my life); no pressing need for the *aprés ski* ensemble.

About the only thing I'll be needing now, besides a clean collection of nightgowns, is one decent outfit in which to be cremated—and how demanding can the criteria be for that? Burns quickly? Ignites easily?

Well, that's a dreary path I'm meandering down, even for me. Surely there's something a little more elevating I could think about. There's my jewelry to think of— though I was never much for gaudy rings and such. Still it would be nice to distribute it before my demise, just so there are no tawdry fights over any of it after I'm gone. I'm most inclined to give it all to my stepdaughter Claire. She would, at least, appreciate it, but would probably never wear any of it, whereas Lisa probably wants it desperately, in which case it might be best to withhold it, I think to myself, smiling wickedly. What a delicious dilemma. What to do, what to do…?

Honestly, though, if I really think about it clearly, I'm tired of the estate distribution thoughts; let them paw through my things at their leisure and do what they like with them—why should I care? Jewelry, clothes, artwork, antique pieces—what do all those acquisitions mean to me now? They have no intrinsic value, perhaps they never did. They seemed to enhance my life at the time, but now they just seem like so many trinkets, yesterday's trash.

No point taxing myself at this stage of the game. Can't I find something to look forward to? I ask myself. There's always Laila; she interests me and always manages to spirit me away from my dismal thoughts, pulling me into her world without ever intending to do so. Yes, I'll wait for Laila; things will be better when she's here.

When Laila finally does come in this morning, she seems guarded, uncomfortable in her skin. Eventually, she sits down in the chair next to me and says, "I feel so embarrassed about yesterday. I'm thinking that I should not have told you about all those terrible times in my life. It sounds like I'm looking for sympathy, but honestly, I'm not. And it's all so gruesome. You didn't need to hear any of that in your condition. It was not very professional of me; I apologize," she says sheepishly.

"Oh please, Laila, you have nothing to apologize for. I feel honored that you shared your story with me." I reach out for her hand and hold it in mine, noting the contrast between her soft, young skin and my shrunken, bony appendage. "You've been through way too much pain for such a young girl. I'm so sorry it had to happen to you. But I can tell you this: you are a brave, resilient young woman to be able to bear all of this as well as you do."

Laila seems embarrassed, and I let go of her hand, looking her straight in the eye. "But look at you now, after all of these harrowing events, after all that death and destruction, here you are, standing on your own two feet, working, supporting yourself, helping other people—like me, for instance. What courage you have shown to come this far, to triumph over your fear and quite natural resentment..."

Laila lowers her eyes. "I don't know that I've overcome all my emotions the way you suggest. I wouldn't say I've 'triumphed' over my resentment completely, or even my fear; I still live with a lot of both, but I've learned to co-exist with them, I guess you'd say. They are at bay most of the time. Sometimes they creep up on me and get a stranglehold, but most of the time I can keep them down."

"Understood," I say, pushing myself back onto the bed where I'm more comfortable. "So now, what plans have you got for me today?" I ask genially, switching the subject to something less weighty. "Let me guess: breakfast, the taking of vitals— very important; the ever-trendy bathroom visit, meds, more meds, a bit of massage, a quickie dry shampoo, the de rigueur—that means necessary—walk around the apartment—or should we call it a shuffle—the..."

"Yes, yes, all of the above," Laila laughs gaily, interrupting me. "Where should we begin? With the shuffle or with breakfast, or perhaps the—as you put it—trendy bathroom visit?"

"Ah, well, let's take the latter first, then breakfast, and then we'll tackle all of the rest. Deal?"

"Deal," Laila says, reaching over to help me out of bed.

An hour later, having gone through our usual daily routine, I am settled in again. I am feeling more clear-headed than usual. It is only eleven o'clock in the morning and the day looms ahead of me with way too much time to fill. Might as well take advantage of my mental clarity since it is an unexpected visitor, I think to myself.

"You must finish your story, Laila—unless you don't want to, in which case, just say no to me, and I promise I'll move on."

Not having expected to be called upon in this fashion so soon after the last batch of stories, Laila sighs heavily. She arches her eyebrows at me. "Are you sure you want to hear more about my pathetic life?"

I smile. "Of course, I do. And believe me, you are not pathetic in any way. Your story is certainly raw and difficult, but it's your reality, and you can't change the facts. In any case, you can't leave me hanging like this. I'm an old lady, and I haven't got much more time on earth, so for God's sake, let me, at least, hear the end of this story!"

She giggles. "Okay, you've persuaded me. I can't deny you a dying wish, right?" "Exactly. So, let's see—the last I remember you had left the American hospital, gone to live with your reluctant aunt and uncle and their two hundred children, and you were being chased and bullied by your new classmates because of your physical and emotional scars. Does that about cover it?"

Laila had the grace to laugh at the thought of the two hundred children. "Substantially less than two hundred, but getting up there for sure," she says. "Well, let me think. I need to put myself back in that space and time. Okay, yes, I was being bullied and teased at my new school because my scars made me look like a freak to them."

"My uncle's house was in a completely different village than ours, some forty kilometers distant from my parents' home. I knew no one except my relatives, of course. I still had pain from my injuries, difficulty walking and hearing, trouble trying to concentrate and, more importantly, I felt terribly isolated, lonely, ugly and just plain miserable. Quite a recipe for depression, don't you think?"

I nod. "The perfect storm."

"Well, I felt isolated not only because of the scars on my face and body but also because of the scars on my soul. Outside of my time in the hospital after my parents' death, it was the worst time of my life. I was suicidal without even knowing what that meant. But there I was, barely living, going through the motions, hating every day that passed. Maybe if I had had a single friend, just one, it might have helped, but there was no one, not a soul to turn to."

"The other children either taunted me or were frightened of me. My aunt was too busy with her husband and her brood to worry about my psychological problems. And my cousins shunned me because of my scars and, quite simply, because they didn't want me there. You know how children are, they can be cruel, and they don't tolerate others being 'different'—especially not in the society I lived in. I was, quite simply, an outcast."

"I think I can relate," I say, then immediately regret saying it, realizing how preposterous it is to think I could relate to any of the events in her life. "No, cancel that, I can't relate, not on any reasonable level. I apologize for even saying it."

"Don't worry Miss Olivia—sorry, Olivia—we don't have to compete over which of us had the most misery in her life..."

"No, we don't, because you win hands down," I say.

"Well, yes, probably, but who's counting?"

"So we agree, you're the clear winner here. Go on, Laila. Here you are, your life is abysmal and not showing signs of getting better anytime soon, right?"

"Right. I don't know what abysmal means, but it doesn't sound good, so it's probably true." She smiles as though we have shared a secret, then continues. "So then one day, out of the blue, I got a letter from the American Captain, Ben. It was written in Pashto, so he must have had it translated and then sent. I got several letters, actually. They were simple letters, basically: 'Hello, how are you doing, are you making progress?'—that type of thing."

"He would throw in a few lines about himself, vague things like: 'I'm in Kandahar,' or 'we're going north now,' or 'it's cold here, I hope you are doing well.'"

"He would always end the letters with something like: 'I think of you every day and pray that you are getting healthier.' Or he'd say 'I pray for your long life.' And then sometimes there would be something to the effect of: 'Please try to find a way to forgive me. If I can ever help you, please call upon me. I'll do whatever I can.' They were always signed: 'Captain Ben.'"

Laila pauses for a moment as if remembering those letters. Then she continues. "There would always be a cell phone number at the end. He would include a couple of Afghanis in the letter—an Afghani is like the U.S. dollar. Sometimes he would send the equivalent of ten dollars, which was a fortune to me. Along with the letters, I hid the money under my bed, lest my cousins find it and steal it from me."

"Later I found out that he was sending money to my aunt and uncle to help pay for the cost of keeping me, but I did not know this at the time."

"And did you keep the letters?" I ask.

"I did. At first, I couldn't bear to even look at them, and yet, I surprised myself by not throwing them away and re-reading them later. I kept them in a small box tucked way under my bed, where I also hid the money he sent. I showed them to no one, although my aunt and uncle knew I had received mail from him."

"They were too disinterested in me to care what was in the letters and didn't like even coming near my bed. They treated me like a diseased animal. I was embarrassed to even have the letters. But at the same time, this man was literally the only person in my life who seemed to be concerned with my welfare. Strange that the creator of all my misery was the only one who showed any interest in me."

"I would secretly spend some of the money, buying treats for myself, but I never let my relatives know about it. And I never answered any of his letters, not a single one," she says with a slightly defiant tone.

"This went on for how long?" I ask.

"Oh, maybe six or seven months. And then one day, in the winter, with an interpreter at his side, he knocked on our door and asked to be let in. My aunt and uncle were terrified. They stood on the other side of the door and begged the two men to leave. They thought it was a raid of some sort. The interpreter said, 'We are not here to harm you. We only wish to speak to Laila.' Once they understood that the American Captain wished them no ill, my aunt and uncle looked relieved and were more than happy to offer me up as long as they were not in trouble. So they pushed me roughly towards the door and opened it. Then they backed into a corner, leaving me there to deal with the two men. They would have liked to leave the house, but in Afghanistan a young girl would never be left alone with two strange men, so they stayed."

"Captain Ben asked in English, 'Please can I have a word with you, Laila?'"

"I said nothing; I only glared at him.

"'You look better,'" he said, again in English. "He could tell that I understood him by my shrug. He said something like, 'You're healing, aren't you?'"

"Again I said nothing, only looked up at him with fear and distrust."

"He reached over and very gently touched my face where the scars were. I pulled back from him as though he had touched me with a branding iron. He looked embarrassed. 'Sorry,' he said, 'I won't touch you again, I promise. Let me speak to you in your language.'"

I interrupt her. "Why didn't you let him speak to you in English, since you understood it to some extent?"

"Because I didn't want to have any kind of relationship with him. And it seemed too intimate to me to have a one-on-one conversation with this 'murderer' in his language, not mine. In some way, I didn't want to give him the satisfaction of communicating with me on his terms."

"I see. So you wanted to make him work at it, then?"

"Exactly," Laila agrees. "So then he nodded to the interpreter and started telling him what he wanted him to translate. I remember almost exactly what he said. It sticks with me even now. It went pretty much like this:

'You must wonder why I'm here. But I need to talk to you. I understand why you don't answer my letters, really I do. I don't blame you. I keep trying, but I can't get that night out of my mind. I'm sure you can't either. I feel so terrible about what happened. It was a mistake that took the lives of your parents and pretty much ruined your life at the same time. We are in a war, and wars are like tanks that just plow through the land, crushing whatever is in front of them. It doesn't matter whether it's good or bad, innocent or guilty, war just crashes through without regard for anything or anyone. I am a soldier engaged in a war, and this is how wars go. Can you understand that?'"

"I remember I crossed my arms over my chest and glared back him, tears spilling out of my eyes at being forced to relive that awful night and at being compared to the crushed landscape left behind in the trail of a tank. I remember that I was trying not to shake, trying to rein in my hatred for him enough to hear his words. While he was not speaking directly to me, he was looking at me with sad brown eyes. I could tell that he was sincere. But I didn't much care."

"'Ask her if she understands what I am trying to tell her?' he finally said to the Interpreter, looking frustrated and exhausted."

"I nodded sullenly to show that I understood. And then I spoke to him in Pashto. I told him: 'But it doesn't change anything! Don't you understand? Nothing changes because you are sorry or because you explain to me what war is. Why do I care? Why should I listen to anything you have to say? I am an orphan now because of your war and because of you. My life is ruined forever. Do you really think your words matter to me?'"

"The interpreter relayed this back to Captain Ben. He replied, again through the interpreter: 'No, I'm sure they don't. I accept the way you feel. Anyone would feel the way you do. Nothing about it is fair or right; I know that.' He shook his head for a while and rubbed the side of his face as though he were searching for words and couldn't find them. Finally, he said: 'I can't change what happened in the past. But I am here to try to change your future; that's my only option.'"

"I glared at him and finally said, 'I don't have a future! You took everything away from me.' I remember I was crying by now."

"'I know you think that,' he said, 'but I want to offer you an alternative.'"

"I was shaking my head at him, trying to will him to go away. 'An alternative to what?' I asked him."

"'To all of this...' he said, gesturing to the room we were in, to the squalor of the place. 'Listen to me, please. Think about what I am about to ask you. You need physical help with your wounds; you need psychological help from the trauma; you need someone to care for you and nurture you, the way your parents would have wanted you to be raised. I want to take you away from here, offer you a new home in America, fix your scars, give you some hope, give you an education...'"

"I remember being stunned by his words, wondering what on earth he could possibly be saying. By now he had my attention. The thought of being plucked out of my current life was not unattractive. In fact, I dreamed of it every day and every night, but I never thought it was even a remote possibility, so I never entertained the fantasy for very long. And now, suddenly, my archenemy, the architect of all my misery, was proposing a way out? I could scarcely believe what I was hearing."

I interrupt her. "He must have been an extraordinary man— soldier—to have such a highly developed conscience—despite the circumstances, don't you think?"

"I think that now, in retrospect," Laila says, "but I certainly didn't think it at the time. In fact, I remember just staring at him blankly, not saying a word."

"'Don't give me an answer now,' he said. 'Just think about it. Pray on it. Consider the new life you could have. Try to imagine it. We can get into the details later, but think about whether you would let me offer you a new life...as a way to...in some way...pay for the life and the lives I took from you. This is something for both of us, and I want you to know that I mean every word of what I have said. This is not idle chatter. I have been thinking of nothing else since the day it happened. I need to fix this somehow, and this is the only way I can think of. It will be hard to accomplish—lots of red tape, lots of paperwork, lots of persuading, lots of waiting—but if you are willing, I am too, and I will put my whole heart and soul into accomplishing it. In six months my tour of duty is over, and I will return to the States. Let me take you with me. My wife Lauren and I will adopt you. Please, let me take you with me…'"

"I'll bet you never saw that coming!" I say.

"No, never. I was dumbfounded. Such a thing had never occurred to me in my wildest dreams. I didn't know how to react at all. On the one hand, I was tempted, and on the other hand, this man—and his country—were the reason my parents were dead. Wasn't I betraying them to even speak to him? Those were the thoughts racing through my head. How could I consider letting him take me to America, of all places…? The things I had heard about America, both good and bad were swirling in my head. Before the Americans came, I had a normal life in my native country, had a family, had a home, had a normal face, had some hope of a future. America was my undoing, and yet, here I was considering his offer. I hardly knew what to think or how to reply. "

"Well, I can only assume that, in the end, you made your decision—he brought you here."

"Long story short—of course that is exactly what happened. There were many, many roadblocks, as he had forewarned, especially getting my aunt and uncle to agree. But money greases such transactions in my country, and this ended up being no different. In the end, they considered it a 'win/win' for them, as they not only got paid for their efforts, but as an added benefit, they got to unload one more hungry mouth from their household, so for them the net effect was positive."

"But what about you?" I ask. "What about your resentment towards the Captain, your quite natural hatred for the man and the country responsible for the death of your parents? How did you square all of that?"

Laila pauses before she answers. Finally, she says, "Well, it didn't happen overnight, that's for certain. It was a process, as they say. I fought hard to hold on to my anger towards Ben—almost thinking it was something I owed my parents. But in the end, he was the only one who could rescue me from the wretched situation I was in. He was the only one who was willing to try to change my circumstances, who gave me a slender hope that maybe, in the future, I would not be such a *piranha*—good word, right?"

I laugh. "Very good word if you're talking about a carnivorous fish. I think you mean pariah."

Laila giggles, looking sheepish. "Oh, okay, pariah then."

"Laila, I can tell that you have gotten a good education, maybe even done some classical reading, haven't you?"

"I did get a good education, thanks to Ben and Lauren. They were so very kind to me in the end. And yes, I love to read. But I'm jumping ahead of myself. After he had posed the question to me, I turned his offer over in my mind, and I thought that it would take me a long time to come to a conclusion. But, in fact, I made my decision quickly. It seemed like the only way out of my despair."

"So one day, after all the details were finalized, almost a year from the time he first brought up the subject, Ben came back to fly me to America with him. My cousins were half horrified and, I think, half jealous at the notion of anyone—let alone me— going so far away and to such a strange land with this foreigner, and worse yet, this 'murderer' in their eyes."

"My aunt and uncle seemed pleased with themselves for having managed to find a lucrative—I think that's the word—solution to their problem of taking care of me when they had neither the means nor the desire to do so. To be fair, I think they thought it would be best for me to go, both for their sake and for my own."

"As for me, I had nothing to hold me there, no one to beg me to stay. The truth is, once I had made up my mind to look forward, I barely looked back. All I could see behind me were the faces of my mother and father and the life that might have been. I had to turn the page or go mad. And so I did. And I found a way, in the end, to be grateful to the man who, in essence, killed my parents and the life I had known."

She continues, "He—and his wife too—made an effort every single day to make me feel wanted and to eventually make me feel loved. He did that for me, and I will never forget that. He taught me that people can make mistakes in their lives—important, tragic, epic mistakes—and still be good, atone for their sins, repair the damage. He did all of those things. I came to regard him as a father, strange as that may seem—never to replace my own, but still someone of great importance in my life. In fact, he was a father to me, and still is a father to me today. I have come to love him and to respect him—impossible as that once sounded to me."

"That's quite a revelation, don't you think?" I asked.

"Yes, it has been a long hard road, but we have made the journey together, he and I, and I am grateful to him for what he has given me. It took many years, but he saw to it that my body was healed and my scars diminished. He watered my soul, which was perhaps the most in need of being restored."

"That's quite a story," I say reflectively, "and beautifully told, Laila. It's been a long time in the making it seems. So here you are now, a transplanted American, with an Afghan heart, 'livin' the dream,' as they say." I wink at her, letting her know that I see the irony in all of this.

"Yes, that's me, living la vida loca," she smiles.

"Do you ever think about your old life?" I ask.

"Of course, I do, from time to time, usually unintentionally, because it brings me pain to consciously think about it. Sometimes a fragment of a song or a memory will float through my head, or I'll remember some phrase from my mother or a piece of advice from my father, but mostly I try to keep my eyes straight ahead of me. It's the only way I can have any peace."

"I have much to be thankful for, and much to anticipate. Someday I want to fall in love—experience what that is like—have my own family—that is my dream. And my goal in life is to do my part in pulling someone else out of the mire, much as I have been pulled out. There are many 'Laila's' in Afghanistan, most of them with no one to lean on or to help them. Someday I want to go back there; I will go back there. I want to 'pay it forward,' as they say here."

I smile indulgently at her young wisdom, her naiveté, and her generous heart. She smiles back at me, implicitly understanding my compliment to her. "I don't like to think of my story as tragic anymore, you know. I like to think that I've been given an opportunity to grow and change and see the world for what it is: a strange combination of cruelty and kindness."

I nod in agreement. "That's a good way to put it. There's no other way to describe your situation. You've seen the best and the worst of people all in one capsule. I applaud you for finding a way out of your bitterness; most people would have had a hard time of it."

Laila looks thoughtful. "I had a hard time of it, too—it's taken many years. I just managed to crawl out of the hole I was in because I couldn't handle the darkness anymore, and I finally decided that the only way out was up, if you know what I mean."

"I do know what you mean, and I agree with you."

"So here I am today," she says, taking my hand again, "sitting in this room with you, trying to take your mind off your *own darkness*."

"Ah, you can see it, too? Is it that obvious?"

"I can tell you are disturbed about something; that much is clear."

"Well," I say, letting go of her hand and smiling wryly, "there is the little problem of my terminal illness…"

Laila looks sheepish, and I immediately stop her from feeling awkward by making light of it: "Don't worry about the elephant in the room, I'm dealing with that. And you're right; there is something else nagging at me—besides the elephant—but I can't quite put my finger on it. When I figure it out, you'll be the second to know, okay?"

Apparently the unnamed anxiety that has been roiling me for the past week is not completely invisible to the outside world.

Laila still looks embarrassed. "Yes, of course. I didn't mean to be insensitive…" "Don't be silly, you're no such thing," I say waving my hand casually at her to dispel the notion. "It's not your fault that I have cancer! It's not anyone's fault, it's just my time, that's all."

"I understand—more than you know," she says kindly, appreciating my affable tone. She begins to gather her things. "I'm off to my next appointment then, but we'll talk again tomorrow."

"I'm counting on it," I say, rearranging myself on the bed, trying to find a new position that will cause me less pain than the previous one. I smile and wave at her weakly as she leaves the room, feeling as though my last friend has just departed.

All of this reality is leaving me deflated and on the verge of depression. I start to think about some of the things Laila has said and then remind myself that the future is not a good place for me to go traipsing around in. And the present certainly doesn't hold any bright promises, either. Better to turn around, deal with the past—at least, it's manageable and a *fait accompli*. If Laila were here, I would tell her that I simply meant that the past is a done deal.

On the other hand, I think to myself—somewhat schizophrenically, perhaps—that I need to see to that nasty little chore the hospice people keep reminding of: "putting my affairs in order."

I suppose that might be entertaining for a while—take my mind off the elephant before his heavy feet begin to crush my chest again. Ouch.

Chapter 5

DOLLARS AND SENSE

I'm richer than they think.

While Charlie was alive, he handled most of the money matters, and I rarely intervened. Not that he kept them a secret; I just didn't have much to do with it at the time. I kept my accounts; he kept his; we had little reason to involve ourselves in the other's business.

We had an estate plan drawn up where the money passed seamlessly from one to the other upon either of our deaths. We had both worked for many years before we retired and Charlie had a knack for good investments. Thank God, because I certainly did not. Plus which, Charlie had inherited a nice-sized portfolio from his mother when she died. But it came as somewhat of a surprise to me that we had amassed such a goodly sum.

I know this because I recently had my estate lawyer, Howard Chavez, fill me in on all the details of my holdings. He was more than happy to oblige; at $400 an hour, why shouldn't he be? He rattled off the different totals: over a million in stocks, another $800,000 in bonds, two pieces of real estate—being managed by my son—both with positive cash flows, plus some money market funds. Throw in the townhouse I'm living in, and you're looking at a reasonable financial package. All that money, I thought, and nowhere to go. All that money and no way to fix the mess I'm in.

Howard would be amused to hear me say this. He's of the opinion that most things can be fixed with money. And while that is certainly true much of the time, clearly, it is not always the case—as I can willingly attest. In fact, Charlie used to say, "Pray for problems that can be fixed with money; it's the ones money can't solve that will bring you down." How right he was.

Howard Chavez is an interesting sort. Formerly a junior partner in a large Miami law firm, he moved to Seattle some ten years ago to be near his brother and with the intent purpose of setting up shop on his own. In the end though, he succumbed to the pressure and joined up with a local firm that specializes in estate work, and now has his last name neatly appended to the two that come before it. I always like to remind him of the joke about "Dewey, Cheatem and Howe." In this case, it would be Dewey, Cheatem and Chavez. He is sufficiently evolved to smile when I bring this up. He came highly recommended to us from one of Charlie's friends at work; we hired him to write up our wills and a living trust and have stuck with him ever since, with no regrets as of the present.

He is Cuban, medium height, with curly black hair cropped fairly short. The hair gives him a cherubic appearance until you get to his eyes, which are sufficiently feral that you give up on the angel idea. He is just beginning to acquire a paunch that has a comfortable look to it, as though it's settling in for the winter and will be enhancing itself as time goes on.

His clothes are expensive, well-tailored, never too casual, as befits an estate lawyer used to encountering somber scenes without too much warning. He is scarily clever when it comes to nuances of the law and has just the right touch of humor to keep me in his thrall.

He has a superior intellect that he likes to toss around so that others can praise it, but overall, he is the kind of man who is far too entertaining to get rid of, either as a lawyer or as a friend, and I consider him to be both.

He would be pleasantly surprised to know that I consider him a friend, but in fact, I do—and I know he's fond of me as well. So Howard is pretty much a fixture in the household at this point.

He has the look of someone equally at home in a funeral parlor as in a law office. And in fact, he has a habit of turning up at wealthy clients' prayer services as a matter of course. It goes without saying that this is the perfect chance for him to cruise the grieving relatives for burgeoning legal opportunities while they have their guard down.

I always marvel at how something so obviously opportunistic is so successful. While shaking the hands of the recently bereaved he can be heard saying, "Yes, of course, George, I can help you with that; just give me a call at the office when you have recovered from the terrible shock. So sorry for your loss..."

Charlie and Howard had gotten on rather well together, which surprised everyone but me. We managed to hammer out a living trust, which kicked into gear after Charlie died. Despite his high rates, I was too enamored of Howard to find someone new.

They've always got you by the short hairs, these estate lawyers, since you're convinced that changing horses during the period before the estate taxes get paid would do nothing but cost you more by the time you brought someone else up to speed. Plus which, it's like changing dentists who have been wandering around in your mouth for years. Why break in a new one at this late date?

They also know you've got the inertia and haziness that comes with someone's death muddling your mind and keeping you from making sharp decisions. By the time you emerge from the fog, it's way too late. They understand this and exploit it, for which I can hardly blame them. I would do the same thing in their position; in fact, I would question their competence if they did anything other than that.

And who understands any of the drivel they write, pages and pages of it, mountains really, with hardly a recognizable word amidst it all. I once tried to read through the latest trust papers but gave up when I hit the section entitled: "QTIP Election with respect to Property." It is specifically designed to numb the mind and succeeds beyond the author's wildest dreams, a point that is hardly lost on estate lawyers. This is the bedrock of their profession, the foundation upon which it is built.

At one point I forced myself to read the entire trust document from cover to cover without skipping a single paragraph. I'm not stupid; I understand English better than most. But apparently that is not the prerequisite for comprehension in this case, as I failed to grasp more than 20% of what I read. And even after Howard laboriously explained it to me twice, I must confess that there are parts of it that continue to totally bamboozle me.

How very clever of them (lawyers en masse) to deceive me like this. Still, I am complicit and share in the conspiracy to defraud myself. It's like fighting City Hall; I just don't have the will or the energy to fight them, so I collude by paying their bills and filing their bilious documents in my desk drawers. The deceit perpetuates itself; no one wants to admit that they have no idea what they are signing, especially since everyone else is apparently signing similar paperweights themselves.

I cannot be alone in this. Note to myself: ask other widows (or other humans for that matter) if they have understood the wills and trusts written up for them by their so- called solicitors. But remember when you do so that ego might force those you ask to lie about their comprehension level, so that would undoubtedly be a waste of time as well.

Further note to myself: give it up. Let them write what they like. It still all comes down to the same basic story line—who gets what, when, and what's the catch?

But Howard doesn't know everything about my financial life; he only *thinks* he does. In point of fact, I have a secret asset—one whose existence only I am aware of. Charlie knew about it, but he's gone now, and so the secret is mine alone. I've been figuratively "sitting on it" all this time, but to what end? I've always thought the right time would present itself, and perhaps now it has, what with the sand in my hourglass getting perilously close to the bottom. Since time is no longer in my corner, perhaps this will force my hand.

All of this is swirling through my head when I realize that Howard is actually in my bedroom talking to me—has been for some time now apparently, which makes sense, since I was the one who asked him to come over this afternoon. I'd better get with the program; I tell myself: *focus!*

"…the revised trust is pretty straightforward, Olivia," he was saying in his deep voice—he liked to call it mellifluous though I thought ridiculous was closer to the truth. "But you still need to clean up the bequest list and decide how you're splitting up the bulk of the estate between your son, your stepdaughter, your grandchildren and the various charities. We had it divided equally in the last draft, and I assumed you were happy with that until you sent me an email saying that you've changed your mind— again!—as to the final distribution."

I sigh deeply, then shoot him a long, annoyed look. He is perched awkwardly on one of the lounge chairs in my bedroom while I lay modestly robed in my bed. I had asked him to pay me a house visit as the likelihood of my ever leaving my room again, let alone the house, was slim to nonexistent. He was only too happy to oblige.

Tick-tock, tick-tock, I think.

"The bequests are easy, Howard, I've made you a list—here take it," I say, pulling a handwritten page out of my night table drawer. "There are three people here, people who have stood by me—more or less—for the last thirty years, so I suppose they're entitled to some sort of reward for their perseverance and their uncanny ability to get along with me for this long. Give them all $20,000 apiece and be done with it. As to the split among the 'prospective heirs'…I just can't seem to make up my mind. I suppose their spouses, or 'spice,' as I prefer to call them, will also get to put their sticky fingers on the loot?"

Howard purses his lips and searches for the right phrase. "Olivia, I know you're not serious, so I'm going to ignore that remark. If it's any consolation, as I'm sure you already know, inheritance is always considered separate property, so your heirs can choose not to share their expectancy if they are so inclined. And I'm sure they know that as well, having been brought up at Charlie's knee. Hell, he made them both sign a prenup when they got married, so I wouldn't stay up late worrying about sticky spousal digits if I were you."

He continues, "But my question remains: after the bequests and the charitable donations and any taxes are paid off, we'll force the sale of the houses—that's what you told me you want to do. So then, how do you want me to split the resulting estate? Into equal per capita portions, as we had originally drawn it up, or not? It's your call, of course, but deviating from the per stirpes norm can always cause problems."

He puts his chin down and peers at me ominously as though to reinforce his point and to see if I am paying attention, and also, of course, to see if I know what per *stirpes* means.

"Aye," I nod wickedly at his warning, "there's the rub. And yes, I know what per stirpes means; I took Latin for four years, for God's sake—'By the branch,' if you want to be literal. It means that if an heir dies before my death, his or her heirs take the proportional share that the deceased would have been entitled to if still living."

"Yes, exactly," he says, with a note of admiration in his voice. "And by the way, you're not in as steep a decline as some might think, are you?"

"Yes and no, Howard, it's all very subjective—difficult to quantify deterioration, I would think. It sort of depends on who you're talking to and whether or not they have a dog in the fight… But back to your point: you have to understand that I'm still rather inclined to leave the entire remainder to the Petting Zoo." I smile slightly, pause for effect, then continue. "To tell the truth—which that was not—of all of them, I think that I prefer my stepdaughter and my cat the most, not necessarily in that order, though this won't go down well at all with Brian."

I pull my longhaired tabby cat higher up on the bed when I say this, patting down his thick tail so that it lays coiled perfectly against his body. Merlin preens contentedly while I stroke him, as though the prospect of the petting zoo and his inheritance has somehow brightened his day.

Charlie had been married briefly before we met and this union had produced a daughter named Claire. She was smart, funny, charming and everything I would have wanted in a daughter. Only she wasn't mine, in fact, or legality. Her mother had kept her close, and Charlie did not see her as much as he could have/should have during her formative years and during the years when he and I were first together though he helped her financially all along. By the time they did become closer, she was a fully formed adult with her own wants and needs, no longer craving or soliciting the approbation of dear old Dad.

Nonetheless, she was the apple of Charlie's eye, and he had always made me promise if he should die before me, to take care of her and any of her children as though she were my natural child. This was a promise I had no trouble making or keeping.

After all, it was mostly Charlie's money, not mine, and while most wives would not think of it this way, I always did. It was his financial savvy that had made our investments double and then triple. He was the one who bought the properties and saw their potential. He was the one who had the foresight to buy the tech stocks that catapulted us into the higher tax brackets. We would never have gotten there on our salaries or my financial advice. And finally, he was the one with the inheritance, not me.

Our salaries would have been fine for maintaining our middle-class status, but it was his portfolio that paid for all the extras and made us semi-rich, for what it was worth. I was good at spending it while he knew how to make the numbers work. And then, when I lost him, I no longer cared about spending it anymore. Without him, the numbers had no meaning.

When he was alive, he would get the brokerage statements in the mail, and we would be thrilled when the numbers swelled. But without Charlie what use do I have for all that money? A vacation without him seems meaningless; there is no place I want to go without him; clothes that he will never see on me no longer interest me. Everything has lost its luster.

There were so many things we wanted to do when he was with me, and now anything I can think of seems dull and lifeless and leaves a metallic taste in my mouth. So the money just sits there, quietly churning, racking up interest, splitting, compounding itself, growing—not unlike the cancer inside me, I think grimly.

Ironically neither of my main heirs-apparent needs my monetary assistance. They have both done well on their own. Brian, the doctor, has a thriving practice, owns his home, and knows how to invest his money. Plus which, when Charlie died, he left a tidy sum in a life insurance policy directly to both of his children, so neither of them was left wanting—financially at least.

Brian's son Tad attends a posh private high school, is enrolled in nothing but advanced classes, and has his own car now, so no one is overly worried about his prospects in life. Knowing Brian, he will somehow finagle his son into Stanford with or without the SATs to go along with it. No one will go wanting there.

And of course, Macy—his daughter, his first-born, our sweet granddaughter—is gone now. I can't bring myself to dwell on this for even a moment, or I won't be able to think. She is a subject for another time and place.

Claire works for a large credit card company and seems to get one promotion after another. Not only that but when she first started with the company, she had wisely enrolled in the stock purchase program and managed to build herself an admirable stockpile of equities that has doubled and tripled over the years so that now she is sitting on a small goldmine.

During those years, she had also acquired a husband and a son, but only her son Kevin had made the cut, though she eventually remarried and, this time, did a better job of it. Kevin is a high achiever and a charmer to boot. I adore him. He is winsome and funny and wickedly clever, as one would have expected from one of Claire's progeny. He could read by age four, had a rock 'n' roll band by age seven, and was writing computer apps at ten. I'd have to be sure to leave him something meaningful from the old lady. He'd like that, and I would be happy to oblige.

In case I haven't already mentioned it, I adore my cat. Merlin is one of the few creatures in my life (besides Charlie) who has never betrayed me. He bit me once, but it was admittedly provoked, and furthermore it was curiously endearing—as it was most decidedly a "love bite," so how could I possibly be offended?

Aside from that, Merlin has been fiercely loyal and the least covetous member of my family. In general, if the question were put to me, I would have to admit to preferring his company over most of those whom I know that are currently alive. Luckily, no one has ever asked me the question out loud; still I'm sure they suspect this to be true. Furthermore, he is blessed with more natural beauty than my offspring, and he's done the best with what he was given.

"The petting zoo does have its allure," Howard is pointing out languidly, bringing me out of my reverie on Merlin, "although your heirs-apparent will probably tear me to pieces post-mortem if you do that."

"There's a pretty picture," I retort. "I vacillate between thinking my heirs are deserving to thinking they shouldn't get a penny. Please tell me what they ever did to warrant having a fortune just slipped into their laps like oysters out of shells? Did they help earn it? Good God, no. They pretty much just helped spend it. Did they ever thank us for the sacrifices we made sending them to those bloody expensive schools, or providing the world's most exhaustive medical and dental care? I think not. Did they ever…"

Howard groans heavily. "I must interrupt you, Olivia, since you seem to be warming up to this line of thinking. And even though I am happily charging you by the hour, I still think you're missing the point. Furthermore, you're becoming schizophrenic; just yesterday you were telling me how much you loved your family, how hardworking and industrious they were, and how much joy they had given you. Do you remember that?"

I shrug sullenly. "Perhaps, but that was yesterday; this is today.

My head is killing me. You can't expect me to be altruistic when I feel like someone just poured my brains into a bucket. What's the point of being miserable if you can't spread the misery around?"

Howard sighs loudly, ignoring my last question. "To your point, Olivia, it's not a question of logic or gratitude or deservedness, if such a word exists, it's just the way of the world. Your parents gave to you, you give to your children, they give to theirs, and so on; that's how the formula works and how it's always been. Trickle-down wealth, if you like. Worthiness is not really the issue. If it were, no one would ever get anything. As a general rule, the trickle-down makes sense. Sometimes, at a specific level, it's a bad idea or even a disastrous one, but we need to take the tried and true path, follow the curve. At least, that's my best advice to you."

"Please continue, oh wise one. I can see you're on a roll."

"I will, and I am," Howard continues, ignoring my tone. "You'll leave a righteous mess behind if you go against the curve. Cut one of them out and they'll be bickering and backstabbing each other like hungry vultures, gnashing their teeth and countersuing until they're cold in their graves. Trust me; it happens like clockwork; I've seen it over and over. People never rise to their highest selves at these times but invariably sink to the lowest common denominator and stay there until they run out of energy. This is my world; I know of what I speak…"

I yank the covers up to my neck and shove one of my bony hands into the air in an effort to stop his harangue. "Holy crap, Howard, enough already! I'm not interested in what the rest of the world does, nor am I interested in your advice on this highly private issue. I should think you'd have gathered that by now. It's my money, and I'll do what I please with it. Won't I, Merlin, my wise pussycat, my furry co-counsel, my most worthy heir?"

I scratch roughly behind Merlin's ears, which makes him crane his neck in my direction while purring noisily. But I'm not finished with Howard yet.

"And by the way," I continue, pulling myself back into a sitting position, "I insist that you put in one of those—what are they called—no-contest clauses, that's it. I want a stiff no-contest clause that limits the distribution to one dollar if they try to fight the terms of the will and lose. I read about this in a legal thriller recently," I said proudly. "Sounds like a bloody good idea to me."

"So noted," Howard replies. "Standard fare—and good fun at the same time, so well worth the effort. Sometime, remind me to tell you the story about my client that had that exact thing happen. You can't believe how satisfying it was to write the check out to one of his relatives for one dollar." Howard smiles indulgently at the memory, clearly an estate lawyer's idea of good fun.

"Yes, well, you can share the delicious details with me some other time. But listen, I'm not done with my rant yet. Let's get back to me: I mean you can do what you like with your own money, Howard, I couldn't care less, but stay out of this one. I've let you push me around on everything else—distributions here, lump payments there, yearly tax-free gifts, the whole nine yards. Those two have already gotten more 'gifts' than I dreamed of in a lifetime. You think they appreciate it? You think they deserve it? You think it makes them better people? Think again. They resent the money I spend on myself and call me stingy for not giving them more…"

I take a deep breath to reload and then continue, noting Howard's stony silence and disgusted look. "I know how their minds work; I know what they say behind my back. Don't think I don't have my spies. But anyone with half a brain would see their mindset. They think it's their birthright. They think they're entitled. They think some accident of birth grants them rights and benefits whether they deserve it or not. I don't happen to see it that way."

Dear God, What fresh hell is this: I have turned into my mother! I think to myself, suddenly feeling guilty and deeply embarrassed by my little speech. When did that happen? How is this possible? What happened to the sensible, even-tempered, non- judgmental Olivia I used to know?

Howard is simply staring at me, waiting to see if I have completed my harangue. I fold my arms across my chest to indicate that I am done.

Merlin yawns languorously and finds a new position on the bedspread, fanning out his tail in a perfect arc.

Howard glares at the cat menacingly. "I assume you are finished now? I don't know why I'm letting you jerk my chain like this, Olivia. I don't believe you for a second. But go ahead, rant and rave like some lunatic fishwife and pretend that you believe every word that you're saying when I know you don't. I've had conversations with you in the past that negate everything you're saying now. You sound like a bitter old battleax—excuse the expression—but it's not really you, it's not your style. Go ahead, be dramatic, leave it to the cat and let the lawyers spend years litigating. Oh, and by the way, that should go a long way to proving your competence," he says, the tone coming out more sarcastically than he means it to sound.

This actually gets my attention. "Competence? Who's questioning my competence, pray tell?"

He stands up now, trying to smooth out his rumpled appearance and clearly attempting to rein in his gathering emotions, lest he aggravate the woman who is admittedly his client, not his adversary.

He ignores my question completely for the moment. "Listen, Olivia, putting my ideas aside, let's at least, get the will and the trust finalized," he says, trying to sound more conciliatory. "I'll write everything up and just leave a blank where the name of the final inheritors will go. Then you can fill me in when you're good and ready. Deal?" "Sure, Howard, sounds great. Less pressure that way," I say, also trying to ameliorate the situation. "Why don't you get some flash cards that say: Brian, Claire, Howard, Merlin, Tad, Kevin, Laila and the Petting Zoo. You notice that I stuck you in there near the cat and the grandchildren? Then if I get really rummy towards the end, you can hold up the cards, and I'll point to the ones I've chosen. Instant heirs. Who knows, you might get lucky in the inheritance lotto, the little issue of 'conflict of interest' notwithstanding." I smile at the thought, knowing that, in reality, there is zero chance of any of that ever happening.

Howard looks apprehensive, even defeated. "You think this is a game, don't you? Why on earth are we even seriously talking about the cat and a nurse that has only worked for you for seven or eight weeks?"

"Laila may have only been with me for a short time," I say defensively, "but I happen to feel very close to her. I can't explain it, but I feel as though I have known her my whole life. She is the kindest girl—so gentle with me, so sweet-natured, so wise, like an old soul, and, after all she's been through—born in Afghanistan, orphaned by the war, adopted here in the states, feeling like an outsider…"

Howard cocks his head to one side and looks at me as though he thinks I have gone completely, stark raving mad. "Good Lord, Olivia! Who cares what she's gone through? It's got nothing to do with you! She shouldn't be a part of this conversation. She's not even in the running! Don't you know this is why estates end up in lawsuits over medical personnel who get too close to their ailing patients and take advantage of their situations? Don't even joke about it! As an estate lawyer, it makes my skin crawl."

 I can't help but smile at his discomfort. "Oh, Howard, relax. I'm playing with you, and you're turning out to be a much easier target than I ever imagined."

Howard seems to visibly let go of some of his tension and looks slightly ashamed of himself for taking me so seriously. "Admittedly, Laila has had a rough go of it, from what little you have told me. And it's very endearing of you to want to help her. But when you mention putting her in your will, it gets my hackles up, even if you are, as you say, 'playing with me.' But this is no game, Olivia. I mean, what would Charlie think about that?"

"You're right, Howard, this is no game. Trust me; games don't normally cost me $400 an hour—sorry to keep harping on that, but you did bring it up. I know you're dead serious—oops, also hate to use the 'D' word these days, especially in my current state— but I'm not making fun of this, believe me. I'm thinking about it, so don't rush me. I'm not going to do anything stupid or rash. After all, it's only a life or death decision…" I manage a crooked smile and look at him coquettishly, which, in my current state, is not easy or even successful.

Before he can interrupt me again, I continue. "I'm joking about the petting zoo and the cat, and certainly about leaving anything to you, really I am, you must know that. You take me much too seriously. I realize it looks like I've only got several hours to live, but reports of my demise have been deliberately exaggerated. Don't believe everything you hear from Lisa in the kitchen! I'm mulling it over—reflecting, okay? I'll come up with an answer sooner or later. And believe me, whatever I decide, Charlie would back me up on it, I know that. But I expect you to follow my wishes when the time comes and not give me some boilerplate, knee-jerk attorney response. Got it?"

Howard nods curtly, pursing his lips together in an attempt to register disapproval. "*Sooner* would be better than *later*; you wait too long—if you haven't already—and your mental competency really *will* be challenged, and you know we don't want to get into that. It's not like you're in tip-top physical shape, you know—no offense meant."

He takes a deep breath. "You need to be able to speak, or at least write, cogently, or the flash cards won't do you much good. You don't want some attorney crawling all up and over your estate after your departure, do you?"

I shudder at the loathsome picture this brings to mind, remembering earlier colonoscopies. "Goodbye, Howard, thanks for the little visit," I say deferentially. "Go back to the office and charge me more money; you know I love supporting your habits, puritanical though they may be. Come back in a few days and we'll talk again. And don't worry, I'll still be here."

"Have Lisa set up an appointment for me; she'll like that. It always makes her think she'll be getting something soon. I do love leading them on…" I say, smiling weakly at the thought.

"Oh wait, Howard, I just remembered, there's one more thing we need to discuss. I'm truly sorry to throw you a curve so late in the game, but I've been mulling over what to do about this and I've finally come to a conclusion. I had thought about simply handing this over to someone as a gift, but after listening to you drone on biliously about tax consequences and avoiding probate and blah blah blah, I've decided to do it properly so that everything is kosher and there are no last-minute squabbles. I want you to put something on the asset list, but not in the trust. I want you to do whatever is necessary to set this up as a 'transfer on death' account. Tell me what to sign and I will do so. I will let you know how I want it disbursed when we have our next meeting."

He looks at me curiously, trying to figure out just exactly what this "something" could be.

"Just a moment, let me show you what I'm referring to," I say, reaching gamely under the mattress. I pull out a tattered-looking envelope, sealed with just a small piece of tape that looks yellowed and insufficient to keep its seal.

"What on earth, Olivia?" Howard says as he reaches out for what he assumes is a letter of some sort.

"Go ahead, open it," I say, fixing my eyes intently on him, waiting impatiently to see what his reaction will be.

"Wait, stop! Before you open it, let me give you a short history. It's a good story."

Howard obliges by laying the envelope flat on his lap.

I smooth down my bedcovers and sit up straighter so that I can look directly at him when I speak. "I have had this envelope in my possession since my mother died. I left a box of my things at her house many years ago. The box held small personal items that had been mine when I lived with my mother and stepfather, Nelson. Someday maybe I'll tell you the whole story of Nelson, but not now. Suffice it to say that we had a somewhat unusual relationship. The box contained pens, rulers, ornamental boxes, a few school books, some scarves and a ragged copy of *Gone with the Wind* that I must have read twenty times when I was a young girl. Nelson knew it was my favorite book. I often read it when I took a bath. I had meant to take it with me when I left there, but I was in such a rush to get on with my life that I left the entire box behind. Honestly, I never gave it another thought after that."

"Where are you going with this, Olivia?"

"Be patient. I'll get there. I had forgotten about it completely until my mother died very unexpectedly—that's yet another story for another time. So when it was time to clean out the house, her live-in boyfriend Albert—it gags me to say his name—told me I could pick up what few belongings I had there. So I went over to the house with Charlie, snatched the two or three boxes that Albert had stacked up for me, and left. When I got home to my place, I pushed the boxes to the back of our hall closet and never thought about them again for years."

"Dear God, bottom line me, Olivia, what has this got to do with anything?" "Oh, ye of little faith. I'm getting closer. Bear with me. So when Charlie and I moved, these boxes naturally moved with us, and again, I thought nothing of them and never had occasion to get into them. It wasn't until my granddaughter Macy was eight or so that I started to think about books that she might like to read in the future." I pause here. The mere mention of Macy's name makes me catch my breath, and for a moment, I feel my chest tighten with emotion. Don't cry, I tell myself, wait until he's gone. I take a deep breath, lick my lips, and force myself to continue.

"I had given Macy various children's books, of course, like The *Secret Garden,* but I was thinking that when she got to be older—remembering all the pleasure it had brought me—I should start her on *Gone with the Wind.* So it was not until then that I suddenly recalled the book that had been sitting in the closet for some thirty years. I thought it might be fun to give her my old tattered copy, but if it were in terrible shape, I'd simply buy her a new one. So I broke open that dilapidated box. And there was the book, just where I'd left it, just as I remembered it. I picked it up and turned it over in my hands."

"But then I noticed something just peeking out of the top of it. I pulled it out and opened the front cover. There was the envelope I am handing you now."

Howard groans. "I feel like I'm an actor in a bad soap opera. Are we approaching the End Game?"

"We are. In the envelope you will see a stock certificate and a short note that says the shares had been transferred to me and are now registered in my name. If you open it, you can see the note. It's on the top there."

Howard dutifully opens the envelope and extracts the top sheet. He reads it out loud:

I think these will do well for you over time.

I have confidence in the management of the company.

I hope you will think of me kindly someday.

Always, Nelson

Howard looks intrigued. "Okay, I'll bite, what have you got in here?" He pulls out the second item in the envelope: an old-fashioned but official-looking stock certificate in the amount of five shares. At first, he shakes his head derisively, then as he takes a closer look he realizes what he is holding.

"Oh my God!" he gasps. "You have five shares of Berkshire Hathaway Class A stock? Do you have any idea what this is worth today?"

"Actually, I do. As of the close of market yesterday, they were worth $592,000 a share, so close to 3 million dollars in total." I paused for this to sink in. "The beauty of it is—and I looked this up on my iPad—Nelson paid approximately $76 apiece for those five shares when he bought them. Thank you, Nelson. Thank you, Warren Buffett. His faith in you was well-placed."

Howard drops the certificate into his lap. "I'm speechless. Really, I am. And you've been sitting on these shares all this time?"

"Unwittingly for most of the time, but yes, I suppose I have. But they certainly haven't been just sitting around! What a story they have to tell—these fiveca little shares. The real question is, how did Nelson have the incredible prescience and foresight to buy them in the first place?"

"How, indeed. And why did he leave them to you?"

"Ah, well, I can't speak for the prescience, but the 'why did he leave them' part is not such a mystery to me. However, it will have to continue to be a mystery to you. In any case, here they are, and they need to be dealt with. I assume I don't pay any tax on it if I don't sell them myself?"

Howard rubs his face. "Correct. I'll look into the details when I get back to the office. So you want them transferred to someone upon your death?"

"Exactly. So now, did you enjoy my little surprise? I thought I'd spring it on you at the last minute just to spice things up. Now you'll spend the entire weekend wondering who's going to get it, won't you?"

Howard smirks. "You are so bad, Olivia. I really do think you are enjoying this. No, better yet, I *know* you're enjoying it…You seem to think this is some late night quiz show."

"Not enjoying it so much as just savoring it. There is a difference, and I'm ignoring the quiz show comment as it seems overly tacky."

I turn over heavily in my bed, finally weary of the conversation and yearning for a quick nap. "I'm so very tired. I think you must leave now. Nighty-night, Howard. Don't let the screen door hit you…"

Howard looks surprised at the sudden dismissal, but takes the hint, backing out of the bedroom quietly, closing the bedroom door behind him, briefcase in hand. I hear him conversing with Lisa as he passes through the living room, though I cannot make out what they are saying.

The sound of his deep bass voice nudges me right into the

dreamless sleep I had been yearning for in an effort to escape.

When I awaken, once again I am alone with my thoughts. As visions of the present begin to recede, the past comes trickling down to fill in the spaces. In many ways, I am more comfortable living there.

I turn my mind's eye back to my review of the senses. There is one that I have no pretty lists for: yes, I could name a thousand beautiful things that I have touched and so many different people in so many different ways. But that is not where my mind goes. No, there is one particular touch that never leaves my thoughts, one particular touch that haunts me—one touch I would give the world to undo. But even the world won't undo this one.

Chapter 6

TOUCH

It seemed an inspired idea at the time. Charlie had always wanted to go back to Australia. He had been there once before on some journalistic mission and had always wanted to return when he could concentrate on the landscape and not his work. He claimed that the beaches were "sparkling white and unparalleled," the parks were spectacular, that the "sky was closer there than it was here," and that the people there were friendly and welcoming. My opinion about it was that the plane ride all by itself would be insufferable and that you could find astonishing beaches in plenty of more geographically desirable areas. But Charlie was bound and determined to see the Down Under again.

He was indefatigably upbeat about everything while I always sensed danger lurking just around the corner. He usually wore me out with the arguments for why something was advisable (his opinion) versus why it was way too much trouble (my opinion). In the end, he was the captain of our marital boat and normally led us into safe harbors. But even Charlie was not always a match for the universe, which had its own ideas about who was in charge and how things were decided. This was one of those times and one of those decisions that, as we were soon to discover, had a life of its own.

"Well, you make all of the arrangements, tell me what time to show up and we'll go. Oh, and I suppose you'll expect me to go snorkeling while we're there?" I said, wondering vaguely where the word "snorkel" ever came from and not really looking forward to the prospect of being seen in a bathing suit on a public beach.

"That would be a normal expectation, yes. I absolutely think we should go snorkeling. You're never too old for it, swimming attire notwithstanding," Charlie said, anticipating my thoughts about bathing suits. "They have some mind-blowing, spectacular fish down there, like nothing you've ever seen. Colors you've never even imagined—electric blues, heliotrope, goldenrod—more exciting even than your childhood goldfish Oliver—I believe that was his name. Besides, I haven't told you the best part yet: I've decided we're taking Macy with us!" Charlie waited for my reaction.

"Really, Macy, and not Tad or Kevin?"

Macy was nine years old. She was sweet and cuddly and precocious and good company, even with adults. She had a sassy, smart way about her and a sunny disposition. We all adored her. Things were never dull with Macy around. She made us feel young again, as simple as that.

Charlie smiled. "Tad's too young, and he's a boy—he'd be nothing but trouble. Too many bathroom incidents, too much seat kicking, temper tantrums, the works. We'd be fed up after the first hour. Furthermore, he's intoxicated with his LEGOs at the moment. He won't even notice we're gone. And Kevin is a teenager now—too old to spend that much time with his grandparents. Macy is different; she's easy, she'll put a smile on our faces, and we'll see everything through her eyes. It will be a vacation we'll always remember. And she'll look back at it someday and be glad she spent some quality time with the old folks. Don't do you think?"

"Oh, I suppose it's a good idea, maybe even a stellar idea. I wouldn't have thought of it. But yes, I like it, especially if you do all the organizing. You'll have to talk Brian and Lisa into it. I don't know how they'll feel about sending their girl child off to a continent halfway around the world. I think Macy would like it, though. She loves the water, likes going places with us, enjoys different foods. And she's always up for a good adventure. Why not? Let's do it!"

"Alright, it's settled then," Charlie smiled, pleased to have gotten the upper hand. "Leave Brian and Lisa to me. We'll go in April. It will be beautiful, the perfect temperature, not too crowded—I've researched it. You'll be glad we went."

After some world-class cajoling and sweet-talking—he told them it was our heart's desire—Charlie persuaded Brian and Lisa to let Macy travel with us. It took a heavy dose of charm to pull this off, but Charlie had charm in abundance, and he used it unflinchingly when necessary. And for whatever reason, he thought it was necessary here. He truly believed this would be a dream vacation, one that we would talk about for years. He was right on that point. We did talk about it for years.

And so the die was cast. The threads of the story began to be spun. One event cascaded into the other, and slowly the whole chapter morphed into being.

There was much preparation, planning and research that went into the trip—most of the details lovingly taken care of by Charlie, who was a planner by nature. He always liked to say that the devil was in the details, but there was no devil here, just the careful compilation of lists and accoutrements that went along with the trip. I took care of some minor details, but the bulk of the work fell to him.

His work as an editor had made him careful and meticulous about minutiae, and he always did his homework, no matter what the subject. In this case, the subject was Australia, the seashore, the parks, colorful fish and beachside hotels. He was eminently up to the task.

He purchased the tickets, reserved the rooms, organized the cars, printed out maps and itineraries, made lists of items to pack, and figured out everything down to the last item. Macy was excited beyond belief. She told all her friends she was going to "'Stralia" and mocked Tad behind our backs when he pouted that he was not going. She spent weeks packing and unpacking the same little suitcase, unable to decide what to bring. It seemed the departure date would never come, but then it did come, and the three of us took off that April morning for parts unknown—at least unknown to us.

Brian and Lisa stood on the porch waving as we pulled out of their driveway on our way towards the Great Barrier Reef and the majestic continent of Australia.

I had, of course, been prescient about the plane ride. Human beings weren't meant to sit in airplanes on and off for twenty-six hours, and certainly not your average nine-year-old, who become bored after the first half-hour. It's uncivilized at best and unbearable at worst. Still, we somehow survived the sheer boredom of the flight, thanks to modern electronic devices, and stumbled our way off the plane, thrilled to be once again on terra firma and sitting on seats that didn't vibrate.

From that point on, the trip promised to be delightful. Our hotel was within view of the water and the white sands stretched out as far as the eye could see. It was tourist season, but not the height of it; we were in the ideal venue. The weather was perfection, hovering around 75 degrees Fahrenheit the entire time we were there—warm and balmy without being too hot or humid.

Charlie and I were religious about wearing hats and sunscreen. The sun seemed stronger here for some reason, closer, as though— as he had suggested—if you reached your hand up far enough, it would be singed from the sun's heat. But despite that, the heat was not oppressive; like everything there, it seemed just right.

We spent the first few days wandering around Sydney, like many a visitor before us, taking in the shopping and the monuments, the parks, the gardens and the restaurants, acquainting ourselves with this new space in our world. The parks were indeed magnificent and impeccably manicured, sporting every species of flower and tree you could imagine. Victoria Park enthralled us with its ponds and fountains, its breathtaking red trees, the exotic flowers, the exquisite birds.

Macy was in her glory. She would examine some new showy blossom, touch the leaves, rub her fingers on the petals, press flowers into her pocket, all to be collected and then carefully put into her "memory book" when we got home.

She wore a different sundress every day, confident that each new outfit was better than the last. And in fact, it was. She wore yellow hats with streaming ribbons and red and white sandals. She was all bare arms and shiny knees and wide-open green eyes that took in everything she saw. She felt ever so grown up, "like a girl in Seventeen," she said, referring to her favorite magazine, even though it was light years too old for her. She so completely enchanted us. She could easily have been the girl on the cover of a children's book. Macy takes 'Stralia, it would have read.

"Oh Macy," I would say conspiratorially, "you don't really read Seventeen now do you? That's for teenagers, or tweens, or whatever you call them these days, isn't it?"

"Yes, tweens. And I do Gram. I read it, and I know what it says. And now I am just like the girls in there that travel all over the world."

"Oh, really? They travel all over the world, do they? Is that by themselves, or with a little help from their mothers and fathers?" asked.

"Well, sure, they have help, and they go with their parents—or maybe their grandparents—because come on! *They* don't have any money, so how can they pay for things? That's why the grown-ups have to go. Everyone knows that." Macy shrugged in exasperation, as though you'd think that by now I would understand how things work.

Charlie and I laughed indulgently, as grandparents will do. We were at an outdoor restaurant for lunch, one that we had just discovered and that seemed like a great find. He and Macy had both ordered shrimp and chicken wings, drizzled with some sort of red sauce while I dove into a fruit salad that looked as though it had just been flown in from paradise.

Macy picked up each piece of shrimp and chicken with her fingers, one after the other, forgoing forks, knives or napkins, much to our horror. By the end of the meal she had smudges of barbecue sauce on her hands, her face, and the tabletop, not to mention the front of her dress. I begged her to slow down, use her fork, wipe her face, the usual things adults say to children at the table, but nothing could dampen her pleasure and enthusiasm for the meal. Charlie liked it just as much as she did, but managed to resign himself to the use of utensils for the most part. It was a sumptuous meal, one of many we had there.

The plan was to spend the next few days on the beach.

First thing in the morning, we bought tickets for a boat tour around the area, just to get a feel for the environs. The temperature was perfect again; the air felt warm and silky, the water was azure blue, the boat a sparkling white against the waves. There were perhaps forty people on the boat, all of them tourists like us, most with young children.

We had thought that Macy might mingle with some of the youngsters, but she did not. She didn't have a shy bone in her, but for whatever reason, on this trip, she stuck close to us. We were perfectly happy to have her all to ourselves and made the most of her unadulterated attention, something we did not usually have. Absent her parents, she turned herself completely in our direction, like a plant to the sun, and seemed to hang on our every word. We basked in her affection, appreciating the rarity of this time for the three of us to be completely isolated from the rest of our world. So far, we all thought it was, indeed, the perfect vacation.

On the second afternoon, we packed up several bags at the hotel with all of our beach gear and then installed ourselves on a patch of sand that we had carefully picked out in the morning. We each had our own giant-sized multi-colored beach towel, and each towel was meticulously laid out on the sand in a perfect rectangle as our designated spot.

We pulled off our street clothes, revealing bathing suits underneath; in my case, there was also a white, oversized man's shirt as a cover-up. We had brought the always popular canvas beach chairs for something to sit on if we were so inclined. I, of course, had brought a stack of books, a gigantic sunhat and a lifetime supply of sunscreen for all of us—not to mention the cooler, handled strictly by

Charlie, that contained all of the snacks, drinks, and ice that we had carefully assembled beforehand.

Macy flopped onto her beach towel, stomach side down, already slathered with sun lotion, then inched herself down until her feet were completely off the towel and buried in the sand.

"This sand feels smoother and warmer than all of the other sands I have put my feet in," she announced.

"Oh, and how many other beaches have you visited, my little world traveler?" I asked, amused at her grandiose statement.

"Well not *that* many, maybe, but I am telling you that this sand feels different. I know why: it's finer—you know, smaller—than the sand in Washington."

Charlie propped up in his beach chair, considered this thesis thoughtfully. "It's possible," he said. "She may be onto something. Perhaps it's finer here because someone sifted it all before putting in on the beach, but in Washington, they simply didn't bother. After all, it's colder there, so it wouldn't be nearly as pleasant to sift all that sand when the sun wasn't out."

Macy pondered this. "I think you're teasing me, Grampa, but that doesn't change the facts. The sand is definitely smaller and much warmer here."

"Don't you think that's simply because the temperature, in general, is warmer?" he asked, without commenting on her accusation.

"Well, maybe, but there's no question that it just feels better in 'Stralia,'" she said, languorously sifting the sand through her fingers.

"Well, who could argue with that," I said turning over on my back and adjusting my shirt to cover my chest completely.

We spent at least an hour lying on the beach, sipping cold drinks, eating chips. Eventually, Macy wanted to test the water and Charlie and I both went down with her to the shore. She splashed around in the shallow waves for five or ten minutes, acclimating herself to the temperature, then strode forward until she was waist deep in the Australian ocean.

I reminded her of the warnings posted periodically along the beach cautioning swimmers of the dangers of sharks and various jellyfish.

"I'll be careful, Gram," she said. "I don't think they come in so close to the beach."

Even at nine, she was already a good swimmer, a strong swimmer. Lisa had insisted she learn to swim when she was just a baby. They used to take her to the communal pool in their condo complex where she eventually learned the crawl, the butterfly, and the backstroke, so she had no qualms about pushing her way into the languid waves. We were directly behind her, slightly less assertive than she about getting ourselves wet, but nonetheless, gamely following in her footsteps.

The water, which at first had felt cool to me, soon felt comfortable and soothing. I dragged my hands through it, feeling the liquid resistance on my arms. The sand under my feet felt smooth and squishy.

"Don't go any farther than that," we warned as we could see her eyeing a buoy further out in the water.

"I won't," she said, flipping onto her back and letting the waves rock her. An unexpected spray of salt water caught her by surprise, and she jumped up, sputtering and wiping at her eyes. "Wow, that one really got me," she laughed.

I pulled up next to her and held her waist, marveling at her lightness in the salt water. "The water feels pretty good doesn't it?"

"Yeah, when you don't have a mouthful of it!"

"Oh, you're fine," Charlie said, coming up behind her. "No worries, as they say here in the Outback."

"I know," she said, kicking her feet to move to the side of us. I could tell that she was in her element, happy and strong, secure with us just beside her.

All three of us stayed in this small patch of ocean for another twenty minutes or so, taking in the slow rise and fall of the tiny waves surrounding us, enjoying the lift and the buoyancy the salt water provided. I had kept my hat and sunglasses on the whole time, so I was relatively protected, but Macy was completely exposed to the beating sun, as was Charlie.

"That's enough for today," I said, grabbing her hand and pulling her towards me. "And next time we go in the water, try hats and glasses, would you?"

Both Charlie and Macy gave me sour looks.

"No, I don't want to go yet. Let's stay, please, please," she implored. "I put on tons of sunscreen…"

"Absolutely not! You're going to end up with a right nice sunburn if you're not careful, and I don't want to have to answer to your parents for it, so march that way!" I said, pointing to the shore.

Macy was still at the age when obedience was the default response, so there was no real arguing about things. That would probably come in her teen years. But for now, she was pliable and easy to deal with.

She groaned and rolled her eyes, the way nine-year-olds do, and finally righted herself and began the trek back to the dry shore.

Eventually, we packed up our things and headed back to the hotel, where we all felt exhausted and ended up taking a nap for the rest of the afternoon, Macy in her twin- sized bed, Charlie and me in the adjoining room. I don't think I'd ever seen Charlie take a nap in the afternoon before, but the combination of the warm sun, a few drinks, and a small dose of jet lag had taken its toll.

One day followed another, with new gardens to explore, new buildings, new restaurants, new beaches. We had planned for five days in Sydney, and four of them had already flown past us. Charlie had mapped out the fifth day for snorkeling. He had spent some time researching the best way to do this with the least amount of hassle.

The gear he assembled was minimalist—rubber fins in three different sizes, face masks, short air tubes, paddle-boards. We were to go out on a tour boat that arranged for snorkeling parties. This was not the professional type of scuba diving boats with people lugging oxygen masks and heavy diving gear, just a small boat for amateurs who simply wanted to look at pretty fish relatively close to shore.

We lined up ahead of time at the dock with about ten other people and took off in the jauntily-appointed boat for one of the small coves not too far from our hotel. We all signed waivers before leaving, holding the boat company harmless in the event of a long string of dreadful catastrophes that might occur in the ocean. Macy was breathless with anticipation, convinced that this would be her most exciting adventure thus far.

When we got to the cove, the captain turned off the motor and set up ladders on the side of the boat for us to climb down into the water. Charlie and I put on our gear, such as it was, and followed Macy and the others down the rope ladder. The water felt warmer here than it had the previous day, and it didn't take long to feel relaxed and comfortable. By the time I got down the ladder, Macy already had her goggles on and her head buried in the water, her reddish-brown hair spread out behind her. She knew how to use her breathing tube and floated confidently out from the boat as we watched.

"Come look at these ones, Grampa," she said, pulling her head up. "Big bunches of them swimming together, you should see them!"

"Not bunches, schools," Charlie mumbled in her direction. We moved closer to her and put our heads in the water. The goggles seemed tight to me, and I couldn't quite adjust them properly, plus I found the breathing apparatus clumsy, but I forgot all of that when I saw what Macy was staring at: a massive number of shimmering, brilliantly colored fish only a few feet from the top of the water.

The sun filtered its way down through the ocean in long white sheets of light, illuminating the incredible life and movement going on right beneath our noses.

"Wow, pretty bloody amazing!" I managed to say, thinking how inadequate that was to describe the beauty of these undulating aquatic colonies that represented just the tip of the iceberg as far as life in the ocean was concerned.

We were floating within five feet of each other so that whatever Macy saw was what Charlie and I saw. I felt happy that Macy could experience this glorious day on the other side of the world and hoped that she would treasure these memories and think of them in her life to come; I hoped that she would have an appreciation for the variety and majesty of the world around her.

I remember thinking that I, too, would always remember this day and these underwater splendors.

As I put my head back into the water, floating contentedly in my space, I felt something silky nudge me. I yanked my head out of the water, thinking it was Macy bumping into me, but she was still several feet away from me.

Again I felt something warm and almost gelatinous touch me, and I recoiled. This time I looked down in the water in time to see a bundle of floating tendrils just passing by me. I lurched backward, remembering what I had heard and what the boat's captain had said about jellyfish.

While the touch itself had been soft and non-threatening, my mind suddenly began sending out distress signals. I knew that they could be dangerous, and all I could think about was making sure that nothing touched Macy or Charlie. Charlie was off to my left, placidly floating on his stomach, his breathing tube bobbing just above the water line. He seemed serene, comfortable, not in any danger.

Macy was on my right, and I could see that her head had come up out of the water. She still had her face mask on so I could not see her expression. But something about her body language told me all I needed to know.

"Macy," I screamed. "Move! Get out of there. Don't let them touch you." I swam as fast as I could to her. She pulled off her mask, and I could see that she was terrified. "Gram, they're stinging me.

Help me; they're hurting me!" Everyone could hear her screams now.

She was clearly agitated and was flapping her arms on the top of the water. "Get away from me," she keened in a high-pitched frightened voice. "My arms, they're stinging my arms!"

I could see Charlie powering his way towards us. I was on top of her now, and by the time I could grab her, I could feel the silky tendrils of the jellyfish near me as well. But for whatever reason, they did not sting me. I pulled her to me and headed for the boat, screaming to the boat's captain as I swam. Her arms were already beginning to swell, and her skin was turning an angry red.

The captain jumped into the water, fully clothed and helped me pull Macy to the side of the boat. Then several sets of hands pulled her swiftly onto the deck. Out of the corner of my eye, I saw Charlie racing towards us, his face mask and breathing tube having been tossed behind him. He looked petrified. He pushed me out of the way so he could see for himself what had happened.

"Dear God in heaven," I heard myself saying. "What have they done to our child?" *This can't be happening,* I remember thinking to myself. This can't happen to us, not to Macy, not now on this perfect day.

Macy lay on the floor of the boat, shuddering, shivering, her breathing more and more panicked, her body pulsating. She clutched my hand and looked at me with uncomprehending eyes.

"What's happening to me? I can't breathe right, I want Mommy, I want Mommy," she wailed inconsolably.

"Do something!" Charlie screamed at the captain, who was wildly rummaging through a cabinet on the deck. "You must know how to deal with this. Get us back to shore, call an ambulance. Do it NOW," he yelled in his most commanding voice.

"I'm looking for the anti-venom kit," he yelled, but I thought he had a panicked look on his face as well. I heard him tell someone named Jack to turn the boat around and call the ambulance. The other snorkelers had heard all the commotion and returned to the boat.

Charlie pushed himself up next to the captain. "Well, where is it? Hurry, we need it now! Do you know how to administer it?"

The captain jerked his head around and snapped, "Of course I know how to administer it, I just have to find the damn stuff, that's all. Now get out of my way so I can look for it!"

I was cradling Macy's head, trying to comfort her in some way, but nothing was working.

"Don't you have any fucking anti-venom on board?" Charlie screamed again in the direction of the captain, his face contorted in a rare show of rage. "You must have it; you're required to have it! Have you called the medics?"

"Christ, we used it yesterday, and it was supposed to be replenished, but I don't see the new batch. Jack!" the captain screamed at one of his crew, his face contorted, "Where the hell is the replacement kit? Don't tell me we didn't get it?"

Jack shook his head, and it was impossible to know whether he didn't have it or just didn't know the answer, but in any case, neither of them seemed able to locate a medical kit with the antidote to the poison from the jellyfish.

"I've got vinegar," Jack shouted, "we can use that."

"Yeah, great, put it on her, but we need the anti-venom!"

Jack rushed over to Macy and began to gently dab vinegar onto the spots where she had been stung, being careful not to massage the arm, which can push the venom higher into the veins. This seemed to have no effect whatsoever except to make her scream even more loudly, though in theory the vinegar is useful to help counteract any poison remaining on the surface of the skin. The problem was that the poison had probably already entered her bloodstream. And once inside, it would begin to make its deadly circuit through her body. Charlie and I knew that you could die within minutes if left untreated.

By now her skin was shiny red, hot, inflamed and swollen. I could tell that she had been stung in several places. She looked up at me with glassy eyes, gasping for breath. I pulled her upright and into my arms as best I could, but nothing we did had any effect on calming her.

Finally, the captain rushed over with a syringe that he said had a half dose of antitoxin. He wiped her skin briefly with a piece of alcohol-soaked cotton, then plunged it into her arm. I wondered to myself whether it should have been released directly into her vein, or whether a simple intra-muscular shot would do. "Are you sure you know what you're doing?" I screamed at him.

"We have to get her to shore," the captain said urgently, ignoring my question. He looked around the boat.

I couldn't focus on what he was saying. Charlie was standing next to him now, yelling at him to hurry, pushing him towards the steering wheel and forcing him to gun the engine. Charlie looked furious, his face dark and foreboding. But I couldn't deal with any of that. I felt completely out of control, bordering on hysteria, distraught that I couldn't do a single thing to help Macy at that moment.

She had stopped screaming, which was good in one sense, but almost more frightening to me, as she seemed to be sinking into a sort of delirium. I could see that she was shivering, almost convulsing, and her eyes seemed glassy and unable to focus. She was clearly in pain and was moaning softly. I could feel tears streaming down my face.

I took one of her arms and started to rub it without thinking, and the captain immediately lunged at me and pulled my hands away. "Don't touch her arms; it just helps move the poison around. The less you move her, the better." He glared at me as though I should have known this, but I was too angry with him to even respond.

The boat was closing in for the shore now. No more than five minutes had passed since he started the engine. We could see that there was an ambulance at the dock. I felt the tight band of tension that had been wrapped around my chest loosen just slightly.

"We're going to make you better, darling, I promise," I said to her, though she gave no indication of hearing anything I was saying. "This will fix you, sweetheart. Hang on Macy, just a little longer," I urged her in a broken voice.

She looked terrible to me by now. Her arms were swollen and red and shiny with lesions. She was perspiring fiercely and shuddering constantly. Her breathing seemed choppy and labored. Her head lolled dangerously, her eyes rolling back. I was paralyzed with fear.

Charlie was next to me again, trying to stabilize her head, arranging blankets on top of her to try to keep her warm. He kept closing his eyes and muttering something under his breath, which at first I couldn't hear. And then I realized he was saying over and over again,

"Dear God, don't take her. Please don't take her."

I started to cry now, hearing him begging for Macy's life. I had tried to convince myself that this was something we could deal with, that in the end, everything would work out, but now I realized that this was not necessarily going to end well. If Charlie was begging favors from a God he wasn't even sure of, it was not a good sign.

Neither of us was particularly religious, but suddenly we found ourselves beseeching this same God that we had been so distant from for all these years. This rarely-called-upon-God suddenly sprang into existence and became the one focal point we could cling to.

I too threw myself upon his mercy and begged him to hear our prayers. Like so many desperate souls before me, I promised anything in return for this one favor, just this one. "Save my little girl," I cried. "Just that, nothing more. I won't ask anything else for the rest of my life, just that one thing. Oh please, be merciful, have pity on me—don't take this child from us. Don't take this life. Take mine, not hers, just not my Macy, she's too young, too precious to us…"

Tears rolled down our cheeks in rivers. Strangers' hands reached down to try to console us, but we were oblivious to all of them. Our universe had shrunk to this tiny patch of space where a nine-year-old child fought for her life. Nothing else existed but this moment in time.

We finally reached the dock and Macy was placed on a stretcher and whisked into an ambulance. Charlie and I rushed to the back of the ambulance and demanded that they let us ride with her. They reluctantly let us into the cramped space, where they had already hooked up an IV to hydrate her and were preparing a syringe with anti-toxin to put in her arms. But the doctor fumbled around for try after try in an attempt to put a needle into one of her badly damaged veins.

Macy's whole body was swollen by now, and she was convulsing wildly. Her breath was raspy. I found myself sobbing at the sight of her in this state. Charlie had his arms around my shoulders, trying to shore me up. His face was wet with tears as well, but he seemed to have control of himself where I did not.

"Doctor, what's happening, is this going to work?" Charlie pleaded, grabbing the doctor's sleeve.

The doctor looked at him, shaking his head over and over again, as though he was finding this hard to believe. "I won't lie to you. It doesn't look good. She's too young, too small, too frail to take all this poison at once. She's not responding the way I had hoped."

"Meaning what?" Charlie screamed, "Meaning what, tell me?"

"Meaning that I don't think I can save her. It's too much poison, it's too late, it's too strong. I don't know what to tell you beyond that. Must have been a box jellyfish to have this bad a reaction. They're the most dangerous of them all. I don't think she will make it; that's the truth of it. I suggest you say your goodbyes."

We stared at him in disbelief. "Goodbyes? That's what you're telling us? Just say goodbye?" He was shaking the doctor's arm now as though that would somehow change something.

The doctor gently pulled his hands away. "I'm so sorry, really I am. I understand that you're not prepared for this, but there's nothing more we can do. These things happen. I've seen it before..." His voice trailed off.

The horror of his words struck me like a lightning bolt. I tried to talk but could not find my voice. It was stuck somewhere in the hard knot of my chest. I felt so constricted by fear that I could only clutch at Macy's cot. I could feel the hot sting of Charlie's tears falling on my hands.

Macy was no longer convulsing as before. Her body was mostly still now. Her eyes were closed and fluttered occasionally, perspiration beading up on her forehead, her mouth clenched as though she was feeling pain. I took her hand in mine and recoiled at its lack of warmth. I touched her legs, and they too were cool to the touch.

Then I saw her feet and noticed their mottled blue and white appearance. A sense of dread overcame me. I remembered reading that this was the tell-tale sign of a body right before death—a sign that the circulation was failing, that the body was dying.

I turned my head away from the inevitability I saw. Charlie knew it, too, I could tell. He had put his hand on her ankle and could feel the cold spreading up from her feet. He leaned over now and kissed her gently on her cheek, then tried to push back her hair.

"Goodnight, sweet girl," he said, his tears cascading on her cheek. "I will never forgive myself for this until the day I die. Never."

And then I saw him turn his head upward. "How could you do this? Is this how you answer a prayer?"

But I was too deep in my own sorrow to deal with his.

"She's not gone yet," I tried to say, but no words came out. She's still here, I still feel her, I said to myself, knowing that it was a lie and that with every breath I took she was one step closer to the abyss. I touched her skin again and knew that whatever warm spirit had once lived there was now departing. I will never forget that touch and the horror it brought to me.

The redness that had flushed her skin before was now giving way to a bloated whiteness. She was almost unrecognizable. I searched for Macy and could not find her anywhere. I was distraught, inconsolable.

In the end, it was the machine that told me. I had blocked out most of the sounds around me up until this point, but I somehow knew that something had changed. What had been a series of staccato beeps in the background had suddenly turned into a long unbroken tone. That was the tone of her death. That was the tone of our undoing, a sound we wanted forever to un-hear.

Our sweet little girl, our nine-year-old grandchild, that joyful soul that we loved so much, had been taken from us, wrenched from our arms, pulled into a place where we could not follow. And we—who had been entrusted to care for her, to protect her—had failed beyond our wildest imagination. How could we ever face her parents? How could we face the future without her? How could we face ourselves? How had this gone so terribly wrong?

A sheet of gun-metal gray grief dropped over me, turning my limbs to concrete. The sheer weight of my pain seemed to crush me. I wondered how it was possible that I was still breathing.

The rest of that day is a blur to me now. Charlie somehow took over and saw to the gruesome details. He was always a man you could lean on in a crisis, and I leaned on him now in a way I never had before. I remember nothing of what happened from the time we lost her to the time we returned to the hotel. Nothing except for the searing pain in my heart and a sense of loss so deep it could not be touched or described.

I suppose there were a thousand more details involved, none of which I participated in. There were reams of paper to fill out, arrangements to be made for the body, bills to be paid, reservations to cancel, new reservations to be made. I did nothing, I said nothing. Charlie did it all by himself, with not a word of complaint. He knew I could not function. His strength stunned me. He carried me in every sense of the word, with not even a simple "thank you" from me.

It took every ounce of courage he had to function for the two of us. But he did it.He was such a warrior. I knew better than anyone that his heart had shattered into a thousand jagged pieces, that he was crushed like broken glass. And I knew that the worst of it was about to happen. He was about to make the call to Brian and Lisa. My mind shut down completely at the thought of it. I found the very topic unbearable.

How on earth do you tell a parent that their child—the child they brought into this world, the child they entrusted to you because they had faith in you to act in their place— was now lost to them forever? How do you say that because of you, the light of this child's life would no longer shine?

No one has the words for that. Not me, not Charlie. Not the God we had prayed to who saw fit to turn a deaf ear to our pleas. There simply are no such words.

I wondered what Charlie could have possibly said when he made that call. I'll never know because he never spoke of it, and I could not bring myself to listen to the words he would have to use. It was bad enough she was gone, let alone that we must make it official with words like "death" and "her body" and "the coffin," and on and on with things I could not bear to hear.

You might have thought that we could share our grief, but grief is not something to be shared. You can't split it in half and bear your half while someone else takes the other. It never divides, if anything, it multiplies like cancer, getting bigger and more amorphous with time.

We were not able to comfort each other. Each of us took the body-blows separately. It was the only time in our marriage where we felt apart and separate, though we would come back together eventually.

We grieved differently, but compassionately, wishing we could tamp down the other's sorrow, but incapable of so doing.

Those days, those months—eventually that year—printed its dark stamp on our souls. Time finally played its desired role and mercifully blunted the edges of our agony. Eventually, we found ourselves again, found a way to breathe again without aching, found a way to allow ourselves to enjoy small things again. The grayness that painted those days slowly began to gain color that did not numb the mind's eye. But it was agonizingly slow.

The day came when we could speak with each other of the loss of Macy. We spoke of our guilt, our horror, our depression, our shock over the whole incident, and the way it unfolded in such a blinding rush. We knew intellectually that we were not to blame, and yet we blamed ourselves every day, at every turn. Why this, why that, why not this, why not that. But in the end, the story was written, and much as we would have given our lives to change the ending, the writing was over. The chapter was closed. There was nothing left but to accept it. And over time, we did. It became a dark closet of grief that we closed and tried not to visit, lest it consume us.

But nothing was ever the same for us with our son and daughter-in-law. Hardly surprising. We understood—of course we understood—but it was painful nonetheless. We slowly rebuilt what we could of our relationship with them, and, to be fair, they eventually accepted it—at least on the surface—as we did. We forged a fragile peace but it was always tenuous and tinged with dark resentments that occasionally bubbled to the surface.

They, too, knew in their hearts that it was not our fault, but they needed someone to blame, and we were certainly the perfect candidates. They didn't realize that the weight they threw upon us was insignificant compared to the weight we already carried on our own advisement. If it helped them to hate us at some level, then so be it. We would hardly notice the extra pinpricks of their judgment compared to our own.

Still, like all living creatures, we eventually adapted to the new reality. The cruel corners of our pain began to soften. There came a time when we could all be in the same room together and look like a normal family—at least from a distance. Eventually, we were able to interact with Tad again, because like most children, he was more adaptable than we were, and the daily realties of his life became more interesting to him than brooding about his sister.

When Christmas dinners took place again, we could even look at family photos and laugh over silly gifts. Tad was a child, so he was more able to live in the moment than the rest of us. He and I eventually resumed our close relationship and he presumably did not notice the awkwardness between the rest of his family. But Tad needed to feel close to us as a way to deal with his loss. We all tried our best to normalize life for his sake; how well we succeeded I never knew.

Brian even came to us one summer some eight years later and said he had had an epiphany of sorts, a "Come to Jesus" moment, and that he wanted us to know that he forgave us. But I knew that it wasn't true. Nor did I expect it ever to be true. And I understood that not all sins are forgivable in the eyes of the beholder.

As parents, we had failed Brian and Lisa on the deepest level possible. *Mea culpa, mea culpa, mea maxima culpa.* We could never forgive *ourselves*, so Brian's forgiveness was like a snowflake on our consciousness. We thanked him for his effort and hoped that it would in some way help *him*, but we had no such hopes for ourselves.

And so slowly and painfully we lifted the dark veil that covered us. But Charlie and I had a love that was not easily diverted. It was like a stream that had difficulty maneuvering around a large boulder of grief, but which eventually found its way around the barrier and came back together, to flow unfettered along its path.

We had shared great happiness and now a weighty sadness, but every night we still lay side by side, and there was an energy and constancy to our love that kept us conjoined throughout our marriage. On some level, Macy's death and the events that took place seemed to deepen our intimacy in a way that only the two of us understood.

Ours was a love that only his death interrupted.

'Til death do us part…and then it did.

Chapter 7

LOOSE ENDS

I have been feeling strangely detached these last few days. My mind seems to be hovering somewhere between two distinct worlds with no particular address of its own. My body, with all of its pains and weaknesses, seems stuck in the old familiar world while my mind is starting to slip into the next realm—whatever the hell that is. At least, that's what I tell myself, having no other explanation (except the obvious) for the disembodied sensations I'm beginning to experience.

I suppose I could blame the medications—God only knows what they are. Doctor Brian has me taking all manner of concoctions, some of which he says are meant to tame my disobedient cells now that the chemo is behind me, and some, per him, are meant to ameliorate my pain, though the latter is arguable. I still have plenty of pain to spread around despite his claims to the contrary. Question: what makes him think he knows how I feel on the inside? Answer, he doesn't, it's that simple, Doctor or not. The source of all this trouble, he tells me, has something to do with my lymph nodes misbehaving—or perhaps it's my spleen, or more likely those pesky, deviant blood cells, but who really knows? I can't keep track of all of my miscreant organs and body parts. They clearly have a mind of their own. But I do know that the net effect of all the drugs I am taking is that I am constantly narcotized. I'm reminded of my twenties when I dabbled in various hallucinogenic drugs; but they, at least, were colorful and exotic and occasionally quite entertaining. These current drugs simply make me feel alien and slightly out of control. I can find nothing endearing about them.

When I was first acquainted with my diagnosis, it was hard to swallow, both literally and figuratively. It was the last thing I was expecting to hear. I've been so unaccountably healthy all my life. I never had measles or mumps or chicken pox or even ear infections. Never broke any bones, never got mononucleosis or stomach flu or all the usual ailments that young people normally succumb to. I never even had a bladder infection or pink eye. I was always lucky with my health—until now, of course. But luck is capricious and undependable. I remember from my blackjack days at the casino: the House always wins.

Evidently, I have used up all of my good karma and health bonus points, and now it is time to pay the piper. Cancer in my sixties—not so unusual, really; and, after all, something was bound to bring me down eventually. I just didn't expect *eventually* to come so soon. So here I am, apparently at the crossroads of cancer and old age. And now I have been formally and personally introduced to Leukemia, a venerable, long-standing, fear-inspiring disease. Pleased to meet you. Not.

I once read a magnificent book, Cancer, the Emperor of all Maladies, and since then, I have had a healthy respect for the disease in all of its forms which, without even blinking, has felled kings and commoners alike throughout history. Now I am just another one of its statistics. How quaint; how humanizing, how deeply disturbing. Still, better to be taken down in the arms of the Emperor, I should think, than some more common assassin. And now he's my personal Emperor and apparently I am doing his bidding. I don't usually subscribe to the "Why me?" line of thinking. "Why not me?" always sounded much more reasonable, but I can't help but think that I would have been happier had we never met—the Emperor and I.

So now I'm linked with the throngs of people who turn up in data files at the National Institute of Health, and I'm one of those victims that T-shirts and marathons and fundraisers are meant for. I would have been happy to skip this step. I don't need the publicity.

However, as someone who always felt somehow separated and alienated from the rest of mankind, I guess I can relax now, knowing that I'm in good company, just one of the crowd. Now we all have something in common.

I have to console myself with the thought that having cancer is somehow better and more dignified than just fading away at age ninety or so. Fading away is much too nondescript. After all, who wants to see "Cause of death: Old Age" on their death certificate or, worse, in their obituary? Certainly not me. I prefer something a bit more dramatic, more robust. I never wanted to live a bland life. Give me adjectives with color and sound and vibrant pulsing sensations. I want to go out kicking and screaming, but at least thoroughly alive until I am dead. Let my white cells wage war, all shock and awe, until they are spent—a feast for the senses, not a bowl of meal.

Really?

These overly dramatic ruminations makes me shake my head in wonder at the preposterous conversations I sometimes have with myself. All of this hyperbole finally serves to jolt me back into the present reality. Putting my currently soliloquy aside for the moment, it occurs to me that I need to reassess my situation in light of my realistic options, no matter how limited they may be—starting with my doctor and my relationship with and to him…

My oncologist: the good Dr. Calvert. I often wonder what is going through Brian's head these days. It must be difficult for him to be both Son and Doctor to his mother; it puts him at such an awkward nexus. And yet from the beginning he has insisted on being in charge. That's Brian, always the alpha male. And for the most part, I am submissive with him in this new relationship that we share.

He has a prickly personality that does not allow for a lot of give-and-take. Brian likes things done *his* way because, as far as he's concerned, that is always the *best* way. I do not always share that opinion, but I have generally bowed to his wishes in these circumstances, sensing that there would be no peace and no victory in trying to argue with him. And for the most part, on average, he appears to be content with that arrangement.

But I do see more than his flaws. I am his mother, after all, and I cannot help but be proud of him for his accomplishments. He has made a good life for himself, carved out an excellent career, juggled a marriage and fatherhood along with his growing practice and, for the most part, been a loyal son, father and husband along the way. What mother wouldn't take pride in such a journey? What more would a mother wish for her son?

Obviously I might have wished for a better relationship between the two of us. But, of course, the truth is that everything changed after the accident. The world turned upside down after that; everything went topsy-turvy. Without a word ever being said, the ranks we had established before Macy's death changed irretrievably from that point forward. Positions, attitudes, affections—they all rearranged themselves after that.

The old order was destroyed while a new order established itself, with or without my consent—mostly without. That was among the multitude of penalties—too numerous to list—that we paid for the event simply classified by all of us as "Australia." But many years have passed since then, and I have come to accept my revised role in our family life, albeit reluctantly and resignedly.

Australia notwithstanding, we have been getting along reasonably well of late—at least, so I thought—especially as long as I keep my complaints to myself, which, as a matter of habit, I normally do. I was well aware of my psychological problems after Macy died, and again after I lost Charlie. But I had not been mentally prepared to deal with my physical problems as well. They definitely caught me by surprise and threw me off my game. Somehow I never saw them coming.

I had originally chalked up most of my physical problems—especially after the accident—to classic depression: the fatigue, the loss of appetite, difficulty sleeping, sudden weight loss. But I hadn't really seen them as a constellation of symptoms. Brian, on the other hand, saw it differently—and more perceptively—than I.

"Mom, what's going on with you? You seem awfully lethargic these days," he had said to me one weekend in the middle of winter, roughly nine months after Charlie's death.

"Oh, I blame the weather," I said listlessly, pointing accusingly at one of the big picture windows in the den. "Look at that horrendous sky out there, not a hint of blue, no color whatsoever, just relentless gray. It's no wonder I'm tired. It's depressing, it's demoralizing, it's—lots of words beginning with D. I just haven't felt like myself in some time. Hardly surprising, what with everything that's gone on, wouldn't you agree?"

Brian shrugged his shoulders, then looked at me more closely. "For how long haven't you 'felt like yourself'?"

I pondered the question for a moment. "Since your father died, I suppose, which can hardly come as a surprise…"

"Well, that would make sense as far as your feelings go, but what about physically?"

I shrugged. "I don't know. I suppose the two go hand in hand, wouldn't you say? It's nearly impossible to feel healthy and cheerful when your mind is a train wreck. It hasn't been that long, you know. I'm still grieving, and everything hurts, from the top of my head to the tips of my feet, since you ask. It's painful all the way down. Don't you think that's normal under the circumstances?"

"Yes and no," Brian said, still looking at me with a doctor's eye. "Specifically, what physical symptoms do you have?"

"Well, I don't know that I'd call them symptoms at this point, Brian," I had said somewhat defensively. "That would suggest that I have some sort of disease, and I don't think that's the case. I have your typical aches and pains, probably no more so than most women in their late sixties. And I don't seem to have much energy for anything anymore. But, seriously, I chalk it all up to depression. It's very predictable, really."

"So you say. But why don't you humor me and see a doctor?"

"I'm looking at a doctor right now," I said, winking at him.

"Very funny, Mom. I'm serious. Call your G.P., what's his name—Patel, right?

"Yes, Dr. Patel, and I like him, so don't start calling him 'what's his name.'" "Whatever," Brian said dismissively. "Go see him, have him run some blood tests and have him copy me on the results."

"Yes, Herr Doctor, right away. But you know how I hate having my blood drawn…"

"Yes, I know you hate it, but I don't understand *why* you hate it."

"No, you wouldn't. But trust me, I have my reasons. In any case, I'll get around to it in my own good time, so don't pressure me."

"Wouldn't dream of it, Mother," Brian said, still looking at me more intently than usual.

It was another month before I reluctantly decided to take his advice. When I informed him of my decision, Brian seemed both surprised and pleased that I had actually listened to his suggestion. My fatigue level was beginning to worry even me, and I had become aware of a nagging pain in my abdomen. The fact that I was beginning to lose weight and was not consciously dieting was even more disquieting, since I'd spent the last fifteen years trying to keep my weight down and usually not succeeding. Something was clearly awry and it was time to find out what it was.

Good God, I thought, next thing you know he'll be asking me to get a colonoscopy to see what's going on with my stomach or bowels or whatever it is that comprises your abdomen. That can't possibly be good. *Don't get ahead of yourself,* Olivia, this could all be very simple. Low blood sugar, iron-deficiency, something like that. Don't be asking for trouble. Start with a blood test; maybe you're just anemic. That's probably it: eat more red meat. But I couldn't deny that Brian's offhand suggestion had rattled me and started me thinking in a new direction—a direction I didn't particularly want to take.

Eventually, though, I had given in to the pressure—both Brian's and my own. I made the appointment with Dr. Patel, showed up on time, and took the detested blood test. I let him probe my entire torso, all of which was making me feel singularly nervous and uneasy. I had begun to feel a certain undercurrent of dread and foreboding, as though I could feel a change of tides inside me.

Perhaps it was because I was so alone now—no Charlie to hold my hand in the waiting room, no one to bustle me off to a midday lunch afterward as a reward for "being so brave," no one to quell my rising fears. Charlie would have taken care of all those things, in that order, and seen to it that no harm would come to me. But Charlie had vanished into thin air; my protector was gone. And now I was beginning to think that harm was indeed coming my way— unchallenged by Charlie and unwelcomed by me, but on its way, nonetheless, and at breakneck speed, if the truth be known.

Five days later, Dr. Patel's office called to ask me for a second blood test, which I reluctantly agreed to, even though the reason for it was not clear to me—all the while pushing back a gnawing sense of alarm. The fact that they wanted to run more tests did nothing to ease my growing anxiety, and only fed into my generalized paranoia.

Six days after the second blood test I was called back into Dr. Patel's office. This sounded ominous to me. When I told Brian, he had asked me if I wanted him to come with me. I had said assertively, "No, I'll see him alone. Thank you, though."

I remember sitting in the doctor's mahogany waiting room on that particular dreary Seattle day—there were so many, it was hard to distinguish between them. Clouds were rumbling outside, water pelted the sidewalks, soaking the lawns, dragging down what leaves remained until they looked soggy and gray. I felt like the weather: dark and baleful.

When the good doctor finally ushered me into his private office rather than an examination room, I knew nothing good would come of it. I decided to take the offensive, more in order to unleash my nervous energy than for any other reason: "Well, I assume you have something of import to tell me, Doctor, or you wouldn't have insisted I come down here in person. The fact that I have been escorted into your personal quarters—which I have never seen before—is even more disturbing. So I imagine you have something unpleasant to say to me. Is that true?" I finally took a breath.

He paused before he spoke, sizing me up, looking for the right tone. "Yes, that's true, and I'm going to get right to the point for that very reason—that is, if you're okay with straight talk?" Dr. Patel had a serious but attentive expression on his face.

I nodded slowly, thinking to myself: what would he have done if I'd said no, I'm not okay with it?

I braced myself: here it comes, I thought, the sentences you don't want to hear, the crimson tide from which you can't escape. I felt like an actor in a bad movie during the part where the violins swell, the lights go dim, and the dialogue trails off into absurdity.

He continued now: "When your test results first came back, I saw that you had a high white blood cell count. Also, when I palpated you, I noticed that some of your lymph glands seemed swollen. I knew that we needed to investigate further. I immediately ordered a follow-up set of tests, as you know. They showed an elevated white count and a low red blood count which confirmed my diagnosis of Chronic Lymphocytic Leukemia—CLL; it's a cancer of the blood, Olivia. It starts in the blood- forming cells of the bone marrow."

He paused while I took a deep, if ragged, breath and tried to digest his words, my mind reeling from the onslaught of what he had just said. The dreaded C-word. There it was—naked, raw, unadulterated, and more than anything else, unwanted. When I nodded at him silently, lips pursed tightly together lest he see them tremble, he took it as his cue to continue.

"This is something we still need to stage in order to determine what your prognosis looks like. Your next question to me will be: 'can it be cured,' and my answer is that it cannot."

Again he paused to let the new words sink in, and again I said nothing, too stunned to respond.

He picked up the thread once more. "However, while it cannot be cured, it can be treated with some success. There are several options, including certain types of chemotherapy, blood transfusions, bone marrow or stem cell transplants, gene therapy, or all of the above where indicated, that we can use to manage it."

"Relatively speaking, you should know that it is a slow-moving cancer. Still, we're talking about *decelerating* it, not stopping it. The staging will determine what time frames we are dealing with. But please understand, Olivia, that we are usually talking years here, not months, if that's any consolation."

"Ahh," I managed to squeeze out weakly, thinking to myself: no foreplay today, straight to the point, just as promised. Consolation? I don't think so. I found myself wondering if there was enough oxygen in the room, since suddenly it seemed difficult to breathe. I wondered, too, if I had brought this all on myself by having the blood tests in the first place. What if I had never asked the question? Could I have avoided the answer? Would the conclusion be any different? Was there some way to rewind this tape? Could we go back to the five minutes before I came into this room with its awful revelations?

I noticed that Dr. Patel was still talking. I was unsure of what I had missed but indifferent in any case. He was still droning on: "…I understand that this comes as a shock to you. News like this is always disorienting," he was saying as kindly as possible. "How are you feeling about all of this?"

I took a minute to gather myself before speaking, still doubting the quantity of air in the room. "I think there are many synonyms for how I'm feeling: distressed, bewildered, unnerved. And I can hardly believe I'm sitting here thinking up synonyms for 'disconcerting,' but apparently that's the way my brain works. In a minute, the reality will sink in, and I won't have anything clever to say," I warned him.

He smiled knowingly at me. "Everybody deals with these things differently. It's hard to take in news like this; I understand only too well. You're not the first to have trouble with it."

He pushed his chair back from the desk and folded his arms across his chest. "Believe me, I never relish the idea of being the bearer of bad news, but it comes with my job description. For you—the patient—it's much harder. But while I would like to help you navigate through this, Olivia, I'm afraid it's best if you see a specialist at this point— you'll need an oncologist. I know of your son, and he may want to take over your care if you're agreeable; I'm assuming that's your wish?"

He waited to see if there was any cue from me. When there was not, he continued. "He would be the obvious choice as this is his domain, but sometimes people don't like to treat their own family members and vice versa. It's up to you, of course. Dr. Calvert contacted me and asked me to forward a copy of the tests to him, which I will do—but only if that's your decision; otherwise, of course, I won't."

I tried to find my voice, but it had somehow disappeared into the fog of my mind. "I suppose so, yes," I finally managed to say. "Send them to Brian. I guess he can take over my case. I'll have to speak to him about it in more detail. I wasn't really anticipating any of this…I mean, I was anticipating *something*, just not this. "

Dr. Patel shook his head in tacit acknowledgement, shuffled some papers on his desk, and then picked up the phone and called in his assistant.

"Liz, see to it that all of Mrs. Calvert's records get sent over to Dr. Calvert's office—Brian Calvert, the oncologist—would you?"

"Yes, Doctor, I'll take care of it right away." He nodded and she backed out of the room, ever the efficient employee.

"So, Olivia, I'm reluctantly going to pass you on to my colleague then. You've been coming here for many years now; we will miss seeing you regularly. Really, I mean it…"

Dr. Patel was such a kindly man that, for a moment, I thought it was actually possible that he was completely sincere in saying he would miss me. "I'll miss you as well, Doctor, I will," I said, standing up awkwardly, feeling embarrassed and unbalanced, and still trying to fight the strangled feeling in my throat.

He came around the desk and clasped my arm to support me, understanding how disoriented I felt. "It's going to be alright, Olivia," he said gently. "You've still got time…"

"Do I?" I asked, tears leaking from my eyes—tears that I had been trying to suppress.

"You do, I promise. How much time, I can't tell you. Your oncologist will have to evaluate that, but today is not the end of the road. And there are always new therapies, new treatments. Don't give up hope just yet. Try to stay positive, and just look straight ahead. You're in relatively good health—aside from the leukemia; medicine changes daily, and there are always new possibilities that arise. Listen, if I can be of any help, don't hesitate to call me. I mean that."

He picked up a card from his desk drawer and wrote down a number on it. "My cell phone, in case you ever need to speak to someone, or have any questions…I promise I will take your call."

"That's very kind of you, Doctor," I said, dabbing at my eyes, surprised at his empathetic gesture. "If you're this accommodating to all of your patients, your wife must be insanely jealous."

He smiled. "Indeed, she is—desperately so. You see, you still have your sense of humor; you'll be alright."

"Hmm, I don't know about 'alright'; that remains to be seen. I'll get out of your hair, though, let you get on with your next life-and-death drama," I said, slowly backing out of his office, my mind churning and frothing like the rain outside, my legs feeling weak and jelly-like.

"Do you need some help out to your car, Olivia?" he questioned as I kept walking, trying desperately to leave his building in one piece.

"No, I'm good, really, I'll be fine," I lied, wanting more than anything to be left alone, longing for the dark comfort of my own room, my own house, my own bed.

I remember all of that as though it was yesterday, but, in fact, it was well over a year ago that I left Dr. Patel's office for good.

Brian had said he was not surprised by the diagnosis. He said he knew there was something going on with me and that, while he had several possibilities in his mind, this one did not surprise him.

He could easily have passed me off to another oncologist, but he wouldn't hear of it. I put up a feeble fight and then gave in to him when he pleaded his case. He insisted that it would be best for both of us if he took charge. It seemed easier to capitulate to him than to argue, and so we became doctor-patient on top of mother-son, a new label that was to define us from that point on.

Neither of us was accustomed to being in that position—where he is at the helm and I am simply following his orders—a passenger on a doomed ship. It was a complete reversal of our original relationship, though, admittedly, things had changed in the last ten years. Still, I bowed to his superior knowledge on this subject and put myself in his hands. What choice did I have?

I think he has gotten a certain amount of pleasure out of having me in this new posture, whether he would admit it or not. And I— well, I have had to surrender myself to him completely; yet another indignity forced upon the sick when they no longer have the strength or the knowledge to pilot their own way.

Surrender, of course, is the repeating theme in cancer, the recurring motif, as you begin systematically to surrender pretty much everything you possess, both physically and mentally, to the Emperor of all Maladies and, in this case, to my son, the Doctor.

I have been a good patient, a compliant patient, but hardly a *patient* patient, which I find vaguely amusing but Brian probably does not. Hard to be patient when the thing you are waiting for is going to kill you. Still, I shouldn't be so negative. Maybe the good doctor will find a way to keep me alive for a few more years; is that really asking too much? I understand that he can't "cure" me—since he reiterates this constantly—but I was hoping he would, at least, buy me some time, since Dr. Patel suggested that this is possible. I thought we understood each other on that front, but it's difficult to get a bead on Brian. His mind has always been a mystery to me and he seems determined to be asinscrutable as possible.

In my humble opinion, whatever he's doing now amounts simply to palliative measures, though he continually denies this. I don't see much progress being made in fighting what is undeniably an uphill battle. Apparently the cancer is taking hold and spreading, or so I think I heard him saying to Lisa in the living room the other night. "Spreading" is a word he keeps using behind my back, so I suppose that is my status quo. I'm told this particular cancer doesn't actually metastasize as there is no *tumor*; instead, it just starts infiltrating every part of your body. Clever cancer; insidious cancer, powerful cancer.

But I'm not all that interested in the details of my advancement towards the abyss; I have ruefully accepted that I am sick and will soon die; it's as simple as that. The lyrics of a Beatle's song come floating back to me: *Life is very short, and there's no time for fussing and fighting, my friend.*

All of which brings me back once again to my present condition, terminal though it may be. And of course, what goes best with terminal? Why, the ever-popular tying up of loose ends, of course. I need to put some energy into the tying up part. And this time, I need to put my money where my mouth is, figuratively speaking, of course. Time to call Howard. That should get me out of my current black hole, churn up some of my creative juices. Talking to Howard always revives my spirits and makes me think in a more linear fashion. Yes, Howard is just the man to get things kick-started again.

***

"You can't take it with you, Mother," Brian had said ingratiatingly the next day when he found out I was going to set up an appointment to see my lawyer again.

I had no trouble in squelching his enthusiasm for my rapid departure. "I'm not gone yet, dear, in case you hadn't noticed, but thanks for the timely advice." He gave me a strained look, then turned on his heel and left, which annoyed me even more.

The "dear" I used on him had that lovely acidic tone I have cultivated lately, and which I knew would irk him. I couldn't care less of course since he deserves to be irked. I've made his life a day at the beach—his missus, too, I might add—and he doesn't even realize it. He thinks his casual attention to my properties has earned him some sort of reward beyond the fees I pay him, that I am awash in gratitude, but I beg to differ. I could have run a much tighter ship myself, as I did in the past, but I've been too weary these last months and years, especially since Charlie's death.

All of my bitterness seems to take the fight out of me. For one thing, I don't really understand where all of this internal hostility towards Brian is coming from. He's my son, I gave birth to him, I love him, I even used to love his wife; so the real question is, what on earth has gotten me so exercised that I am constantly berating them and having such caustic thoughts?

I can't believe some of the things I have been saying to Howard about them lately. What is my problem these days? Drugs perhaps? Depression? The onset of dementia? No. I reject that one out of hand; it's simply not true. Bloody hell, what a stew of unpleasant choices! Hmm, this bears some consideration, but not now; maybe tomorrow. No time for a therapist at this stage, so I'll have to figure it out myself.

I force myself to turn the page on all of this psychological wallowing and completely pointless introspection. Taking a more proactive stance, I paw through the mail, open one of the bank statements, then throw it down on the bed in disgust. It used to be entertaining and comforting to look at the revenue summaries, count up the gains, savor the growing real estate empire we were sitting on. But without Charlie to enjoy it with me, and with the cancer diagnosis hanging over my head, how interested can I be in a pile of profit and loss statements? All the joy has gone out of it.

Brian, of course, is blind to any of these realities, having neither the empathy nor the perceptiveness to have noticed my change in attitude. No one seems to understand what I'm going through, Merlin notwithstanding.

The only person left in my universe who is kind to me is Laila, and I barely know her… But back to the task at hand. Someone has to manage the properties after I'm gone, and I suppose Brian is really the only sensible candidate. I'm glad he thinks he's such a bigshot. He likes to tell me how he's "handling" things without ever giving me any details. I shudder to think. I've decided that I'm better off not knowing since I'm dead certain I would disagree with whatever he's doing. Soon I'll just be dead, minus the certain.

God help the tenants, I think to myself. Knowing Brian, he returns their calls, if they're lucky, three weeks after the initial inquiry and then spends another three weeks arguing with them over why they need or don't need various repairs. In the end, I imagine he takes care of the issues, more because he's worried they'll find their way back to me and complain than out of any real desire to appease them or fix the problems. I could wring his neck, but what would be the point? It's all over but the shouting now anyway.

Of course, no sooner has all of this live-streamed through my mind than I am racked with guilt for even thinking such a thing. How do I dare even formulate phrases like "make his life a day at the beach" when in reality I have played a part in ruining his life forever? Has that little fact slipped my mind, I ask myself? Was I really trying to cast Brian and his wife as the villains in this drama? In what universe were they the bad guys and I the helpless victim? What on earth is the matter with me?

I feel myself flush with a combination of shame, anger, and frustration. It is a particular side effect of my illness—or possibly the drugs—that sometimes I like to rewrite my own history, conflate the facts, put my head in the sand, and generally attempt to ignore reality. Well, sometimes it works, but this is apparently not one of those times. On the other hand, I am constrained in my thinking by The Obvious.

Say what you will about Brian and Lisa, they have been the victims of one of Fate's most grievous arrows. And I was unwittingly and unintentionally an actor in that drama that played out so many years ago. It would be the height of naiveté to think that any of it has been forgiven or forgotten—by any of us.

While time has washed over the roughest edges of that story, nothing will ever erase it. It is always playing somewhere in the recesses of my mind. Was it somehow my fault? Could I have done something differently? Should I blame myself? Will I roast in eternal flames for my part in the story?

In the end, I never have any answers for these questions. I always come to the conclusion that there was not one thing I could have done differently. It was a story that seemed preordained. I was no more than an innocent bystander, a bit player in a larger narrative, *wasn't I?*

How often can I repeat the same insoluble questions to myself? Apparently the answer to that question is simply that there is no limit to the number of circular conversations I can have with myself. Over and over again, round and round and round in an endless loop.

I finally tear myself out of the current loop and wait impatiently for Laila to show up. When she does, later in the afternoon, I ask her to call Howard's office for me. He is always good about taking his calls, having correctly figured out that his well-to-do clients expect his immediate attention.

When she finally has him on the line, I reach across the bed and take the receiver from her, then nod my head towards the door to indicate that she can leave the room, hoping she doesn't think I'm just dismissing her for no good reason. She leaves quietly, shutting the door behind her. She's a good girl, I think to myself.

"Howard, thanks for taking my call. I'll get right to the point as I'm told I don't have much time left—that's a semi-joke. Listen, I want to take a more pro-active approach to this 'competency' issue that you raised when you were here last."

When he says nothing, I continue. "As you well know, I still have my wits about me, and I don't really see why I should have to prove it, but just in case you're right about the narrowing time frame, I want to pre-empt all of that. I want you to organize a meeting with Brian, Claire, and the appropriate spice, plus a third party witness with nothing to gain. I'll let you know who the third party should be. Get them all to show up in my bedroom within the next few days and we'll sign some papers that you are going to draft."

"And what papers would those be?" Howard asks more politely than usual.

"Papers that confirm that I'm making an early distribution of $100,000 each to both Brian and Claire and that we are all witness to the fact that I am still competent and capable of making monetary decisions concerning my estate and my will. Explain that I am taking care of the tax consequences to the estate before I die, and expand on why this makes me a considerate and generous person."

I can hear Howard ruminating on the other end. After a pause, he says, "So let me get this straight. You want me to tell Brian and Claire in a letter and in person that you are giving them this money, that the final estate won't have to pay taxes on it because you will, right now, that you are clearly a saint, and that in signing the receipt for this money, they will be attesting to the fact that they agree you are competent and able-minded. Plus you want a third party witness to agree to same."

"You've summarized it perfectly. Good God, Howard, don't pretend that this isn't just boilerplate. I'm sure you could write this in your sleep."

"It's not that…" he intones.

"What then? I can tell you're not happy about something," I say.

"Spit it out."

"Olivia, think about it. When you tie money in with an attestation to competency, you blur the lines. For the sake of argument, suppose you weren't competent. If you offer someone $100,000 and say 'all you have to do to have the money is sign here and say that I'm mentally sound,' don't you think it's a bit fishy legally?"

"Well, what are you suggesting, that I'm not mentally sound? Get real, Howard, I'm as sharp as you are, probably sharper. Do you dispute that?"

His voice now takes on an avuncular tone that I have never liked, and I can tell that he is about to choose his words very carefully. "I'm certainly not saying you're incompetent *today*; I'm just saying that a person in your condition can, in some cases, deteriorate more quickly than one might anticipate. Sometimes these things can change in a matter of days and then you have a more fluid situation. Do you see where I'm going with this?"

"I do, yes. So you admit that as of today, I am still lucid. I guess you'd better hurry up with the draft then, lest we miss this tiny window of sanity on my part," I say unctuously. "Listen to me; I'm not stupid. The whole point here is exactly what you probably suspect it is. I want them to stipulate to my competency as of the date they sign the papers so that it is clear that as of that date I was still *compos mentis*. I don't want to go to court or have doctors showing up here for competency tests. I want my children and an unbiased witness to acknowledge that I am sufficiently 'with it' to give them monetary gifts. It establishes a de facto time line for me that I want verified. Now, the question is, do you see where I'm going with this?"

Howard clicks his teeth over the phone in response. "I'm only guessing, but let me take a stab at it: you want to set up a scenario where your children agree that you are competent to give them something so that if you take something away from them at the same time—even if unbeknownst to them—they cannot simultaneously argue incompetence?"

"Howard," I coo appreciatively, "your Ivy League education is finally paying off. I could not have put it more perfectly. That was so poetic that I won't even mind your charging me for this half-hour, even though it will in fact only be about 15 minutes."

Howard has the decency to chuckle. "Okay, Olivia, I get the drift. It's pretty snarky and underhanded, but I admire a good undercut. So does that mean you're ready to decide on the final heirs to the rest of the estate plus the dispersal of the stock?"

"That's what it means, Howard. "Pack up the babies and grab the old ladies," (I'm hoping you remember that song) and bring the flash cards with you when you come. And don't forget all the pretentious prose and signatures in triplicate, all the usual drivel. Have the papers ready for me to sign, leaving just the blanks where I fill in the names for the final distribution—which you and I will do in private."

"Also," I continue, "I'm going to give you my neighbor's number so you can call her and have her act as a witness. Her name is Marla, and she's always home and has nothing better to do than to show up here and see how incredibly decrepit and cadaverous I look—which will please her no end."

I take a deep breath. "Now, Howard, this is really tiring me out, so why don't you get on with the drafting part and call me if you have questions. But call me tomorrow, not later this afternoon; I've had all I can take for one day. Capiche?"

"Roger that, Olivia. Talk to you soon. Pleasant dreams…And yes, I do remember the song."

Chapter 8

SIGHT

The next morning, I drag myself out of bed, let out a deep sigh, and crack the shutters open to a forty-five-degree angle. It is yet another nondescript morning in Seattle: dark purple clouds scudding across the sky, fat with rain—the winter of my discontent and then some.

Sleep had been hard to come by, despite the capsules Brian had brought me, so that I feel no more rested this morning than I felt when I first lay my head down last night. I remember tossing and turning fitfully half the night in a futile effort to find a position that did not make my bones ache, though the physical discomfort seemed minor in comparison to the turbulent mental storm I was experiencing.

Another day ripped off my calendar, another morning of malaise and generalized anxiety—that's the way I characterize most of my mornings these days. Chin up, old girl, where's that positive attitude you used to possess, the one you guarded so fiercely, the one that seems to be deserting you now, just when you need it the most?

As usual, there is no answer to this rhetorical question. I am at least eager for the break in routine, knowing that Brian will be coming by to see me before his flight to Chicago for a medical conference. My ambivalence towards him does not mean that I do not appreciate him, or love him in my way. And anything that breaks the monotony is certainly welcome these days. Also, I continue to nurture the fragile hope that somehow we can begin to repair our tattered relationship.

At mid-morning I hear him turn the key in the front door and call out my name to announce his presence. I tell him to come into the bedroom. He walks in carrying his briefcase, a raincoat folded over his arm. His thick brown hair is combed carelessly over his head, giving him a tousled look that belies his esteemed profession and even more serious mood.

Brian is tall and lanky like his father and still rakishly handsome despite his standoffish air. In a strange way, he has always intimidated me—something which, as his mother, I am loathe to admit but about which there is little doubt. Without saying another word, he lays his things down on the loveseat across from my bed, nods at me casually, as though in greeting, then sits down on the couch and starts fiddling with his cell phone, looking uncannily like my grandson Tad.

I notice that he seems more edgy than usual, not to mention less communicative. Because of his prickly nature, I generally try not to irritate him by inquiring into his mental state but for some reason, on this particular day, I put that directive aside.

"Good morning to you, too, son of mine. What's bothering you?" I ask in my most congenial voice, trying to conjure up the aforementioned positive attitude.

"Nothing's bothering me, Mother, why do you ask?" he says, barely looking up.

"Well, you've hardly spoken a word, you're playing with your phone, and you seem distracted. Or did you just come over here to browse through your text messages?"

He looks up from his phone as though seeing me for the first time. "Text messages? Hardly. Sorry, Mother, I've got a lot on my mind right now," he says, reluctantly putting down his cell phone but looking neither apologetic nor unharried. "My mood aside, how are we feeling this morning?" he asks, attempting a more affable tone than his face suggests, but the patronizing tenor is difficult to ignore.

"Well, I don't know how you're feeling, but I'm a bit under the weather since you ask."

"Anything specific?"

"No, just the same old laundry list of complaints: tired, achy, sore, the occasional dizziness, swollen ankles—you know, the usual suspects."

"Ah, yes, the suspects. You know you have to expect these kinds of symptoms with chronic leukemia…"

"So you've told me repeatedly," I sigh. "I've accepted my diagnosis, but I was hoping you might have some magic potion to ameliorate some of my symptoms."

"No magic today. Are you taking the methylprednisolone I ordered for you?"

"Yes, of course. But I can't help but think it's the source of half of the symptoms I just listed—oh, and did I mention overwhelming depression as well? I looked up the drug on the internet, and everything I just described is considered typical of its side effects and…"

With a dark look on his face, Brian interrupts me before I finish my sentence. "Why don't you leave the doctoring to me? Of course, it has side effects; it's a powerful drug—steroid drugs are like that. But you need to take it, which is why I prescribed it. And quit looking things up on the internet; it's only going to confuse you—feed into your already overactive imagination."

I glance at him, wondering what has brought on this dour and patronizing mood.

"Yes, Doctor, whatever you say," I respond listlessly. "But I can't see that the steroid is doing me much good. Hmm, perhaps I need a doctor who's not related to me…" I try to smile while saying this.

Brian furrows his brow. "What are you suggesting, Mother?"

"I'm not suggesting anything; I was teasing you actually. It's just that I've heard that it's not always a good idea for doctors to treat their own families—no perspective, that sort of thing…"

"I have plenty of perspective," he retorts defensively, "and I think I'm the best person to handle your case, which is why I suggested it. It's only right that I should treat you; this is my specialty, after all! We already agreed upon this, and besides, in the end, blood is thicker than water, you know."

"If you say so, though I don't know what that's got to do with anything. Oh, I'm just giving you a hard time; I'm sure you know what you're doing. After all, this is your 'métier'—you do remember your French, don't you? So, let's get back to this medical conference you're attending. Is that what's got you so irritable this morning? Are you nervous because you have to give a speech at the conference, or make some sort of presentation?"

Brian glowers at me. "Nothing of the sort, and I resent your calling me irritable, I'm just preoccupied, that's all. There's no real pressure at the conference; it's just a chance to catch up on all the latest data in my field. I need to stay current. You know how it is with doctors, always chasing the latest research."

"Yes, well, on that subject, maybe you'll find out about some new treatment or drug that will improve the quality of my life, or even extend it…that would be some good news you could bring back to me, wouldn't you say?"

He shrugs. "That's not likely to happen at this conference, Mom. Besides, we're already doing everything we can for you; I've told you that. You've had all the state of the art treatments and therapies that exist right now for your particular situation. How many times can I repeat this? There's only so much we can do with your condition. I know it's hard to accept, but I've exhausted the possibilities. Those exotic treatments you keep dreaming about aren't going to help you in this particular situation; you need to get over thinking that."

"Right. But I'm always reading about people having bone marrow transplants and stem cell therapies and being in clinical trials with all of these cutting edge treatments…Why can't we try some of those things? Is my case so different from all the others?" Even I was conscious of a whining tone to my question, but why should I have to conceal my feelings?

"In a word: Yes, your case is different, Mother. I'll tell you one final time—and I know you don't like me to sugar coat these things, so I'll just say it straight up: you have a chronic, ultimately fatal disease. We can slow it down—which we have done as much as possible—but we can't stop it. You need to let go of the notion that I can magically turn this disease around; I can't," he chafes, seeming even more unapproachable than before, his face darker by the moment.

I sigh deeply, at a loss for words. He seems to be in an even worse mood than when we started, which was not my intention. In an effort to change the subject, both for his sake and for mine, I take a different tack.

"So, you're flying direct to O'Hare?"

"Yes. You know I never take connecting flights if I can avoid it." He seems glad to change the subject.

"I know. Lisa going with you?"

"She is. In fact, I expect her in a few minutes—she had a few errands to run, then we'll leave from here. Tad is staying over at his friend's house and Louise will be in to cook your dinners. We'll be back in two days. Should be a miserable flight out of Seattle though, what with all the snow."

"True. It's a shame you have to travel in this weather."

"I hate to travel in any weather if the truth be told," he says, shifting uncomfortably on the couch.

"I understand completely, believe me. I feel the same way about airplanes that you do. They never bothered me before, but now, of course, it does nothing but bring back terrible memories. It makes my head hurt just to think about it," I say, sitting up straighter in bed, trying to find a more comfortable position for my legs. I am suddenly aware of a familiar anxiety creeping over me, like cold water being poured down my back.

"Terrible memories? That would be an understatement," Brian says quietly, looking at me intently, but using a different tone than he had been using up until now. "I can't believe it's been nearly two years since your father's accident," I say slowly, pushing the hair back from my face and breathing sharply, trying to ignore the palpable feeling of coldness in my veins.

"Two years and counting," Brian says. "It *is* hard to believe it's been that long. It seems like only yesterday that it happened. Of course, it's pretty difficult to forget losing your father…especially the way it happened, with no warning, gone in an instant…."

I feel my pulse start to quicken as it always does when the topic of Charlie comes up. "Sometimes I can think about it rationally and other times it's so painful it's like cutting myself with glass to go back to that place."

Brian looks at me almost sympathetically. "Same. But that doesn't stop me from thinking about it. It's like what happened to Macy. I'm damned if I do and damned if I don't. If I try to imagine what it was like for either of them at the end, it makes me want to scream. But on the other hand, it's like watching a train wreck in my mind: I'm pulled in by the desire to know what they must have experienced, all the while knowing that I can't possibly put myself in their place. Whatever terror they experienced died with them and we'll never be able to share that. And maybe that's a blessing; I don't know."

"That's some blessing," I say sardonically. I decide to ignore the reference to Macy, but pick up the thread about Charlie instead. "And naturally, they've never caught the bastard who caused the plane to go down. Nor will they ever, I'm sure—it's impossible to chase them down; it could be anyone—a needle in a haystack."

Brian sniffs, "Of course they've never caught anyone; that would have been too satisfying. Could have been a million lousy punks anywhere in the city. Who knows which lowlife, in particular, decided to have himself a grand old time pointing a laser into the eyes of a pilot—and a student pilot at that!" he says bitterly. "What a success that venture was! Two people died, two birds with one stone as it were—what were the odds?"

I can tell that Brian is beginning to feel as emotional as I am as the sights and sounds of that day come roiling up in our minds like an icy wind.

I pick up where he left off. "And why did it have to be that time, that place, that plane? Why my husband, your father? I'm sorry to indulge in the *why* questions—I'm usually stronger than that—but for God's sake, what was the point? He was so loved, your father; we had such a good life. And it was all just snatched from us in an instant— for *nothing*, for some whim, some asinine prank! Entire lives detonated in a matter of minutes—for no particular reason—just because it seemed like some counter-culture, badass thing to do…."

Anger and frustration start constricting my throat so tightly that I can hardly speak another word.

"Take it easy, Mom. I know how you feel, believe me," Brian says soothingly. "I have the same questions you do, times one hundred, I think. I remember Dad telling me how much he loved learning to fly, how he loved the freedom of it, the different perspective it gave him, being up in the clouds like a bird. I always thought it was strange, his wanting to be a pilot at his age, but he said it was something he always wanted to do—and, well, you know how it was with him; I'm sure you know better than I do. Who were we to dissuade him, right?"

"Exactly. I couldn't have stopped him even if I had wanted to— which I didn't, at the time. I figured he had worked hard his whole life; if he wanted to do this for himself, who was I to interfere? And he was doing so well up there until then…"

By now I am too choked up to continue so I look to Brian in the hopes that he will change the subject and pull me out of my tailspin.

Brian gives me a pointed look and narrows his eyes as though suddenly remembering something. "He loved those lessons that you bought for him. Let's not forget that you were the one who had the bright idea of giving him lessons for his birthday. You just had to do that, didn't you?"

I feel the anxiety grip my chest as my heart begins to race. "I can't believe you're bringing this up as though it was my fault that he crashed that day. That's so unfair of you," I cry, my voice thin and quivering. "Do you think I haven't gone down that road a thousand times myself? It's not fair to blame me. I can't take that on, Brian, not with everything else; I just can't!" I could feel my face crumble with the despair and heartache I was feeling.

In an attempt to ignore my clear discomfort, he looks down at his hands and shrugs. Then he cocks his head at me. "Well, I'm not saying the crash was your fault per se, but you certainly have a proclivity for picking activities that end badly now, don't you?"

The silence in the room seems to echo. He pulls his eyes up even with mine and stares at me unabashedly as though defying me to respond.

I lower my eyes and just shake my head in disbelief, unable to form a sentence, unable to defend myself with words. I feel a tear spill down my cheek and leave it unchecked. Several more follow in rapid succession. It is difficult to say whether I am more hurt by the implication itself or by the fact that he has chosen to accuse me in this way at this time in my life.

Finally, I look up at him. "I'm sorry you feel that way. I don't think I should have to defend myself for something that I never intended. Accidents happen, Brian; life happens. And I think it's cruel of you to suggest otherwise. God knows I torture myself enough with these questions without having you piling more on," I say bitterly. "Perhaps we should table this discussion."

But, unfortunately for me, Brian does not seem inclined to stop there. He clearly has more on his mind and, now that the floodgates have been opened, he has every intention of outing his feelings. "Well, we don't need to discuss your part in all of this— whatever that may be—but there are still things that need to be aired out despite the fact that you seem to think the subject is taboo. I mean, at least Dad had the benefit of having lived a full life before he disappeared out of ours. I wish I could say the same of Macy. What chance did *she* have? Her dance card hadn't even been filled out yet. She had so much ahead of her, so much promise. I had so many dreams for her. She was my princess, my first-born, my little girl…" His voice trails off as he lowers his eyes, a look of abject pain on his face.

When I say nothing in response, he continues. "You and Dad— you had your life, you had your chance at happiness, but what about my Macy? What chance did you give her, hmm, what chance…?" Brian halts mid-sentence, as though there is something more he wants to say but is forcing himself to stop.

I can see that he is holding in a raging tide of emotions. Then he gives me a look that makes me wither. It is a look that betokens sadness, grief, bitterness and worst of all, judgment. The sheer weight of it crushes me. I turn my head away, unable to sustain his glare and the impact of his words.

I open my mouth to reply to him, but can find nothing to say that has any meaning. I sigh deeply, then finally mutter, "I know, I understand how you feel, I do, but don't you know how sorry I am? I thought we had put this all behind us…?"

"Behind us? What a concept, what a great solution, why didn't I think of that," he snaps sarcastically. "But, in any case, what difference does it make, Mother, how sorry you are? Do you think that helps me any? Do you think that helps Lisa? Do you think *sorry* fixes anything? Do you think there is a statute of limitations on grief?" His eyes seem to pierce the space between us.

I shake my head back and forth, tears raining down my cheeks. "What do you want from me, Brian? What can I possibly say or do?"

"Nothing, Mother, absolutely nothing. I don't expect you to say anything. I don't expect you to do anything. Indeed, what could you possibly *do* that would make any difference to me at this point? What do *I want?* I want justice; that's what I want. I don't see anybody paying their karmic debt—not for Macy, not for Dad. It makes me feel powerless and enraged. I don't know where to put all my anger. I don't know that there's a place big enough to hold it all. I don't know what to do with it...it just hangs over me like a big toxic cloud...."

With that he abruptly stands up, gathers his things, and storms out of the room, leaving me feeling shattered and helpless. Lisa must have just shown up at the front door at roughly the same time because I hear a brief conversation between the two of them, followed by the thud of the door closing behind them.

If I had felt a generalized depression before Brian's visit, now the feeling is acute and overwhelming. I have never heard him express these feelings before in such a pointed way. Granted, right after each accident, he had acted out and blamed nearly everyone around him, but I had taken that as nothing more than unfettered grief and a desire to lash out at those closest to him, for lack of a better target. Everyone was behaving badly in the aftermath of those tragedies. But I had never before felt all of his anger directed at me in such a blunt, laser-like manner, especially after all this time, and especially after I thought that we had made some progress. It shakes me to my core.

It's not as though I don't share his frustration; it's just that we each come to such a different conclusion at the end of it all. Brian's conclusion is rage and a desire for retribution while mine is more sorrow and acceptance of a fate that I recognize as a rule of the universe: a universe that, when I'm thinking clearly, I know owes me nothing—a universe where life is not fair and has never claimed to be.

What is it people always say when confronted with the inexplicable? God works in mysterious ways? Yes, that's it; that must be the answer: short, simplistic, one- dimensional, trite—fit for a greeting card. Mysterious ways indeed.

I try to jerk myself out of the rabbit hole I have fallen into. Thinking about either Charlie or Macy at this level is always a mistake. It is crucial that I try to pull myself out before I go so deep that there is no return.

It is usually at this point in my one-way conversations that I try to reset the monologue. I tell myself that this road leads to nothing but tears and recriminations and that there is never any solace or "closure" that comes at the end of it.

I have a heavy enough load without Brian adding to it, I think to myself. I don't need the additional burden of my son's accusations for acts over which I had no control.

Go down a different path, I tell myself, feeling frantic to escape. Don't let yourself get pulled into this vortex.

Desperate to distract myself, I know I have to replace one set of thoughts with those of a different stripe. I wrack my brain for a new topic that will pull me back from this downward spiral. Anything but what I am doing now, anything but this gnawing, pointless guilt.

Think about the sights you have seen, I cajole myself, go back to your review; anything is better than re-enacting the dark history of Charlie and Macy for the hundredth time.

Like a large cruise ship attempting a ninety-degree turn in a constricted space, my mind slowly, reluctantly turns away. My will is strong, as it has always been. The ship is turning—albeit sluggishly. Soon enough I will be tacking in a different direction, hopefully escaping the strong and violent winds pushing me toward the dark seas of my mental torment.

Sights. Think about that, I keep whispering to myself, eager to change my mental landscape. Eventually, my mind obliges— showing itself to be the agile thinker I knew it to be. The ship now slowly rights itself, setting a new course.

I feel the anxiety loosening its grip on my throat, feel the icy fingers untangling themselves. You can do this, Olivia. You're in charge.

What have I seen in a lifetime? Too many things to chronicle, that's for certain. Too many gorgeous, magnificent things, and just as surely, too many painful, ugly things.

I've been lucky to have traveled in my life, seen all the major sights that everyone agrees must be seen—Paris, Venice, the Greek Islands, Scotland, South America, Africa. Every country had its own spectacular and unique splendor, each one more perfect than the next. I can recall the different panoramas like postcards in my mind, the pictures overlaying each other in a rich tapestry of color and texture.

Some I visited by myself, some with Charlie. Those I saw with Charlie had an even more jewel-like quality when I look back at them for I find the memories of those places intertwined with the memory of my sweet life with him at the time. I remember being in the Blue Ridge Mountains with Charlie, a place so majestic and awe-inspiring that to this day it gives me chills to remember it.

Unbelievably—in light of my recent distress—I find myself smiling at the thought of all those exquisite places on earth that I have seen. I marvel at one's mental ability to shift gears. Yet more proof that the mind—unlike the physical brain—is not constrained by its components. It adapts to every situation in real time, with no boundaries, no limits. It is perhaps the greatest work of all, the most perfect creation, the most mysterious and complex entity on the face of the earth, and yet it is invisible.

It is, simultaneously, both a Servant to the senses and the Instigator and Master of all senses. All of this from something that cannot even be seen. Yes, we can see the brain in an autopsy or pictures, but there is no portrait of the mind, no organ we can hold in our hand, no gray matter we can dissect that would bespeak its breadth and depth. And yet, from birth to death, it is the link to ourselves. It is the mind that sees and thinks and forms our identity and our responses to life on earth.

But places and landscapes are not the only things of beauty these eyes of mine have beheld. Once you've looked up at the Vatican ceiling, is there anything more— artistically speaking—that one could see? Well, yes, a stroll through the Louvre yields other masterpieces, beautiful in different ways than the Sistine Chapel. But still, some things are so spellbinding that they never fade from your mind. That ceiling is emblazoned in my memory forever. I like to think that the ceiling of heaven will look like that. Perhaps I shall soon be testing this theory…

But sight has to encompass not just the exquisite but also the mundane—the everyday, run-of-the-mill sights that we take for granted but which hold a special place in the pantheon of sights worth remembering, for they are tattooed on our hearts. There is the sight of your home, first glimpsed as the car rounds the corner when you return from a trip. Home—wherever it is, whatever it is—always has a pull on your heart. It is the place you return to, the place that is, hopefully, a safe harbor, a place that shelters you from the storms of life, the place you always want to be when the world turns against you and the winds of fate buffet you relentlessly. A place, hopefully, where love exists in some form or other.

And there is the sight of sunlight glistening on wet grass in the mornings, of diamond-cut stars in the evenings, of sheets of grey rain and blankets of white snow, of purple rocks and chocolate mountains, tall redwoods and tender young blossoms, the glint of an iridescent cobweb stretched between two branches, lightning cleaving the heavens, the magenta sunsets and golden sunrises that bookend our lives—all of these, I carry in my mind's eye.

Then there are the faces of the people in my life—the sight of their smiles, their tears, their looks of surprise, the light of their affection. I can see an endless looping film in my mind of the people who have touched me—some lightly, some deeply. Some of them, like my parents, have been gone so long now that they barely seem real to me, and yet all are unforgettable in their way.

But each face seems precious to me now that my time is winding down, now that these faces will fade from my life like an ebbing tide. I want to remember everything I have seen, from start to finish, birth to death before it all just disappears into thin air.

But not all sight is experienced with the eyes, nor is it all exterior to us. Some portion of sight is internal and has nothing to do with our physical eyes. That would be insight, the things we see with our mind's eye, or perhaps even our heart's eye, if such a thing exists.

And perhaps it is insight that guides us through our lives just as surely as our eyes do in the outside world.

Then, too, there is dream-sight, the things we see while we sleep—things that are sometimes hauntingly real and other times so surreal as to seem like science fiction when we wake. There is that split second when we gain consciousness when you question which one is the dream and which the real world; but wakefulness usually clarifies the reality.

Would that I had some insight into the mysteries of this life and the unanswered questions that plague me night and day. But in reality, I have very little. Some things I understand with clarity; others will likely always be out of my reach—unknowable, unfathomable, unreachable. It reminds me of when I try to understand the concept of infinity—where I cannot even adequately fashion the question, let alone determine the answer.

I can only hope that these and all my other questions will be answered on the other side of this veil.

Really? Did I just say that to myself? How delightfully trite. I must be getting soft in my old age. Perhaps it is time to "lift the veil?" I find myself smiling at the thought.

At this point, sure of his reception, and tired of my self-absorption, Merlin jumps up on the bed, demanding attention. After a few moments, I find myself grinning at him and begin scratching him under his chin. He yawns lazily then stretches himself out on top of my legs. "You couldn't care less about any of this profound philosophical discussion I'm having with myself, could you?" I say to him, as though we are having an adult conversation. "Just as well. I was getting in much too deep, believe me, kitten," I say, smoothing the top of his head with my hand.

Merlin closes his eyes contentedly, signifying the level of interest he has in anything I have to say. Saved by the cat, I think to myself.

Several minutes later Laila suddenly pokes her head around the bedroom door. "I'm late this morning," she announces cheerfully, pushing her way into the room and automatically starting to straighten things up. "Been up long?"

"I think I've been up way *too* long," I say, wiping my hands across my face, hoping the stress and the tear tracks of the last hour aren't still written there for anyone to see. "Brian just left for the airport. I'm afraid he took a toll on me."

"Why, what happened?" Laila asks, moving over to sit at the foot of my bed so she can observe me better.

"I don't think I want to relive it in much detail, believe me," I answer. "Suffice it to say we had a very heavy conversation. He's still dealing with a lot of emotional baggage, and he wasn't very easy on me. I knew he still had deep feelings about the accidents—you remember, I told you about Macy and Charlie—but I guess I didn't realize how acute his pain still is. It's as though no time has passed; it's as though he lost them yesterday, not years ago. The sting of it doesn't seem to have worn off in the slightest. He still likes to blame me, but I'm not in charge of the universe…I have no idea how to help him with it. I'm at a loss."

Laila nods. She knows the broad strokes of what happened to my husband and my granddaughter. She is no stranger to sorrow, so I know that she has ample experience to understand the situation.

"There is no timetable," she says knowingly. "It can take years; it can take decades. Some people never get past it. I think because I was very young when I lost my parents, the natural resilience of youth helped me. I mean I was probably catonic for quite a while—is that the right word…?"

"Catatonic," I smile, "but keep going. It's good for us both to talk about these things."

She nods. "Okay. I think I was *catatonic* for the first few years, just sleepwalking through my life, but then I finally snapped out of it when I moved to the U.S. and my whole life changed. Sometimes that's what it takes. Big changes, big moves…"

I sigh, nodding in agreement. "Yes, big changes. I don't know what that will be for Brian, but something needs to give where he's concerned—something needs to change.

"Someday," I continue, in an effort to change the topic, "you'll have to tell me what exactly changed your mind about coming here to the U.S."

Laila takes a few seconds before answering. "You know, it's all very complicated, and something I haven't analyzed very well myself. But in the end, I think 'desperation' probably sums it all up; I was just desperate for something to change, and I didn't care how or what or why. I just needed my life to be different than what it was. And so I decided to take a leap into the unknown. And I don't regret it, not at all. Under the circumstances, it was probably my best move. My life rearranged itself completely after that. I had new places to see, new problems to solve, new people to connect with. All told, I think it was a good thing to make the big move, especially given the limited choices I had. Not to be dramatic, but I think it probably saved my life."

"Yes, probably so. You certainly didn't have much of a future in the situation you were in."

"No, not at all. But you know, it's funny," Laila says, smiling slightly, "well, maybe not funny so much as interesting, but I learned so much more from the hardships I endured than from any of the easy times I have had since."

"That's true for everyone," I say, nodding sagely. "Life's lessons don't come to you while you're sitting on the couch watching TV, they come when something hits you hard in the gut, and you are forced to react to it. Tears have a way of making you think about things that laughter does not. In an effort to make you think that you got something positive out of it, we usually call this 'character-building,' though in fact, it really just means that something was deeply painful. But in any case, you and I should have plenty of character by now, don't you think?"

"Totally," she laughs. "But are you saying that you think God teaches us lessons with pain, then?"

"Well, I don't know if I would have put it that way, but yes, I do think pain is a *catalyst* for thought and *introspection*. Sorry, that's two big words in a row: catalyst is like an agent for change and introspection is—let's see—it's self-examination. So painful situations make us look into ourselves in a way that normal, everyday activities do not. I know that the hard times have taught me many things I did not know before. My goodness, but we're being awfully academic here. I didn't mean to turn this into a Sunday school class."

Laila giggles. "No, that wouldn't do. I have a better idea: tell me what you want for breakfast and I'll fix it for you."

"I wish I could say I was hungry," I say honestly, happy to change the subject and at the same time thinking how distasteful the thought of oatmeal or toast seems at this moment. "But maybe I should eat something…?"

"You should, really," Laila replies, "I don't want to give you medication on an empty stomach. That's a recipe for disaster..."

"I suppose you're right. This is no time for disaster. Toast then, with jam, nothing elaborate."

"Toast it is. And then your favorite—a sponge bath!"

I groan disagreeably. "I don't know who you're cleaning me up for…"

"For you, Olivia, strictly for you. I want you to look pretty and polished in case the film crew shows up…"

I have to smile. "Ah, that's a good one, Laila. They'll be here any minute now to film my life story, is that it?"

"Exactly. So let's get a move on. I'll rustle up the breakfast while you pick an alluring outfit."

"Alluring, that's a good word. You mean more alluring than the one I'm currently wearing?"

"Hopefully, yes." We both laugh, contemplating the tired old nightgown I have been wearing for the last four days.

"I'll start working on that," I smile. "Oh, and Laila, thanks for dragging me into the present. It's exactly where I need to be."

"It's where we all need to be," Laila says softly, with a wisdom beyond her years. "It's the only place we *can* be".

Chapter 9

HEARING

Another dreary afternoon by anyone's standards, though not as bad as yesterday; admittedly, the sun is trying to peek out from the clouds, but its half-hearted efforts have not produced much to cheer about. On a scale of one to ten, I give it a four.

Laila has left for the day, the hospice nurse has come and gone in record time, and the place is as quiet as a morgue. No point even dwelling on that thought.

Clearly the time has come to move on to the last of the senses, though this seems somewhat ominous in and of itself. *Is it deeply significant that hearing may be the last of the senses to go?* I ask myself, wryly amused that I am even having this mental tête á tête. Don't get too metaphysical, Olivia. Plenty of time for that later. Just take it at face value and get on with it. Hearing, one of my favorites.

I vividly remember all the music I have loved over the years, the soundtrack of my life, pitching and changing with each decade. It started in the Sixties when I first discovered the kaleidoscope of sound that was produced in those throbbing, explosive years: Bob Dylan, James Brown, Janis Joplin, B.B. King, Van Morrison, Ike and Tina Turner, Motown, the Beatles, the Rolling Stones. Then there was Phil Spector's wall of sound that rolled over us, bathing us in its rich tones and pulsating vibrations. Things went downhill after that, but what a concept. Those tunes will always be my favorites. These are the sounds that have stayed with me through all my years, music that reverberates in my head and forms a backdrop to my life.

While I went on to appreciate the wonder of more somber music—the symphonies, the operas, broadway, in truth, it was that early music that always played in my head. I appreciated the *Four Seasons, Beethoven's Ninth and the Maple Leaf Rag*, but it was the tunes of the Sixties that continually riffed in my mind.

New decades sailed by, and while some of the later music was sweet and new, some of it seemed strange and discordant to me. Like many of my generation, I had to struggle to accept the current forms of music. Rap and hip-hop, for example, were difficult at first, but eventually, I found a way to embrace them—maybe not with the fervor of the young, but with a certain grace. Some of the lyrics were too much for me to swallow, but once I opened my mind to the concept, I came to find a basic grittiness and truth in certain Rap anthems. I could see the poetry in some of them, despite my original condescension for their language and tone. While they were laid out in a different form from the lyrics of my youth and had a different 'affect', I had to admit that they were unequivocally *present*, and for that I came to appreciate them—not all, but some. And I give myself credit for that.

I surprised my family and some of my friends by liking Eminem and Jay-Z and Drake, to name a few. "I can't believe you listen to that trash," a friend I went to school with once told me dismissively.

"I understand your point of view, really I do," I said. "But some of it is whimsical, some of it is lyrical and some of it is right on the money," I told her. "You have to open your ears and push back your bias; then you can hear it. I love some of the new music; it's raw, it's real, it grabs you—you just need to listen to it with your guard down. Trust me, I don't like all of it, but there are some jewels among the trash, you just have to be willing to look." She wasn't having any of it, and I knew there was no point in trying to convert her.

Music is like food and literature; you should sample all the different cuisines, tap into the various cultures to really experience the resplendent menu in front of you. And that is, in essence, the challenge put to older minds: to see the beauty in new forms, to be able to move and grow with time and not solidify all of your opinions into granite, as we are wont to do with age.

The music of the twenty-first century flowed into new channels in my brain, and I accepted it as one accepts the tides rushing onto the sand. But the early music never let go of me. And like the shells we gather when the tide ebbs, the music of my youth still sits on the shelves of my mind.

How lucky we are to hear such a cornucopia of sounds in our lives: the sounds of nature all around us—the shriek of hawks, the rush of a river over rocks, the whispering of wind through the trees, the sharp crack of lightning, the deep rumbling of thunder, the patter of rain on a metal roof, the buzzing of bees, the rhythmic thrum of crickets in the evening.

Then there are all the sounds we have created with our technology—the cacophony of ringing phones, streaming videos and TV shows, the alarms, the clocks, the buzzers, the sirens, the cars, the trucks, the trains, the planes. A limitless carpet of sounds and noise blankets our earth—that is what we have spawned and what we have come to accept as normal.

And, of course, there are the sounds and the noises we make in our lives—our own personal soundtrack that we have recorded in our head and that we can retrieve at will. I can remember my mother singing to me when I was young, right before I went to sleep. I remember my father reading to me as a rare treat, again, when I was no more than four or five. He would read from a simple book because his English was not that polished. But I remember it well. He half-read, half-sang the lyrics to *The Teddy Bear's Picnic* with his thick accent:

"If you go down to the woods today,

You're sure of a big surprise.

If you go down to the woods today,

You'd better go in disguise.

For every bear that ever there was

Will gather there for certain because

Today's the day the teddy bears have their picnic."

My parents' voices—one of my few memories of them that always sticks with me. I don't remember them being particularly affectionate with me, or even kind, but I can still hear them speaking to me, reprimanding me, interrogating me, punishing me, pleading with me, cajoling me—such familiar sounds that never flee from my memory.

And I remember the sound of Charlie's voice. I always loved his voice; it was mid-range, calm, solid, warm, melodious, and it always struck me as very masculine— whatever that means. He never screeched or yelled or barked; that wasn't his style. He always spoke to me with respect, never swore—at least not at me—rarely argued, and always called me by sweet names. I was "his angel," his "baby girl" (no matter what my age), or "his sweetheart."

It's difficult to be mad at someone who routinely calls you "sweetheart." And I rarely was—mad, that is. I remember how choked up and sentimental we both were when we said our wedding vows, how my makeup got ruined and I could barely speak. Our voices were thick with emotion, and there was a single violin on a recorded tape that played as we walked off into our new life— Pachelbel I think—everyone's favorite wedding piece. For some reason, I remember him saying, "I will never harm a hair on your head. No matter what happens, I will never hurt you."

He said many things that day, and yet that is the phrase I have always recalled. And he never did hurt me intentionally, though, Lord knows, life hurt me many times with no direct help from Charlie. Our life together was a sonata of new sounds and melodies, sometimes sweet, sometimes somber, but always memorable. Unforgettable in fact.

And then there are the sounds that no one else hears, the inaudible sounds if such a thing is possible. There is the language we use when we speak to ourselves—a language that no two people will ever share. There are the voices in my head, occasional whispers from my heart. There is the voice of my conscience, my intuition, my fear, each one a different tenor. And then, ever so rarely, there is the at-once loud and at the same time completely silent voice of God that has entered my consciousness from time to time, always bypassing my ears entirely.

My child made sounds that stick in my memory still—the sugary sound of a baby's laugh, a screech of delight when he first found new words to pronounce, the grown-up monotone he used for his part in a play at school. I remember the way his voice changed from that of a child to the deeper more strident tones of adolescence. I remember him shouting when he was accepted into medical school, and the tone of his voice the day he told me he was leaving home. I remember the day he called me from his new office, so proud, so accomplished, so pleased with himself. And I can never forget his cry of anguish at his daughter's funeral or the sound of his weeping when the news came of Charlie's accident.

These are the sounds I remember. These are also the sounds I am beginning to forget.

***

My life is substantially constricted now; my universe has narrowed itself to the four walls of my bedroom. The only windows to the outside world are often shuttered or only partially open, so that my perspective has shifted inward, and the number of events on my calendar has dwindled to nothing. The only event I have to look forward to is the meeting with Howard and the heirs, something that has been put off for various reasons but which should happen any day now.

Brian and Lisa have gotten in the habit of coming over every other evening to look in on me, with or without my permission. They like to discuss my condition between themselves—my own personal

Death Squad. I feel out of the loop: it's not that Brian doesn't keep me abreast of things, it's just that, in my current state, I sometimes get confused about whether we are in the past, present, or future. They all seem rolled together into my new version of reality. It all seems like the present to me, though I would never let on to Brian and Lisa that this is the case; I have enough problems without them analyzing my mental state.

This particular night, well into my second month of hospice, I can hear them talking in the living room—just bits and pieces of their conversation—but enough to know that I am the subject matter. It is too seductive not to listen. I roll myself out of bed with some difficulty, then creep silently towards the bedroom door. I pull the door in slightly and squeeze myself into the corner so that I can hide behind it, all the better to catch their dialogue:

"…don't know how long it will take, but the prognosis is not good. She's in the final stages. There's nothing much I can do for her at this point except limit her pain. Nature will take its course. We should all be prepared," I can hear Brian saying smoothly.

Lisa says something back to him that I can't hear entirely as she is making some sort of noise in the living room, but I do hear her say something about "…more aggressive therapies." I sense that it is a question, not a statement.

Then I hear him say, "...no point at her stage. Sometimes you just have to balance the karmic scales."

"Well, that's a cryptic statement," Lisa responds.

"It is, isn't it? I don't mean anything by it really; it's just a phrase that sounded good to me at the time," Brian replies casually. Then he abruptly changes the subject.

My mind grabs onto the visuals of his statement. I can see the classic statue of Lady Justice draped in Roman folds with a blindfold across her eyes and a set of scales hanging balanced from her uplifted hand. I try to remember what exactly is on those plates. And how do they perpetually balance each other out? And what has karma got to do with any of it?

And then, suddenly, I know with a searing clarity.

I readjust the door and drag myself back to the bed, my mind focused and clearer than it has been for a long time, a single thought preoccupying me.

I open the bedside drawer next to me and pull out the old tattered address book that Charlie and I used for over a quarter of a century, and once again I become distracted. It contains so many names that are now long forgotten: some of the people are dead, some moved, some simply a footnote in our lives, contacted once and then never heard from again.

Some of the names though make me touch the book with sadness and catch my breath. A close friend here, a cousin there, all gone and dearly missed. Here's a woman I loved my whole life, dead ten years now...was she ever even here? I often ask myself that question as memories fade and the reality of certain people begins to be tangled in my mind. I shake my head to stop the meanderings. Back to the topic at hand, I chastise myself. Remember Olivia; you have forgotten more than some people ever knew... I smile at my own hubris. Humility was never my long suit. What was that thought that seemed so lascr-clear?

I begin to thumb through the dilapidated pages, fondly recalling some of the memories clamped inside it. Finally, I find what I'm looking for. There it is: Doctor Patel, my old doctor, the one I had gone to up until my cancer diagnosis. His card is clipped to the "D" page, for Doctor. And there is his cell phone number, right where it has always been.

You can't call him at this hour, it's too late, and besides, it's not as if it's an emergency, I tell myself. And furthermore, he probably doesn't even remember you anymore, although I find it difficult to believe he could completely forget you...

Get a grip, Olivia, you can call him in the morning like a normal person. I give in to this logic and place the phone book next to the bed. Tomorrow then, I promise myself, tomorrow you can call him.

I sleep badly that night, unable to fall into anything other than a superficial slumber, continually waking myself up with unresolved anxiety. I am glad when dawn finally breaks and the room begins to pick up tinges of light. Only a few more hours now until Laila arrives.

I try one more time—unsuccessfully—to fall back asleep, but my mind is having none of it. The minutes ooze by with no sense of regularity, like molasses dripping off a spoon.

Finally, I hear Laila's key in the door. Thank God, I think. Civilization. Or, at the very least, some hot tea and toast.

"How are you feeling this morning, Olivia?" she chirps as she pushes into the bedroom, a large purse clutched under her arm.

"Don't ask," I smile wanly. "Glad to see your cheerful face, in any case."

"Where should we start then—something to eat, maybe?"

"That would be good. Nothing too heavy, though; as usual, I don't think I could keep anything complicated down."

"No, we'll keep it simple," she says, ditching her purse in the folds of the armchair. She bends over me, presumably to assess my condition with her own eyes. "You look tired to me," she says, gently putting a hand on my forehead. "I don't think you have a fever, though."

"No, I'm alright, just had a bad night and couldn't sleep. I feel like crap on toast, to tell you the truth, but I'm glad you're here. Maybe we can chat a bit after breakfast."

"I'd like that," Laila says, pushing things around on my night table to make some room before heading off for the kitchen.

When she comes back, she has a tray neatly arranged with two pieces of buttered toast, a napkin, and a small glass of juice.

"You'll like this," she says placing it gently on my recumbent lap.

"I'm sure," I demur, picking up the toast more for her sake than mine. While I am doing my best to dispatch the breakfast, Laila is straightening up the room, then portioning out pills for me to take with the orange juice.

"You know, there's something I've been meaning to ask you. You seem open to most questions. Can I ask how you and Charlie met?" she says looking apprehensive, as though I might be offended at the question.

I smile at her politeness. "Ah, everyone loves to hear these stories, don't they? I suppose I could tell you that story once before I die."

Laila looks horrified that I have brought up the subject of death.

"Oh, don't look so worried," I chuckle, warming to the subject. "I'm not dying today or tomorrow I promise. It would be too tawdry, what with Howard and the others coming over at some point. We'll put that one off for a while. But yes, I can definitely tell you the story, though I don't think it's all that dramatic. You can be the judge. I don't know that you would call it 'kismet' (that means fate) or overly sensational on the face of it, but it was a turning point and a clear juncture in my life—and certainly a moment I wasn't expecting."

"It all came about really because of my love of books—certain books in particular. The company I worked for at the time—I was exactly 27 years old then—sent me to a writer's conference in Chicago. In those days I jumped at the chance to travel anywhere, especially on someone else's dime. They put me up at a pleasant enough hotel in the heart of the city and I was in my element. I'll skip the boring details of what went on at the conference itself—since I don't remember anyway! Suffice it to say that I took care of my work assignment during the day and took advantage of being young and footloose once they released us into the jungle of Chicago nightlife. I had no trouble meeting men per se; I had trouble meeting men who interested me intellectually. I was hardly innocent—innocence had deserted me long before that—but I knew I had yet to find what people today like to refer to as *the one.* This of course refers to a romanticized, idealized notion of the perfect Spouse, Lover, Friend, Lifetime companion, etc."

"Why—you don't think that it's possible to find such a person?" Laila interrupts.

"No, actually I *do* think it's possible, because I found one. But I think they are very rare, like unicorns and fairy dust. And I think actively searching for such a one is probably futile. They simply appear in your life or they don't; I'm not sure you have any control over it. I don't think you can hunt them down or conjure them up at will, despite what people think. We got lucky, pure and simple."

I sighed in remembrance and then continued. "But I'm jumping ahead of myself. It was after-hours, the dreary seminar had ended for the afternoon and I had planted myself at a small table in the rear corner of the hotel bar. I ordered some sort of sugary, not very grown-up drink and sat reading the novel I was currently obsessed with, which at the time was *Justine*, the first of the four books in the *Alexandria Quartet*. Just to educate you, the *Quartet* is a remarkable piece of literature, written by Lawrence Durrell, that is comprised of four separate novels, all set in the ancient city of Alexandria—each one telling roughly the same story but from a different point of view. It's a spectacular piece of writing, very deep, very beautiful, very profound, and trust me, I only understood a fraction of what he was trying to say. But even that fraction was worth trying for. His style and language alone is unmatched in anything I have ever read—pure artistry. I could go on and on, but don't let me; I need to finish my story. But I wanted you to have some background about the feelings those books always brought up in me."

"I think you've painted the picture," she said with a rapt look on her face. "So then what happened?"

"Well, I got up from the table where I was sitting for some reason—to get a glass of water as I recall—leaving my book there to hold my place.

"When I got back there was a strange man sitting in one of the two chairs. He was holding my book in his hand, turning it over carefully.

He seemed reasonably attractive, ostensibly friendly, certainly non-threatening, so I sat down in my own chair, reached out my hand and said pointedly, "My book, please?"

"Ah, your book—this book. *Alexandria Quartet*, Book 1? I walked by your table, saw *Justine* and simply had to know who was reading it—that is, what person of excellent taste was reading it," he said, pushing the book back towards me.

"I was reading it. Correction: I am reading it. Why?"

"I was hoping it was a woman. Any woman smart enough to be reading Durrell is worth looking into. I wanted to know, and now I know it's you."

"Well, you're a strange one, aren't you?" I said, or something to that effect. But my curiosity was piqued and my love of all things Durrell overcame my reticence to talk to a stranger."

"I take it you've read them all?"

I said curiously. "Several times. And you?"

"My second time around. I'm still trying to assimilate all four books. I'm not there yet…"

"The layers never cease to amaze me. You can keep peeling this onion and you never run out layers. And as for his vocabulary—I have to read with a dictionary next to me."

"I'm the same. In fact, some of the words are so arcane that even the dictionary doesn't have them, or so unexpectedly used as descriptions that you have to think about how it can possibly apply, and then suddenly you see it."

"Exactly," he said.

"And that's how we met, Laila. Over the *Alexandria Quartet*. He sat with me that evening at the table in the bar and basically, figuratively, never left my side again. It took a while to work out the logistics of a relationship that started out as a long distance affair and ended up as a long-term marriage. But after a time he landed a job in Seattle and then moved here to be with me. There wasn't any question that we would be together; we fit perfectly, like two pieces of a puzzle, his hand to my glove. I loved him 'til the day he died— and still now, if the truth be told."

Laila sighs. "I love that story. I may make you tell me all over again tomorrow Maybe you've left out some details here and there…"

I smile at her, feeling warm and emotional at the same time. "I'll see what details I can dredge up for you by tomorrow, how's that?"

"That's perfect," says Laila. "I'll be waiting.

***

Later that morning, I dial Dr. Patel's number. Soon I am talking to his receptionist. "Yes, I'm sure he's busy with a patient, but would you have him call me when he gets a minute in between? He said I could call anytime, and he'd be happy to speak with me…."

"I'll leave him the message," she says in a clipped tone, all business, sounding like every doctor's receptionist in the world.

"Good. Thank you then, you're too kind…" I say, rolling my eyes.

I don't expect to hear from him until later in the day, possibly after all of his patients had been taken care of. I feel as though I will be constructing every hour until his phone call comes, assembling the minutes one by one, until, finally, the clock moves ahead one more number.

Laila notices that I am more distracted than usual and tries to coax me out of my malaise, but gives it up in the end and writes it off to my lack of sleep.

After she leaves, I try one final time to fit in a nap, but my thoughts are too agitated to afford me any peace. I watch one TV show after another, each one more mind- numbing than the one before it until finally I shut it off. The silence is a relief.

I pick up the Elizabeth Kubler-Ross book *On Death and Dying* that I keep by my bedside and—thinking I ought to bone up on my studies while I still have the chance— start re-reading through the five stages of grief. Not that I am going to be the one grieving, after all, but still it is interesting to read all of her stories about the soon-to-be-departed. Much more pleasant to be the grieving than the aggrieved, I think to myself cynically. It takes some of the sting out of it. Still, I am interested in the process after all—ever the academician at heart.

Then I recall that the five stages of grieving are also the five stages of dying. Time for an assessment: let's see, we're long past Denial; took a brief vacation with Anger—but discarded it as ineffectual; gave up quickly on Bargaining, as I didn't seem to have any chips worth bartering; so I must be cruising into Depression, since I certainly have not arrived at Acceptance yet, which would be the clincher, of course.

Midway through evaluating my current position on the Dying Scale the phone rings. It is early evening now, I think, close to five o'clock: it's unlikely it's him. As I pick up the phone, I glance at the caller ID and am startled to see that it is indeed my faithful doctor.

"Dr. Patel, it's good of you to return my call. Do you remember me?" I say in the most winsome voice I can conjure up.

"Of course, I do," he says in his soothing tone. "It hasn't been that long since you left us. I've got your chart in front of me. How are you feeling these days, or is that a bad question?"

"Pretty much as you might expect. I think the disease is doing quite well; it's me I'm not so sure about."

"Understood," he says gamely. "But how can I be of help to you, Olivia?"

Translation: "why are you calling me?"

I sigh and try to gather my thoughts. "Well, I'm not sure how to broach this, but I should be able to talk to you about my condition, yes?"

"Well, of course, you can—certainly—but I'm no longer your primary physician; that would be your son Brian, no?"

"Yes, yes, it's Brian, but I have a few questions for you. I don't think we're violating any HIPAA rules by talking about my own case just between the two of us, are we?" I say disingenuously.

He laughs. "No, no violations there. What's your question, Olivia? I'll try to answer it as best I can."

"Okay, then. I want to know what Stage of CLL you think I was in when you first diagnosed me."

He hesitates before answering, trying to size up the request. "Well, that's an interesting question. That's something your Oncologist would have determined—in your case that would be Brian, of course. I mean, I had a general idea of your situation at the time. Your white blood count was quite high, your red blood count was simultaneously low, and several of your lymph nodes appeared to be swollen, based on palpation. But your own doctor would have ordered further imaging to pin down just how many of the lymph nodes we're talking about and to what degree of involvement. I'm sure that's already been done, right?"

"Yes, of course," I lie. "I guess I just get confused by some of the terminology. So if several lymph nodes are affected by the cancer, then you're well past stage 0, or 1, right?"

"Well…yes, normally that would be the case if your cancer had spread to your lymph nodes. But I'm a bit confused. Surely you've talked this over with Brian? I can't imagine that he hasn't explained all of this to you?"

I can tell that he is beginning to feel uncomfortable about our conversation.

"Oh, he has, yes, naturally he has. I was just curious as to what your thoughts were back when I was first diagnosed."

"Well, what I thought was that you had a fairly advanced case, but this is not my specialty, and I purposely left the final diagnosis up to your new doctor. It's up to him to decide what types of therapies to use with you in order to slow the disease down. There are so many avenues you can take these days, many of them quite cutting edge. No doubt you've been down several of those roads already. I'm sure I'm not telling you anything you don't already know." I could tell he was trying to cover himself.

"No, you're right. Nothing I didn't already know. We've definitely been down those crooked roads," I assured him while shaking my head. "Well, listen, thank you for your time."

"No problem. Sometimes it helps to talk things through with a third person. Let me know how you're doing from time to time."

"I will, Doctor, thank you," I say, thinking to myself that the next notification he will get will be on the Obituary Page.

Now, with Laila gone and the room still, all my thoughts come cascading down in chaotic layers. I had managed to hold them at bay while she was here and while I spoke to Dr. Patel, but now they rush in like sea water through a hole in the retaining wall.

No matter how hard I try to shut them out, I keep coming back to Brian's words, replaying them over and over again in my mind like a Greek chorus:

Balancing the karmic scales

What's in a word? Or in this case, several words?

Answer: Everything.

I have heard many things in my life: good news, bad news, frivolous things, serious things, cries of happiness, shrieks of horror, but hearing this one phrase cut me to the quick. Because I understood, at the end of that string of words, not what my son had done to me but what he had not *done* for me.

At that moment, I understood it all.

I realize that Brian does not hold me overtly responsible for Macy's accident; instead, he believes that I am passively responsible. He believes it is what we did *not* do that condemns us, not what we *did* do. Sins of omission, not commission. And now he has brought it full circle. I can see the logic in his thinking, at least from his point of view. It's simple enough:

Brian has not made me sick; he simply has not made me well, just as I did not kill Macy, I simply did not save her.

I lean back in bed, feeling as though I hadn't slept for a thousand years—bone weary, I think that's what they call it. I'm searching my mind for a phrase to describe how I feel about what Brian has said. What was the line in Shakespeare? *"How sharper than a serpent's tooth…"*

Yes, that's it.

I pick up the phone near the bed.

"Howard, it's Olivia. I'm sorry to call you at this hour and I'm sorry I've taken so long to get back to you. I know you called to arrange our meeting—the meeting that I had asked for, after all—but I had some final strings to tie up. "

"No problem. Is everything alright? Are the strings tied?"

"Oh, they're tied alright, tied up in one big knot. But that's not your problem, it's mine. To answer your question, yes, I'm fine— well, not exactly, but that's a different conversation. Listen, I'm calling because I wanted to let you know that I am finally ready now. I told you I would call when I reach that point, and that time has come. Bring the Transfer papers and the notary stamp as soon as possible. Get a hold of Marla and the others. I'll leave it to you to organize it. Let's finish this."

"Give me a couple of hours tomorrow morning to clear the decks, then I'll call everyone and gather them together." Howard says, putting his hand on Olivia's file which has been sitting on his desk awaiting the final disposition of the stock. "I've already spoken to all of them in anticipation of this, so this won't come as any surprise. They've just been waiting for me to set a time. So good, tomorrow it is. This should be interesting,"

"Indeed," I say, quietly. "I'll bet they can't wait for a number of reasons. Tomorrow then. Good night, Howard."

Chapter 10

FINAL CHAPTER

Several weeks have passed now with very few notable changes on my part, but today seems different. I wake up this morning feeling visibly altered. I sense it immediately. Today could turn out to be very critical; in fact, it might be the most important day of my life. Like a flag unfurling, I feel something unfolding deep inside of me. I sense a seismic shift in my thinking. A thousand thoughts are swirling in my brain but not frenetically, rather calmly, rationally, and in a disciplined fashion.

What was amorphous and gelatinous before now seems substantive and solidified. It is as though I have laser vision and a clarity of mind that had been missing for some weeks now. I am taking my mental pulse and it is strong.

A weight has been lifted from my shoulders; there is a lightness to my being, a feeling of—what is this really—a sense of freedom? Is that what it is? Freedom from anxiety or, perhaps, freedom from confusion, freedom from guilt, freedom from uncertainty? My mind and body feel uncharacteristically relaxed, elastic, unclenched.

I am aware of my underlying sickness, but the tension around it appears to have fled. The illness still seems to reside in my corporal body, but *I* am not there; I am much lighter than that. The cancer cells are busy fulfilling their destiny, and I am about to fulfill mine. My mind is as weightless as a feather.

What a new sensation this is! A sense of peace and tranquility is welling up in me. A tiny thought forms at the back of my brain. At first, I am afraid to confront it and then its inevitability dawns on me. Is this what I think it is? Is this by any chance:

Acceptance?

And if so, isn't that pretty much the End Game?

Let's face it: I've been drifting down this river for some time now—some would call it "circling the drain" but I prefer to think of it in less cynical terms. Everything that has happened in the last year—in the last 67 years really—has brought me to this place, to this junction, this nexus.

I am not afraid to die; I never really was. I just wanted to postpone it, as we all do—have it take place some time further off in the future. But now death and my future seem to have come to a crossroad, leaving me with no exit strategy besides the obvious. And this does not make me despair; on the contrary, I am finding something pleasant in the realization.

So my answer to today's proposition is: I concur; I accept it. Let's do it; I'm ready now. I've tied up all of the so-called loose ends, put my affairs in order, as they say And, in a way, I'm looking forward to it. After all, this might prove to be really spectacular—cosmic even! Isn't that a possibility? It could be the most daring, courageous, adventurous, thrilling, perfect moment of my life, could it not?

As I find myself having this internal conversation, I feel a smile come to my lips.I remember the old phrase: *"there are no atheists in the foxhole."* I'm sure that's true; and the further corollary to that must be that there are no atheists in the death spiral either. When I think back on my life and my relationship with God, it was tentative at best. But now, in the midst of all these new sensations, I feel the thought of God spreading over me like a warm gossamer blanket. I find myself wrapped up in its heat and comfort.

How perfect it is to be here in this moment, hovering over the bridge between two worlds. How I long to jump across that space, hurl myself into the unknown. The fact that I feel a God-presence, after all of my fits and starts about religion, is overwhelmingly comforting. After all, it turns out I really do want someone to grab my hand when I make that leap across the abyss. I really do want someone to pull me in, someone to give me safe harbor, and who better than God?

I long to see Charlie and Macy again, and others that went before them—that goes without saying—but even more than that, it is clear to me now that I want to see the face of God, and that this, above all else, is my overarching desire.

I am in the perfect place for this, am I not?

Apparently I have now fallen into what would commonly be called a coma, and I seem, for all intents and purposes, to the outside world to be unconscious. But in fact, from my perspective, that is not the case. Contrary to popular opinion—at least the opinion of Brian and Lisa—I can still hear them and can still tell when someone is touching me. Beyond that, it's true there's not much going on in my conscious mind. But my subconscious is vividly alive; in fact, it may even be my superconscious that is at work now—I have no way of knowing.

My mind feels like a hovercraft, gliding effortlessly over my body, taking in the scenery, marking the occasion. I am no longer cognizant of being in physical pain—all of that seems to have dissipated. What I feel now is light and airy, like a bubble on the water, pure spirit, hyper-consciousness.

So this is dying! Thus far, while exciting, it's not living up to all of its press. I thought there would be some celestial music as a send-off, something with harps and angelic voices, and, of course, the mystical "white light," but up until now there's been none of that—though I'm hopeful that there may be more to come. I'm still waiting for the grand finale, after all. Still, I'm not complaining; the transition has been simple, natural and more than pleasant—transcendent, in fact. I am one with the river.

I feel as though my five senses are on the threshold of a new shore. Perhaps they will morph into an all-encompassing sixth sense that embodies all of the old ones simultaneously. Perhaps that was always what the sixth sense was—the penultimate amalgam of all the senses.

I can still just barely feel Brian holding my right hand, and that must be Laila on my left—I know the feel of her hand; it's different from Lisa's and it's the one I prefer. I can tell that she is trying to reach me at some level with her touch. Or am I wrong? Is that Charlie or Macy that I feel? I can't be sure. I see no faces; I only feel their fingers. I can hear what must be voices, but they do not seem to be speaking in my native tongue. Perhaps this is a new language? I would like that.

I'll be there soon enough, my darling.

I know now with razor sharpness that what I really want is not to be here at all in this world, but to shift to the fresco in the Sistine Chapel where Adam brushes the finger of God. That is the Touch I am longing for, the Sound, the Taste, the Smell, the Sight of it. The new address of my soul.

EPILOGUE

Olivia Calvert passed away late that night in February—Brian, Lisa and Laila by her side. It was a fairly unremarkable passing, almost anti-climactic—at least from the point of view of those next to her. There did not seem to be much pain or drama associated with her death, just a few deep, jagged breaths, a long shudder, and then a peaceful transition from breathing to not-breathing that was neither unexpected nor unplanned. As a hospice patient, she had fulfilled her contract. As a human being, her story had ended. Chapter closed.

The next morning, her body was still on the bed. The funeral home had been summoned and would arrive soon to whisk her away. She was appropriately mourned by her family, most notably by her two grandsons and her stepdaughter.

Tad kept murmuring that he "missed his grandma," to which his father answered smoothly, "She's in a better place now, Taddie. Life comes full circle, you know." Tad shook his head at his father and sobbed, "It won't be the same without her; she always understood me."

"I'm sure she did," Brian said sympathetically, throwing his arm around his son. "Now your mother and I will just have to learn to understand you, won't we?"

Tad shrugged off his father's arm and headed for his room, all teenage sorrow and angst. Soon he would return to college; soon he would learn that his grandmother had paved the way for any future studies he might wish to indulge in. His fiscal future looked bright and shiny.

Claire too struggled with Olivia's loss. She had come over in the morning to say her final goodbyes. Though not related by blood, they had always shared a kind of unspoken bond, forged in their mutual love for Charlie. And Claire had always admired Olivia's steely independence, her caustic humor, and her unflinching views of life. In her own way, she had been envious of the love story between her father and Olivia. "How did you manage that, to be in love all those years?" she once asked her father shortly before she lost him. "It's part luck, part hard work, and part serendipity," he had told her. "I don't know how or why we were so lucky, but it's been pure joy—that's all I can tell you."

The picture of my world has lost another color, Claire thought—the same thought she had when her father died. "One less color in my rainbow," she said out loud to Brian, who nodded gravely in response. "I loved her too, you know…."

"I know you did, Claire. We all did," Brian said in a patronizing tone, coming over to hug her as they stood next to the bed.

"Take care of my dad, Olivia, I'm counting on you. Godspeed, sweet lady," Claire whispered when she bent over her stepmother's body for the final time. She picked up Olivia's cold hand and kissed it, tears falling freely onto the bedside as she did so, noting, as we all do, the mystery of flesh without warmth when only yesterday blood was coursing through it.

She, too, would soon discover that Olivia had been indulgent with her and that she had been well taken care of. This did not surprise her; it only made her wish she had expressed her gratitude to Olivia more often. For, in the end, Olivia had been as kind to her as any mother would have been. How she would miss her, she could not count the ways.

Brian and Lisa, outwardly somber and dignified, seemed to be dealing with Olivia's death quite maturely and were bustling around the house making arrangements, notifying friends and relatives, stacking certain items in little piles—apparently for later redistribution. "We'll mourn tomorrow," Brian announced to no one in particular. "Right now, there are a thousand details to tend to. Lisa, I'll call Howard, you don't need to worry about that. He'll probably want to come over."

Lisa nodded. "He told us to call him when the moment arrived, so I guess that time has come. Yes, you call him. I'm making a list of the other calls we need to make— you know, Social Security, the bank, the insurance company…"

Brian nodded absently as he dialed Howard's number.

Laila had stayed by Olivia's side until her last breath, sometime in the middle of the night, both for professional and personal reasons. Since Laila was there, no one had called hospice. Their job was done as well. Everyone could fold up their tent and leave.

Exhausted from her death-watch, Laila had finally abandoned Olivia when there was nothing more she could do. And although she had witnessed many deaths in her short career, this one took her breath away. Later, at home, she found herself bent over with gut-wrenching sobs. Her intense sense of loss did not make any sense to her. I barely knew her really, she thought to herself. Why the anguish? Why such despair? Why does my heart hurt so sharply? She had felt the same level of pain when she lost her parents, so this confounded her. Why was there such a strong attachment? What ties people together like this? She had no answers, only a profound feeling of deprivation.

Even though it was early in the morning, she found herself calling Ben—long before she normally would have done so. "I can't believe she's gone," she cried to her surrogate father. "I haven't known her that long—I told you about her—but she touched me in a way I can't explain. It's as though I've known her all my life. She just took me at face value, with no judgement. She listened to me, she opened up to me. She found a way to make me do the same with her—and, as you know, that is not something that comes easily to me. Somehow she created a space where I felt free to tell her things I had never told anyone, maybe not even you." Laila stopped to wipe her face. "She gave me the opportunity to speak, and I did. She asked me to be Scheherezade for her—you probably know who that is, but I didn't and she explained it to me. I know it sounds silly, but it wasn't, not the way she did it. She made it seem normal to talk about everything and anything under the sun. I shall miss her so. I loved her—I know that. I didn't know you could love someone so quickly and so fully, but I did. And I know she loved me, too, in her way. I know she did. I still can't stop crying…"

Ben attempted to calm her to no avail. "You'll just have to take the time to grieve for her, that's all I can tell you. She probably tapped into some of the feelings you will always have for your mother, so it's perfectly natural. The mother-daughter relationship can sometimes transfer to people other than those we are related to by blood. Give it some time, honey, you'll get there."

Laila sobbed something incoherently, then put down the phone. She walked from one room of her apartment to the other, alternately crying and attempting to stop. Finally, she threw herself on the bed and stared up at the ceiling, trying to reign in her thoughts.

Eventually, she reached into the bedside drawer and pulled out an old tattered notebook. She began to write feverishly in her native language, crossing out words, starting over several times. Finally, when she was done, she carefully translated it into English, a dictionary by her side:

For Olivia,

I did not share your blood, but we shared our memories,

I did not know you long, but I knew you well

I do not know what shifting strong karma blew me in your direction

But I thank those winds that made our lives intersect

Somehow just writing these lines seemed to help. She found herself breathing more deeply, the crying jag seemingly over. "How I will miss you, sweet Olivia," she heard herself whispering. "You will not be forgotten."

***

It was Howard who informed her later of her windfall. He had summoned her to his office several days after Olivia's demise. She had been surprised to get the message from him; he was the last person she expected to hear from. She had gone in, thinking that perhaps Olivia had left her some small bequest. When he presented her with an envelope with a single piece of paper in it, she nervously opened it and frowned while trying to figure out what it meant.

"What is this, Mr. Chavez? This is from Charles Schwab. It looks like it must be one of Olivia's brokerage statements, no?"

"Call me Howard, please. Yes, that's exactly what it is. Except that this account—Olivia's account—had a beneficiary assigned to it. It was a TOD account— that means 'transfer on death'. And you are the 'transferee'—the beneficiary. The final papers will all be mailed to you so that you can take it over, but I wanted to show this to you now so that you would understand what is happening."

Laila bent forward in her chair so that she could get closer to his desk. "Well, I *don't* understand at all. It says that there are five shares of stock here. Why the huge number listed as the total value? That must be wrong."

"No, actually, it's right. As of last night, a single share of Berkshire Hathaway stock was selling for $596,125, which would make those five shares worth close to 3 million dollars."

Howard pushed himself back in his leather chair, grinning broadly, enjoying the look of shock and bewilderment on Laila's face.

"Pretty brilliant, isn't it?" he said, smiling at her and winking at the same time. "You have to hand it to Olivia. She knew how to make an exit."

"But you can't be serious!" Laila exclaimed, her eyes wide with disbelief, still trying to wrap her mind around such an enormous number. "Oh, but I am," Howard said cheerfully. To his credit, he was thrilled to be delivering this news to Laila. "The shares were given to her when she was very young, and I think they were worth $65 or $70 a share at the time—something like that. But as you can see, they've had a rather astronomical growth spurt. Whoever gave it to her either psychically knew what he was doing or was just incredibly lucky. She never shared that particular story with me. But, in any case, you can do what you like with the money, there are absolutely no strings attached—that's how she wanted it. But just so you know, she was secretly hoping you would take it back to Afghanistan and use some of it to help others in your same situation..."

Laila sat quietly for a moment, her thoughts in a daze. "I'm just so stunned. I hardly know what to say! What a remarkable gesture this is. I need to think more about this. But, yes, off the top of my head, that sounds like the right thing to do. It's so uncommonly generous of her to think of me at all… There is so much I could do with this; I can't even begin to think straight…so many people I could help over there…so many lives like mine—so many Laila's in my homeland…"

Howard smiled back at her, pleased that she was going in the direction Olivia had hoped. "Well, she told me several times how touched she was by your story, though she never told me the details. But she believed that you have a purpose in your life, one that she felt she could help you to fulfill. She told me that your story was not finished, that she felt you would accomplish many things in your lifetime. So she had faith in you."

"She did, didn't she?" Laila said softly, wiping tears from her face. "Unbelievable. My life has had so many unexpected twists and turns. This is yet another one. I can't wait to tell Ben and Lauren. They won't believe it! Thank you, Mr. Chavez— Howard—I can't thank you enough…"

"Don't thank me! It was all her idea. At first, I thought it was a bit unorthodox, but I came around to her way of thinking by the time she finished with me. She was quite taken with you, and could be most persuasive, that one…"

"Yes, she was—persuasive, that is," Laila said, smiling through her tears. "But what about her family? Won't they be upset about her leaving me this stock?"

Howard sighed, arched his eyebrows, and then moved a few papers on his desk before responding. "I don't know the answer to that one. At first, she wasn't going to tell Brian anything—which is her prerogative. Then, at the last minute, I thought she might have changed her mind, though I don't know that for a fact. So I'm not sure what she did about informing them before her death, and you and I may never know. What I do know is that she was entitled to do whatever she pleased, and she did so."

He stopped for emphasis. "There are no grounds for an estate controversy here, if that's where your mind is going, so don't worry about that. If you had been an official hospice nurse, there might have been an issue because they usually have a contract that does not allow the nurses to accept deathbed bequests—which makes plenty of sense, if you think about it. But that was not the case here. You were hired by her privately and had no such strictures, though one might have made an argument out of it if she had been incompetent at the time. But that was not the situation, and she took great pains to make all that apparent—and legal, to boot."

"And please, Laila, don't fret for Brian and his family. They have no worries monetarily. Look at it this way: she did not forget them; she simply remembered you."

Howard gazed towards the window pensively, thinking of his friend, remembering his fondness for her. Then he shook his head as though to dispel the sentimentality that was so foreign to him and returned to his train of thought. "I have certainly turned this question over in my mind, though, because it is very thought-provoking. There's no telling what the rest of the family would have thought— well, actually, what am I saying? They most certainly would have been horrified!" he chuckled. "But she kept the stock out of the trust, so to my knowledge, no one knows about it except the two of us. It was a gift to her originally. There are no estate taxes involved, and you have no tax consequence either at this point, though it won't hurt to consult a tax attorney later, as you will eventually have to pay some tax when you sell the stock. All things considered, she did one hell of a job keeping it a secret most of her adult life. I know Charlie knew about it but he considered it her secret to keep. And that's just what she did until you came along.

So, perhaps, now you are the Keeper of the Secret."

"So, you're saying that Brian and Lisa know nothing about this?" Laila asked incredulously.

"What I'm saying is that to the best of my knowledge they do not know. Of course, I can't be sure what she may have told him towards the end. But since she did not see any reason to acquaint them with this information in her lifetime—that I know about, at least—it is certainly not my place to do so now. And my recommendation to you would be the same: let sleeping dogs lie. Take your gift, live your life, and do as much good with it as you possibly can. That will be the way you can thank her. I know that's what she would say because she said it to me in as many words shortly before she died. At the same time, she did not want to tie you down with restrictions on how you should spend the money; she said she wanted to leave it up to you and let your conscience guide you. She assured me that you have a highly developed sense of ethics—'forged in the fire,' I think she said to me, a phrase I don't completely understand, but that's between you and her. From what little I know of you, I think she made a wise choice."

"That's kind of you to say. Olivia was like no one else. She has had a profound impact on my life, and I suppose that will continue as I attempt to carry out her wishes. I have so much to think about and plan now. I hardly know where to start…"

"Indeed. Well, stay in touch, let me know what you decide—not because you are required to do so, but because I'm interested, and Olivia would be interested if she were here."

Laila stood up, straightening her skirt, searching for a Kleenex to dab her eyes with. "I can hardly believe my good fortune. There was a time when I thought my life was cursed; that there was not a single good thing that could come of it, but so much has changed since then. I see my life now as a much bigger pattern than I saw at the time. I'm beginning to see the forest and not just the trees. I hope I will make her proud. Thank you—Howard—and thank you, Olivia," she said pressing the envelope to her lips and then into her bag. "I will stay in touch, I absolutely will."

"Yes, do that," Howard said, moving towards Laila and awkwardly taking her hand. "If you have any questions, you can always contact me. I will be eager to hear of your progress. I think you will use this wisely, and hopefully, you can sprinkle some of Olivia's optimism, hope and well developed sense of humor wherever you go."

Laila's eyes filled with tears again as she nodded her head in agreement and backed towards the door. "I'll take her with me. We'll do some good together. I promise you—I promise her." And then she was gone.

***

Howard had not been able to come to the house when Brian called to announce Olivia's death. He sent flowers to the funeral home and offered the usual condolences to Brian and Lisa on the phone, then made arrangements to meet with them at his office late in the afternoon, one week to the day after her passing.

He was waiting in his office when his secretary showed Brian in.

"Howard, good to see you, especially in these trying times..." Brian said, extending his hand and adopting a somber look.

Howard nodded his head by way of agreement and shook Brian's hand perfunctorily. "Nice to see you, as well," he said sinking heavily into the dark leather chair behind his desk. "Have a seat, please," he said, gesturing to one of the matching leather seats across from him. He wondered silently why Brian was alone, but decided not to ask.

Brian sat down gingerly, then pulled himself forward in the chair. "Sorry, Lisa couldn't make it today, but I'll fill her in on the details. I'm anxious to go over the provisions of my mother's estate. I don't know why she didn't appoint me the Executor, but you know how secretive she could be. Do you know why she didn't? I mean, she told me that you were in charge of everything, and I accepted that, but I did find it strange, being the only biological child and all..."

Howard sighed and clasped his hands together on the desk. "I knew Olivia for over 20 years. I can't say that we were close friends, but we liked each other immensely, and I admired her in many ways. She was a tough old bird, but she was honest and direct—with me, at least—two things that are hard to come by in the legal profession. She also had a wonderful, dry sense of humor that I always appreciated. She was someone who didn't run from her problems; she just stood her ground and let the waves crash over her. She used to tell me that she 'didn't suffer fools gladly.' I liked that turn of phrase; she was always good with words. You know, she didn't trust many people, but for whatever reason, she trusted me. I shall miss her greatly…"

Howard held Brian's gaze for a moment, then looked down. "I realize that doesn't exactly answer your question, but I don't have an answer for you, just my thoughts, really…"

Brian started to say something, then thought better of it and remained silent.

Howard shifted in his chair, fingered some papers on his desk as though they were somehow pertinent, then pushed them aside and finally continued. "We're here today so that I can deliver a copy of her trust and her will to you as she requested. She rarely confided in me about her motives, and I must tell you that I do not completely understand what she was up to when it comes to these documents, but I am fulfilling my legal commitment to her. She did not take my advice as to how to draw up her will, to say the least. But again, I did as she instructed."

Brian seemed unnerved by Howard's last remarks and, after crossing and uncrossing his legs nervously, focused a piercing look in Howard's direction. "I'm not sure what you're getting at…"

Howard responded quickly, "I don't mean to alarm you. Let me finish. The trust itself is boilerplate, nothing special there. The part that is a bit bizarre is that she wanted you to know that she had me create two separate sets of wills and trusts, both signed,

dated and witnessed on the same day. Each will is what's called a 'pour-over will,' which is normal. One directs that her assets be put into a particular trust, and the second directs that her assets be put into another, different trust. She told me that before she died, she would let me know which set of documents she wanted destroyed, and which set she

wanted delivered. They had completely different outcomes with regard to the distribution of the estate. Five days before she died she called me and told me what her decision was. She was still competent—she was always competent as far as I'm concerned—and I took care of it. So what I have here is a copy of the designated will and trust."

Now Brian shifted nervously in his chair, the leather making creaking noises as he moved. "I'm finding this very unconventional," he said, making it clear that he was not comfortable with what he was hearing.

Howard leaned down and pulled a large bound book out of his briefcase.

"The trust papers and will are both in this binder. You are entitled to this copy because you are her descendant and are named in the trust. These documents distribute her estate in the manner she wished it divided. In addition, she asked that I hand deliver this letter to you. I have not read the letter; it was sealed when she gave it to me."

With that, Howard placed a white legal envelope on the desk in front of Brian. Brian picked it up and held it with a hand that Howard noticed was trembling.

"I'll read it later," Brian informed Howard, "when I'm in the proper frame of mind. I think I need some time to myself if you don't mind. I'll take these papers and go through them," Brian said, abruptly picking up the bound document and tucking the envelope into its pages.

"Are you sure you don't want to go over them now while we're here?" Howard asked, surprised that Brian was leaving so quickly.

"No. I'll get back to you. Knowing my mother, everything will be crystal clear when I read this. I'm sure it's all proforma. She talked a good game, but at heart, she was very predictable."

"Well, that's one way to look at it," Howard said as he opened the office door for Brian. "We can set up another appointment after you've had a chance to go over these papers. There are still some details we'll need to work out."

"I'll call you," Brian said, hurrying out of the office with the binder under his arm and a look of bewilderment and disturbance on his face.

***

Alone in his office, Brian fingered the single page from the envelope he had just opened; it was still folded in thirds. Is this what a life boils down to, he thought, one 8- 1/2 x11 sheet of paper?

He unfolded the page and laid it flat on his desk, smoothing it with his hands, both of which felt wet and clammy to him. Apparently, he was about to have his last conversation with his mother. It was typed, single spaced, double sided. He wondered vaguely how his mother had managed, but she was clever about these things, he knew that. Where there's a will, there's a way—no pun intended, he thought. He started to read:

Dear Brian,

You are now in possession of my final—and only—valid will and testament, duly witnessed and notarized. I am of sound mind and dilapidated body. If you are reading this, Brian, my only child, I am gone, but I have several things to tell you.

First, you are my son, and I love you. I have always loved you; please do not question that. That was never an issue, so don't imagine that it was. I understand you better than you think, and I recognize— but do not concur with—the conclusion you came to regarding me. In the end, I must thank you for helping me with what no one else could have done. In my case, sooner was better than later. I realize that this was not your intention—to help me—but still the results are the same. And for that, I am grateful. Only you and I know of what I speak. It is my gift to you as a mother that this secret will stay between us forever.

It is also as a mother that I use this opportunity to be a Teacher. All actions have consequences, even the most benign, and certainly those that are not. I have lived out the consequences of my actions and go to my final destination with a clear conscience.

I urge you to explore the concept of Forgiveness, as I have done, and to let its grace transform you. In this life, intention is everything. My intentions were always good, though my actions may have belied them. You thought that I/we betrayed you, but we did not. Macy's life was not ours to save. Whatever forces were at work that day were far beyond our control. I hope someday you will understand this and accept the fate that took your child—and also your father—away from you. How bitterly I wish that I had never played a part in those epic dramas, but I did, and there's no turning away from it.

As far as Macy goes, we were all caught up in the whirlwind of that tragic day, but no one of us was to blame. Not you for sending her on that journey, not us for choosing that boat and that time, not the doctor for failing to save her life. No one of us could have done any more or less than we did. We are too close to be able to see the broad fabric of our lives with clarity, nor do we have the capacity to see it in its entirety, but in the end, all of the pieces fit together to make a whole. Some of these pieces seem tailored by us while some of them seem to come from unknown and unforeseen sources over which we have no control.

But no one has total control over their lives; we are battered and buffeted by the winds of change, the mysteries of life and death, the hand of God, and other secrets of the universe that we will never comprehend and that I do not claim to understand. You must relinquish your notion that you are in charge; you can only control so much. The rest is out of your hands. With some distance and some time, I hope you can come to accept—if not understand—this.

The only way for you to find peace is to make peace with yourself and to grant those around you the benefits of that peace. I only wish I could have lived to see you grant me the forgiveness that I so longed for, that I so deserved, that we all deserve—even you. And you shall have it from me. I wish you a long and happy life my son, and may you, too, have a clear conscience when your day comes.

I look forward to a joyful reunion between your father and me, and it is my deepest hope that your Macy will be greeting me on the other side. Let us pray that there is, indeed, another side!

I have left you one-half of my estate, excluding some stock that I turned over to Laila. She touched me deeply and was very kind to me in my final days. I was originally going to keep this fact from you, but there is really no reason to do so. I'm sure you won't begrudge her the small quantity of stock that I gave her.

You always believed that blood is thicker than water; I heard you say it many times. But I found, in my later years, that the connections one makes in life are not always based on sanguinity or vows. Sometimes a complete stranger can come into your life and share something primal with you. This was the case with Laila and me. I was not expecting her, but in she came. I think she has a purpose to fulfill, and it is my hope that she does so. Keep your mind and heart open to strangers because sometimes they can become your very best friends.

So, as to blood being thicker than water, I am here to say: Not always.

As to forgiveness, I am here to say: issue it liberally because we all need to be forgiven, and I have been the benefactor of Heaven's mercy and clemency.

Please think of me kindly,

With all my love, your mother

ACKNOWLEDGMENTS

I can't really thank everyone who helped me write this book because the people, places and events that brought me to the point of writing it are spread out over a lifetime and could never all be named. I sometimes think that being sent to my room so frequently as a child (for various infractions) was the beginning of my love of books. My classical background in literature was cast from that vast library that I had to choose from. So thank you to the universe for that; I am forever grateful for the wonder of books.

In the present, I want to thank my dear friend Tom Harney, who led me rather serendipitously to the magnificent editor/actor/writer, Elaine Partnow. She set me on the right path and gave me invaluable advice and superb editing.

Thank you to Kevin D. Sweeney, M.D., Cathedral City, California and to Dr. Nancy Dawson (Lombardi Comprehensive Cancer Center, Medstar Georgetown University Hospital) for their medical advice and editing. And thanks to my brilliant attorney Deborah Breiner for her legal advice.

I owe my lifelong friend Susan Mooers a debt of gratitude. She cheerfully read every chapter and every change I made for well over a year. She helped me in so many ways I couldn't name them all, but thank you most of all for your friendship, which has stood the test of time. She was the one who put me in touch with Kelly through Kathy Rothkop.

Thank you to Kelly Boyette, my project manager extraordinaire, who guided me through the publication maze with remarkable skill and efficiency, and who also turned into a good friend in the process.

Thank you to Caleb Farrell and Hilary Wehr for their advice and editing on the Afghanistan chapters, and of course for simply existing.

Thank you also to:

Leila and Leslie and Dorothy and Alexis and Barbara and Johanna and Linda and Katy and Tressa and Kathy and Renee and Martha, and Mallory, and everyone else who gave me encouragement along the crooked path that took me here.

Thank you to the beautiful Benni, whose life inspired me both then and now. Thanks to Nicole Gee for the back cover photography.

And finally, to my perfect husband Gary, thank you for all of your help and support on this project, but thank you even more for loving me and sharing your life with me all these years.

And thank you Reggie Chaucer for being yourself.

ABOUT THE AUTHOR

Author Holland Childhouse holds a degree from the University of California, Berkeley. For many years, she worked as a professional technical writer. Later she held the position of Vice President of a Silicon Valley Cad/Cam software company. Currently she lives in Colorado with her husband.